CU00592069

CUTI

Felicity Fair Thompson

Cover
Actress Holly Atkins

Photos
Danny Israel
Richmond Studios
Twickenham

Reviews for CUTTING IN

"…hard edged, striking and truthful…"

Best selling novelist Julian Rathbone

"Absolutely stunning… I had to put the rest of my life on hold…"

Ros Sheard   Artist and

wife of Star Wars actor Michael Sheard

"Poignant and believable …the suspense is very well handled…"

Averil Ashfield Transworld Books

"A great gift for portraying the agonies and ecstasies of adolescence…a rare talent…"

Frederick E Smith

Best Selling novelist and screen Writer

"…a tension that carries the reader sailing through the book. Wait for the surprises."

Novelist Gavrielle Groves-Gidney

CUTTING IN

Felicity Fair Thompson

Wight

Copyright 1999 Felicity Fair Thompson

The right of Felicity Fair Thompson to be identified
as the author of this work has been
asserted by her in accordance with the Copyright, Designs
and Patents Act 1988

All rights reserved. No part of this publication may be reproduced,
stored in a retrieval system, or transmitted in any form or by any
means, electronic, mechanical, photocopying, recording or
otherwise without the prior permission of the copyright owner

This edition first published in Great Britain in 1999 by
Wight Diamond Press Carlton House Binstead I W PO33 3RD

A CIP catalogue record for this book is
available from the British Library

ISBN 0-9535123-0-4

Printed and bound
in Great Britain
by Antony Rowe Ltd
Chippenham
Wiltshire

For my mother

Acknowledgements

My thanks to the Vienna Festival Ballet who allowed me to sit in
on their rehearsals and performances,
and to my friends and family whose generosity, knowledge and
effort made publication of this book possible.
The events and characters in it are entirely fictional, though the
seeds of it go back to a childhood filled to the brim with my
mother's love of ballet, theatre and books, and my father's talent
for turning imaginative ideas into reality.

Chapter 1

A spotlight, hot white light. The familiar smell of us, together, our sweat, a gasp for more air, for enough energy, for that extra effort tonight, that final burst of strength before the climax. His hands around my waist, his breath on my back, on my bare shoulders. The last chord of the music rising, swelling, exploding, and then dropping away. Swish. Heavy scarlet velvet curtain plunging down, dragging like a rough anchor chain across the proscenium, muffling the rising applause. He lets go. It's over. My balance disintegrates. I slip out of the posé, magic suddenly subsides into ordinariness. Common tension loosens into individual pain. Stinging feet, aching muscles, throbbing lungs. Exhaustion. No-one's immune, least of all me.

"You missed that pirouette."

Bastard, he knows he lost his grip.

"I made it work!"

Some invisible cue pulls me dutifully back into line beside him just as the curtain divides again, letting in the waves of applause from a darkness spiked with blasts of white light. Pink. Yellow.

A young girl from side stage, one of the students, a crisp crinkle of cellophane. My own applause, center stage, applause for me at last. Finally. Recognition and a future. The sweet smell of these roses. Who's sent me flowers?

I'm pulled further forward, my hand's kissed, he's playing the audience. I glance down at the card, see the handwriting.

"Are you coming to the party?" he whispers, through a wide set smile as he bows to acknowledge his share of the clapping. "Elaine?"

Applause......all this wonderful adulation. Applause, loud, warm, welcoming, yet suddenly now it's sounding like rain. A deluge. Dull, thudding rain. A drowning. What I want is tea. I don't need any party. All I want is tea and tea, with lots of sugar.....

"Smile, Elaine," he hisses. "It might never happen."

But it has.

It's a joke, fate is. Accusation, now! And I can even see it mirrored in my own eyes. You thought you got away with it, Elaine? You had it all under control, did you? Well, where's the cold cream? Wipe away the present, the stage make-up, tonight's success. It's still under there, that old Elaine.

"Going to have drinks with them then, love?" The stage hand leans round the door. He's used to seeing all us company girls naked. Reflected in mirrors. The men too, come to that.

"No."

"First night. You can't not. Everyone else has gone."

I shrug.

"You can have a late car. I can get one."

The tissue, thick with cream and ivory pan stick, thuds into the bin.

"Company rules. Obligatory, first night publicity parties are."

How pale my skin seems without the drawn-on face in this harsh light, rows of naked bulbs.

"He's gone anyway."

"Gone? He didn't wait?"

"Said he'd see you there."

Did he know? Is that why he asked me if I was going?

"Go on. Wait till you see the reviews. It'll be your night."

"Will it?"

The stage hand grins. "Sure it will! Celebrate! What else?"

What else now indeed?

"I'm boiling a kettle. Want tea?"

"Could I?"

"Sure!"

"How long have I got to change?"

"Ten minutes or so."

"Twenty?"

He shrugs. His gaze shifts down and hovers. "Yeah, okay. Just for you."

"Thanks."

Eventually, after an age, an embarrassingly long silence, he uncurls himself from the doorway and goes. Leaves me sitting silently in my nakedness. Padding away in his trainers towards the stage.

The soft crepe of one dress, colour of lapis lazuli, what I planned to wear, swings on the hanger, drapes cool and smooth against my hand. If this is a set up though I should wear the other one. Red, just to prove a point! Yes. But not earrings - let's not overstate the case. And yet, perhaps those diamantes?

I'm always obsessive about the impression I make. One thing, my figure at twenty-one is better than I had at eighteen. It's sleek now, lean, a muscular physique. But real strength? I still search for that in appearance. And I'm needing strength right now. Needing it like I used to, even after all this time. It's funny, I sort of knew. Lately it's been hanging around in my mind that something isn't the same, that things have changed.

Elaine....Elaine.....Elaine.. Had you forgotten?

It's years since Elaine had her recurring dream. She's little. She's in a car, a dusty old blue estate, travelling along in the middle of the night. It's hot, that Australian night, still full of leftover heatwave, and there's a velvet-thick wind blowing over her...me... through the window, with a strong smell of bone dry grass in it, and camphor-pungent oil. Melting eucalyptus.

She's...I'm...let's get this right...it was my dream.... I'm this child, and I'm on two cushions so I can just see over the dashboard but the road ahead is pretty much deserted. My Dad is driving, maybe a little too fast. I've had some sleep so I'm not tired. I'm in that awake, elated-kid state, middle of the night wide-eyed. It's no time since my mother woke me up and helped me dress. We're moving, she says. Moving? People change, people change houses, new people come, she says. At night? It's safer, she tells me, safer to travel at night, cooler. What's travelling, I want to know? Going, Mum says. Her fingers fumble with each button on my dress, as if she expects any one of them to fly off and hit her in the face. Why do I think that?

Going? Leaving, she says.

The fly screen over the back door is propped open with cases, so there are loads of little moths inside, fluttering on the ceiling, excited by their unexpected access to the indoor lights. Mum, with the baby against her shoulder, is still gathering last minute things into a bag with her free hand. Looking over her other shoulder

4

as if she'll be caught out any time now. Gathering, snatching, not tidying. Not tidying. I can't understand why my mother's leaving the house in such a mess. Won't the new people mind? I ask. If they're changing houses, won't the new people mind? She doesn't answer. Instead when Dad appears, Mum suddenly grabs my hand and hurries me out to the car and puts me in the front seat and takes the back seat for herself and the baby.

"I won't be able to see."

"It's dark, Elaine," Mum says, but she goes back inside and fetches the cushions. Then as soon as we're driving, immediately we're moving, she seems to be asleep in the back with baby Jonty. She's put her feet up, has her eyes shut, but is she asleep? I'm four, I'm sure, possibly five. Why am I in the front, awake? I feel I'm awake for a reason, I've been put here for a reason, it's important.

The road ahead seems only as wide as the headlights and straight and flat and empty, and there's nothing much to pass along the way. My Dad is tired. He's worked all day, now he's driving all night. There's a weird feeling of danger in the air. A tingling. And no talking. Nobody's saying anything. I know something of what's happening though, what little my mother told me as she threw all the coathangers on the bed and stuffed clothes into a bag.....

"We're leaving," she says, fighting with the zip. "Heading for Sydney airport. We're going to be London people. In my mother's house." I have a grandmother? Now on the car seat behind me my mother's shifting around. She turns over, turns her back. All I can see of her is her auburn hair straying out of its clips, and the angle of her shoulder, the dip of her waist and the slim curve of her hip. There's no room for her feet on the floor because of the bags, so she's lying, with baby Jonty tucked in between her and the seat where I can't see him. And there's a kind of exhaustion about her, about the way she's lying, that I can't ever remember seeing before. I want to ask her things. I want to ask what's wrong, but I think she really might be asleep. So I can't. Instead I listen to the sound of the road humming the miles away under me, a low rhythmical hum, sometimes broken by the rip and bounce of a pothole, or the rasp when the tyres stray off into the dust along the edge of the tarmac.

When the moon comes out it's full face, surprised and bright. The milky highway starts to zigzag up through the ghost gums into the darkness of the Blue Mountains. Against the black of the night sky the stars seem large and pulsating, as if they can breathe, in and out. Breathing. In and out. As the car climbs higher they come closer. They're so near now I can almost hear them sighing, and feel their breath on my hair. I lie back and watch them breathing.

When I notice where we are my ears are popping, the stars are drifting upwards and we're going downhill, down the other side of the mountains, down towards Sydney. And the lights laid out below are like stars too, and the road is wider, dipping down through the folded foothills. An occasional lorry passes; strange glaring pairs of white eyes loom out of the blackness, dazzle, roar by and then leave trails of dust behind them lit up by red brake lights. Road carriers chugging, muttering away through the night air. Then whistling off into the darkness. My Dad is driving through all this without a word. None of his usual swearing. Just silence. Driving

6

as if he's in a dream, his eyes fixed on the road ahead, his strong hands sweating, clasping and unclasping the steering wheel. I watch that. I'm glad to see it. It's the only real sign that he at least is awake like I am. Now there's a van rearing up on the road in front of us, its red rear lights shrouded by dust and weather and age. My Dad leans outwards a little, to see if he can overtake. His expression doesn't alter. He pulls out.

There's a shrill shriek of horn, a flash of bright oncoming lights. Our car swerves in again, screaming back under me so fast that I have to grab onto the seat and hold tight. There's a gush of air and engine noise and lights shoot past and the horn sound drops an octave, but I don't dare let go - the wheels under me are still veering off the road, on a roll. The van in front may be speeding up and away.....but our car's rushing sideways towards the verge. Dad's hands are fighting the steering wheel, he can't control the swerve. His knee lifts and he slams his foot down hard on the brakes. With a screech the car skids to a halt throwing me forward violently against the belt, then pressing me back hard into the seat.

There's dust rising in the moonlight and an evil burn-ey kind of smell - and silence. Far ahead in the distance the red lights of the old van disappear over the hill.

"Strewth!" Mum says from the back seat. She's clutching Jonty and shaking.

"Shut up."

"Kill us all! Why not?"

"For Christsakes, Kath."

Dad takes a deep breath and with trembling hands reverses back onto the tarmac and then we carry on as if nothing has happened. But now I don't feel safe. I feel stretched and heavy and frightened. My fear makes me chatter, about the house, the one we've left behind in such a state, and then what will it be like in London? Is it very far now? Will I go to school there, and what is school exactly? No-one tells me. They're all in their trances again, my mother curled up on the back seat, the baby whimpering softly, Dad clenching and unclenching his hands on the steering wheel. I keep talking though. Maybe it's what keeps Dad awake enough to go on driving. Maybe if I hadn't.

It wasn't a dream of course, but I kind of remember it that way.

I remember Dad carried the bags inside and up the two flights of steps in the airport terminal. Then he went collect the tickets. When he returned Mum snatched them from him.

"I hope you've organized immediate finance," she said.

"Figure you're due it, do you?"

"Yes."

He looked down at me and patted me on the head. Then he went back down the steps. I thought he was bringing up another case. We found seats and for a while I was fascinated by luggage trolleys, the noise, the announcements echoing, the crowds of people. Then I began to scan the faces. And the longer we sat there the more anxious I became, and the more the question became too terrible to ask.

"Stop fussing, Elaine," Mum said. "Sit still."

An hour and a half later we went on the plane to London without my father. It always worried me that after that I couldn't visualize what he looked like. Okay, his hands, but not his face. I couldn't conjure up his features and see his expression. There was a photograph of him somewhere, but I couldn't remember for myself.

Chapter 2

The London house was disappointing. Small windows
and dark, in a dead end street near the Thames, a grimy
brick terrace in a row of others just like it. Furnished but
not like back home. Television and ordinary things, nicer
quality than we'd had before, but nothing with an old
scrubby comfortable family look about it. No clattery old
fly screen door with night-flowering jasmine growing
beside it. No fig tree or the smell of the eucalyptus. No
sudden screech of pink parrots punching into the
morning air. Nor the infinite silence and shimmering
afternoon heat of the bush under an arc of cobalt sky.
No garden at all in fact. Not even a back yard. And not
much left of the bedridden grandmother either. In that
remembered few seconds of meeting, I was sure I could
see something eating away at those blue thread veins and
tissue thin skin. Bright glass eyes noted me and then
Jonty. A smile which seemed too small for its teeth
followed an acrid smell like vinegar.

"Out!" Mum said, shutting me into a forbidding,
unfamiliar hall.

We'd arrived so early it was dark and I didn't see the
bridge from my room to start with, though somehow I
felt its shadow, and heard the frightening roar of a train
setting out across it. After my mother dragged the zip
bag in and left me to pull out the rumpled contents, I
searched vainly for my old teddy bear, hoping that the
picture in my mind of him still lying among those
abandoned crumpled sheets back home wasn't true. But
it was and I wept, knowing he would never forgive me
for forgetting him. What did come out of the bag I

smelled and held close for a long time, burying my tear-stained face in those few familiar belongings. Then I stuffed them all into the cupboard and while along the hall Jonty slept in a makeshift hollow of pillows, and my mother lay back in a chair next to the grandmother's bed waiting and staring vacantly into space, I stood looking out of the window of my new bedroom at the great gravitational heaviness of that railway bridge, half hidden by a thick pylon of supporting stone which bronzed as the sun rose and the light increased. And in this unfamiliar world which suddenly no longer contained my father, between the buildings there was a glimpse of the river, just a narrow vertical strip like a phial of golden liquid which gradually, as the hours passed and the sky clouded over the English day, turned silver, then into grey, and on into inky shadowed indigo.

But let's cut my father out of this. He cut himself out. Never sent my bear. Never said goodbye. Never wrote or anything. Why should I be the one to include him?
 Besides that's not what I'm talking about. No. That's the little kid. What I'm on about happened three years ago. And everything was so essential by then, all so vitally necessary, so powerfully intense.

In my opinion, there are only two kinds of dancers - ethereal, long legs, the earsplitting arabesque type, the obvious romantic ballerina, and the other, the petite quicksilver dancer, pirouettes and elevation galore. I had a great longing to be one or other. Instead at middle height I'd lost out somewhere in between. Perhaps I should have thought of myself as versatile. There's one thing I had - have - though. Perseverance. And with a big capital P. It's why that night I was standing backstage in the Kings Theatre, amid the clayey smell of Leichner make-up, and the heat and colour of the footlights, smoothing out the stiff red tulle of my tutu, feeling the adrenaline stinging through my veins. And I was connected, powerful. There was a sense of twitching excitement out in front too, out there in the audience, as I flexed the arches of my feet inside my pointe shoes. It was me they were waiting for then, you know. Me. It was my big moment.

But I'm jumping forward. A lot happened before that, before I was eighteen. And built up to that moment. But good things, like bad, come in runs. Just because you've been happy you think it's going to go on. You never expect to be kicked in the teeth.

My mother was always saying you could only be good at English or Maths, not both. One of her theories.

"Why?"

"It's just true." No explanation. No discussion, never any conversation about it. That was Kath Higham....

"Stay and talk to me," she says, switching across the channels on the television. The room smells musty. Nothing ever disturbed. The cushions, crushed, lifeless. The curtains, half closed. Miss Haversham, for God's sake. The cups pile up but otherwise everything remains the same day after day. Once she was tidy. I want to ask what happened.

She doesn't look at me, my mother, when she's speaking. She doesn't look at her teenage daughter. What she means when she says stay and talk is she's waiting to know what you might sit down and watch with her. What's the point? That's not talking. She never tells me what she feels.

But back to that idea of hers. That justified my failing in maths all through school. I never have seen the point of numbers. Can anything really worthwhile ever be reduced to them? My settling for her theory may have proved her point, but it did nothing to improve my grasp of realism, and certainly didn't dampen down my exotic romantic attitudes, my vivid imagination. When I was a kid, like my brother I bunked off school. Disappeared. Not from English though - even if the women who were teaching that were idiots and didn't see half the meaning of the beautiful language they made us study - except one supply teacher who came for two weeks covering for some monster teacher who was having a nervous breakdown from being bullied. This one was pretty monstrous herself, but I can remember her now reading passionately in a low resonant voice from Romeo and Juliet.... stony limits cannot hold love out: And what love can do, that dares love attempt....

"If you're not going to watch, make me a cup of tea?" My mother holds out an empty cup and begins another channel search with the remote. How many million times in my past does that scene occur?

It used to give me a great feeling of freedom flouting school rules, pushing my luck, sneaking off, concocting stories about why I hadn't done this piece of work or that. Good at inventing, I was. Boringly I didn't smoke or do drugs like Jonty, nor did I hang around with anyone then who did. They didn't invite me of course, but who would have wanted to go off with any of those dull girls who popped pills anyway? They were too busy blowing what brains they had to be imaginative. No, the time I spent out of school was mine. On my own.

Walking. Thinking. Dreaming. Sometimes in the streets. Often in the park watching the rooks soaring above the trees. They're never just one, you know, rooks. Always in pairs, shadowing each other, dramatically riding on the wind. Dipping, gliding. Using the wind. Embracing it. Interpreting its hidden rhythms. Part of the elements. I've always wanted to be visually passionate like that. Seen. On display. And more. I wanted... I wanted to be loved. I wanted it, wished for it, craved it. And not just in any old ordinary way either. I wanted the kind of passionate love you could kill for, that you'd die for. All or nothing.

In retrospect, perhaps my mother knew me better then than I realized because that's how it is with me. One thing or the other. I have never bothered to learn any in-betweens. Fractions, percentages, grey areas, all that sort of thing? What does that matter? Anymore than partial success. No, friends or enemies. Win or lose, I believe.

But when I was eighteen....that was the year. A lovely age they said when anything was possible. A dangerous age, when you have to cut your way into life. With a machete if necessary....

So Elaine is eighteen.... and she...I....have been applying the principal of win or lose to myself willy-nilly. I've never been what I deem pretty, so I've lost out there. My brother Jonty is the better looking one. My skin is pale. My snub nose is conspicuous where his is nice and straight and normal. His wavy chestnut hair always vied with my unruly curly. Okay, so I know I'm not the typical classical heroine. Even my name I consider a bad choice. Elaine Higham. Jonty at least got 'Jonathon'. And that's High-am, thanks. Not Higgg-ham. Elaine's bad enough, and don't say it with an Australian accent either - it sounds even worse. That sets me apart too, my accent, though secretly I quite like it. Because my father was Australian, and my mother still speaks a bit that way after spending nearly a decade out there, I do as well. All through my awful school days - at the odd times I actually attended, I was taunted about it. I didn't care though. The school part of my existence was an unnecessary diversion from my true direction in life, something to be endured and got through as quickly as possible. So I never bothered with the people there. None of them. It didn't seem important.

I have always been an outsider.

"Stay and talk to me?"

One Christmas, which registered another year without word from my father - I was nearly thirteen - I remember that because I had considered it to be an unlucky year.... that Christmas was about the only time I ever settled down with my mother and watched television. I had no particular friends as usual, and I was totally bored. Some life! Aimless days, evenings destructively idling the hours away in my bedroom, tearing paper, pulling threads from the bedcover. So Christmas - and the only girl who might, might have done something, gone for a walk or something, was away. I didn't like her much anyway. Outside the frosty light was already disappearing. And Jonty was out, who knew where.

For once the remote was lying out of Mum's reach on the floor. I sat down disgruntled, irritated that I was reduced to watching television. From the Royal Opera

House, Covent Garden, a production of Sleeping Beauty.... but it began and I watched for two hours transfixed and I'm telling you it was like a revelation, a vision. I realized I was looking at my future - because suddenly I knew. All that Grand Romanticism.... that grace. I wanted it, the display of it. Classical ballet. Absolutely nothing less would do.

My mother dismissed the idea as stupid of course.

"It's a whim! After seeing just one ballet? It takes years of dedication."

"And you'd know all about it, wouldn't you!"

How I convinced her to let me take ballet lessons I'll never know. But otherwise what she have done with a rebellious teenage daughter? She had no ideas. And this way I wasn't going to interrupt her viewing if I was out and about. And surely she had some conscience about sitting there doing nothing herself. Maybe it was me saying: "Why not? At least I'm prepared to put some effort into my life," and adding accusingly what was family allowance for then and didn't my father send money for us as well?

"What do you think keeps us, Elaine? He owes me."

"Why?" Predictably no answer. I pushed harder. "So what do you contribute?" But that didn't prick her conscience, not one bit. She didn't even blink. She gave in though. Well, no, she didn't. What she did was, she didn't say I couldn't. The money came from a little bit my grandmother had left me and the shopping fund and though sometimes Mum inquired vaguely where I was going, she never stopped me. I started off at an academy of dance in Hammersmith. Reasonably close and it did give me a beginning, I suppose. And what a discovery! I loved having to force my body into new and difficult

16

positions, and the feeling that suddenly I'd found a direction for myself. And so close too! Just over the river in the bus. But it's a dangerous place to cross the road, where the buses speed past the flyover, unless you use the underpasses. Sometimes I crossed the road though.

I worked hard. And I practiced and practiced at home what I was shown. Monkey see, monkey do. I'd come to ballet very late. Most people there had started earlier and were far better than me, I could see that. But after four years of Hammersmith Broadway and passing exams 'Commended', I finally had the sense to realize that if I really wanted to get anywhere, there was no more time to waste. I was nearly seventeen. If this was the career I wanted I had to work a million times harder and get myself into somewhere much more upmarket. And fast. As a springboard for the theatre and company schools, Orlando's in the West End was the best. If I could get in. If! It would cost much more and I'd have to be out later each night doing classes.

I tried explaining all this to my mother as she watched an early evening soap.

Saturday morning too, I told her, but it would be worth it. I would get a better grounding and have more of a chance in my chosen career.

Her finger flicked restlessly back and forth across the channel numbers. "What about homework? The exams?"

I was surprised she'd noticed I had any.

"I can do that too."

"You need your A Levels."

"I can do it."

When it came to it later, I did too, surprisingly. Perhaps not surprisingly having said I would. Miss

Perseverance, that was me. I scraped through French and History and I got very high marks in English. Funny how by then it mattered, because I was busy proving my equality.

My mother's gaze had drifted back to the television.

"So can I?"

"Can you what?"

"Go to Orlando's?"

"If you go out so much, will Jonty do my shopping?"

I nodded. Bargain. Compromise. Anything. Of course Jonty would take some convincing. And what about her doing it? What about her? You'd think just going to the supermarket, wandering past the shelves might be some sort of outing....

No, not the time for that one. Jonty had better co-operate though, it was definitely time he took his turn.

Her attention was wandering again.

I fought to get it back. If I took a part-time job to pay for my own pointe shoes and practice clothes? Of course if I did that, maybe I could do it on my own anyway, without any assistance from her, but with school as well that would take up so much time....

"Do what you want," my mother said lethargically, and gave her concentration over properly to the remote control.

Jonty was furious.

"You've got a nerve plonking the shopping on me."

"What about me? I've done it for years."

"So you've always done it! Why should I?"

"Little sh...!" I bit my tongue. "Go on," I pleaded. "It's only up the road and we could work out a basic list. I opened one of the kitchen cupboards to demonstrate.

"Why doesn't she do it? Nobody else's mother lazes around like she does."

It was true. She never went out. And nobody ever came into that house to see her either. I thought of her sitting on the shabby sofa in the other room in her creased skirt and woolly cardigan; a bit overweight, bored with all life except what was fed to her on that screen. Nothing special in the looks department, but Jonty's straight nose and chestnut hair. She might even be quite attractive if she would just stand up and get on with her life.

But for some reason I defended her right to sit there.

"She's unhappy."

"Aren't we fucking all," Jonty said, fiddling with the loose handle on the cutlery drawer.

I knew I should hug him, cheer him up somehow, but we didn't have that kind of relationship. It wasn't a tactile household. I resorted instead to blackmail which pleased him better. He capitulated when I promised I'd buy him a new pair of trainers.

Little creep took the trainers I parted with my precious pointe shoe money for, and promptly used the list we worked out to make arrangements with a local shop to deliver weekly.

Chapter 3

I like the area around Covent Garden, so I looked for
my part-time job there. The wider streets like Long Acre
and St Martins Lane criss-crossed by a maze of narrow
lanes and alleys and market streets leading through to
that great covered market, layers like a cake, and all
those glossy shops and the opera house. It fascinated
me, it was my sort of place. Still is even with the Opera
House closed. Brass and spotlights and classy company
names; grubby pavements, rubbish bins in corners.
Colonnades, litter, grand plazas, street musicians, really
good ones, really talented, playing beautiful classical
stuff inside the market building. Coffee counters,
pavement tables. Grimy brick terraces in one street,
pristine cream Georgian town houses in another. Noise.
Traffic weaving through. People - some hurrying while
others wander. Tourists, accents, foreign languages.
Daytime there's non-stop trading: tiny boutiques vie with
big name and specialist shops, offices, sandwich bars,
market stalls. Busy, busy, busy. And then afterwards,
once the working day is ended, the accent shifts. That's
when I like it best. The theatres open, light up, their
names and what they're showing written against the
night sky in thin red strips, and there's the strong smell
of cooking from the restaurants. Good cooking, and
rougher too - herbs, exotic meats, garlic. The people
change their clothes, throw off the daytime work image,
go completely casual or brilliantly elegant. I envy the
way they relax, wander in groups, smile. Above the
streets, first floor, in the grubby terraces, inside the
restaurants, down the lanes, suddenly there's living going

on. Lives happening. Music floats down, conversation, arguing, shrieks of laughter. Still noise, but different.

I walked around for a long time before I decided what I ought to do, where I'd choose. And I remember thinking were the shoes I had on the right shoes for a job. Would they suit what I'd be doing?

Luigi's cafe was in May's Court. You could cut through there from St Martins Lane towards New Row and Floral Street. It was within running distance of the Orlando studios. His was only a tiny coffee bar. It was always packed but Luigi thought May's Court was quiet.

He looked me up and down. I could see he thought me skinny. "I need a waitress?"

His white apron's thin strings strained into a bow on the centre of his belly. The stripes on the trousers below, and the shiny black shoes seemed to edge him back into a black and white movie era that my mother watched in the afternoons.

"A waitress?"

I nodded, trying to encourage him.

He banged the sodden remains from a coffee filter into the bin beside him, then refilled it with fresh aromatic grounds. He glanced at my hair. "You got a bad temper?"

"Hmm?" Oh. "No!"

Outside in May's Court people passed by, back and forth, footsteps echoed, someone laughed.

"In Milano the cars, they drive so close to my door even in the narrow lane. The English do not beep-beep."

I looked puzzled. Beep-beep?

"The cars!" He demonstrated wild steering and honking the horn.

"Oh." I stepped back. Not well in the brain, retard,

21

I thought, but rather a beguiling, if toothy, smile. I persevered. "So do you need one?"

"A car?"

"A waitress."

"I have enough of waitresses."

The disappointment must have really shown on my face because he hesitated and scratched his head. He twisted the filter back into place on the machine, and flicked a switch. Dark foaming aromatic liquid began to dribble into the cup below.

"Nice," I said, sniffing the air.

"Best Italian blend! One day you go to Milano?" He looked up at me and his eyes seemed to mist over, as if he was back there himself. "Bella, bella."

I'd seen pictures of the opera house in Milan. La Scala, even the name delighted me. I clasped my hands together rapturously at the very thought of it. "Oh yes."

"How old are you?"

"Eighteen - soon." I was lying. Fourteen months off was hardly soon.

"Next Saturday? You start, okay?"

"How much do you pay?"

He laughed at my audacity. "Enough," he said. "West End rate."

So, normally Saturday afternoons and Thursday evenings he was saying. Yes? Excellent. How lucky I'd chosen so well. Not right for the shoes but.... And he was fitting me into the pattern of things immediately. Actually one of the other girls wanted two weeks off, so did I want to work that as extra? Starting next week? It was school holidays. Eagerly I agreed - it would give me some money straight-away. I looked round at the tiled tables and pottery sugar bowls and mugs, and absorbed

22

the Europeaness of the place, and felt pleased with myself. I could never have borne some unromantic alternative, handling horrible greasy burgers in polystyrene containers, or the smell of chips frying. At least this cafe was convenient and had some atmosphere.

In fact it was a nightmare working there. Luigi had a distracted temperament, lapsing into his native language at hectic moments. And customers, terse and in a desperate hurry, frustrated with their lives, left brief cases and bags of shopping where I could trip over them, scraped the chairs over the tiles, complained. Only rarely were they pleasant, and none of them ever said please. They changed their minds, altered what they'd ordered, had no patience, wanting what they wanted instantly, and displaying such obvious contempt when they saw me struggling to add up their bills.

At the end of the first week I was convinced Luigi was going to tell me I wasn't suitable. I didn't feel suitable. He sighed and paid me my wages in cash with stubby tobacco stained fingers, browner than the expresso he served. I folded the notes over and waited for the axe to fall. But all he said was:

"Next week, easier."

"Yes?"

Well, perhaps not easier. I mean wiping tables and tripping over people's belongings, and not being able to add up and getting confused on the till was never going to be easy, but I would survive the indignities for the money and, once the other girl returned, the hours would suit me.

The actual entrance to the Orlando Studios is misleading. A glossy green door with highly polished brass fittings at the side of one of the cream Georgian buildings hides an ugly, narrow staircase shadowed by dark walls, which climbs to a black and white tiled landing, quite insufficiently lit. But in the end a draughty hall with bench seating, toilets, with a couple of cramped dressing rooms off, all opens into a huge light, bright studio, with a superb sprung wooden floor, and magnificent, if intimidating, mirroring. Beyond all that is an office and another even larger hall, all beautifully decorated.

I applied in late August. Even by then I wasn't prepared for the sort of fees Orlando's charged so it was just as well I'd already found my part time job and started saving. But you couldn't just sign up, however rich you were. Olivia Orlando had been a principal with the New York City Ballet and you had to audition for her to get a place. Typical. There's always such competition for what I want. She only accepted people she thought had a future. And you had a year to make it. One year! That might make sense to her, but just sometimes don't the oddest people battle on through? I was defensive even before I began. But she was interested in her own reputation of course. There were seven other girls as well as me trying to get in for the new term. Her choice was to be based on an hour's class followed by an individual ten minute interview where she required you to perform enchainments choreographed on the spot and to answer pertinent questions. But she was the best and I wanted that. What of my future if she didn't accept me? I was excited but I was completely terrified too.

So the night before the audition I couldn't get to sleep. I stood staring out over the roofs of Wandsworth, row upon row of TV aerials, and clusters of dark chimney pots, rehearsing in my mind how the class would go, wondering what questions I would be asked in the interview, how to reply intelligently and sound inspired. A bright crescent moon hung in the indigo sky and the sodium street lamp glowed in the street below. The last train, the speeding lights of its windows merging into a sudden streak of brightness, passed across my narrow view of the bridge with a sudden threatening roar. If I wanted to succeed I needed to try and relax. I lay down on the bed. Eventually I closed my eyes.

I didn't hear the alarm. Not even the noise of the early morning trains woke me up.

Chapter 4

I had to run all the way over the bridge to the station and wait absolutely ages for a train. And isn't that always the way? When you want something? You can stare up at the information board willing, willing, a destination to appear, and it doesn't. It doesn't! And then you panic and think how else can you get there. Bus? None that go fast enough that way. Taxi? What about money? And anyway if you give up the train, would there even be a taxi? All those trains running over that bridge, roar after roar after roar. And not one to save my life when I wanted it - and when one did eventually come and I had changed to the Piccadilly line, that stopped on the way in the tunnel. Twice!

So I arrived at the studios hot and in a fearful panic and several minutes late. They had waited but I knew I'd wrecked my chances before I'd danced a step. And it was so embarrassing making them wait even longer while I changed. You know what it's like then too - it's as if everything gets in a tangle just to provoke you. And then all those eyes following me as I found a place at the barre, and their annoyance at having to move up, give up hard won personal space to make room for someone who couldn't be on time. Then Olivia Orlando's dismissive glance. So I began that class keyed up, in a terrible sweat, and appalled at my own stupidity. How could I have slept through the alarm? Worse, I could see immediately, even in the initial stretching, that the Orlando standards were high and the competition was really fierce. I hadn't a hope in hell.

"Plié, first, second and fifth position. Port de bras

forward, demi-pointe and balance," came the orders. "Stand up straight. Deportment. Think about it! This is your future! Imagine there is one contract, one place in the ballet company you most want to dance in. Earn it! Dance for it!"

Well, this is it, some future, I thought, sinking deep into the first plié. They won't take me. But there was nothing else in the world I wanted to do. At least I could say I'd tried. I forced myself lower into the plié, ignored my muscles' objections, tried to forget all the other candidates and concentrated on winning through.

I danced for all I was worth, so desperate to please that I muffed most of the pirouettes, and got one enchainment totally wrong. But there were no second chances. A last sequence to the waltz from Swan Lake, you know, that interminable 'sweet Rosie O'Grady' one.... then whispered conversation between Olivia Orlando and someone next to her, and....

"Thank you."

That was all. Thank you! For once I was glad the class was finished. But the ordeal wasn't over yet.

"Line up. Forward, forward! Don't hang back. I want to be able to see you!" Her thin finger travelled along the line, singling people out, discussing them again in whispers. More pointing. More discussion. The finger aimed briefly at me but passed on without comment, without whispers.

I wanted to slink away into a corner and cry. But we were required to wait out in the dark hall - and there was still the interview to come. Little point bothering with that, but it would be embarrassing to leave now. All the others were perched on benches or standing in groups, eyes down but very aware of any and every movement, all waiting to be called in one at a time.

"Absolutely ghastly, isn't it?" hissed the girl next to me. She was sitting busily sticking layers of plasters round her red raw toes. "Ouch! How am I going to do any more pointe work?" she said breathlessly, "What if I have to do fouettés!" All the same she guided her feet gingerly back into the torturous ballet slippers.

Her name was Diana. I'd noticed her in the very last enchainment when I'd all but given up for myself. She had a kind of exuberance about her dancing that was really attractive. She was sure to be successful, as was the tall, elegant girl with her back to me in the far corner. Even from this angle she looked right.

I was called in before them both. Get rid of the duds first, I thought.

Olivia Orlando sat bolt upright and cross-legged in a cane peacock chair at the mirror end of the rehearsal room. She was studying my application form and smoking a cigarette. The man sat on her right, slightly behind. I'd forgotten him. He'd watched the class too, but his eyes had not been on me. His gaze had followed the tall girl, and Miss Exuberance. I felt giddy and hysterical with failure, sort of mad and throw-away. I stopped caring and focused numbly on Olivia. Her mouth, drawn wider than real with red lipstick, pursed briefly in around her cigarette. There was that little papery sound as the cigarette left her lips and she narrowed her dark eyes to avoid the smoke. Avoiding the smoke over the years had given her lines around her eyes. You can tell how long a person's smoked from that, you know. She'd spent a lifetime in dark theatres too, I could tell that from the colourless skin tone. Black jersey leggings outlined her long slim legs, a red stretch

28

crossover top gave her boobs great shape and her torso freedom of movement. It dated her though; that and the long too-black black hair swept up into a high ponytail. Did I want a teacher who was so definitely past it? The stiletto sandals she'd changed into were an elegant addition to her arched feet maybe, but a definite handicap to any choreography now surely. The man was dressed in black and did not speak. Somehow he was playing invisible.

I stood waiting, the sweat icy on my shoulders as Olivia Orlando turned the form over and read the other side. I tried to remember what was on it. Nothing exciting. Certainly nothing that would make me stand out. Date of birth, earlier training, education - I'd avoided that a bit, just put aiming for A levels. 'Hopes for the future'. Well, what do you put? I want to be a dancer....?

At last she looked up at me.

"Elaine Higham."

She'd pronounced it correctly. That was something.

"Turn sideways," she said. Then: "Now face the back wall."

I did both, wondering which part of me would look the worst. Stand up straight, deportment. She wanted that. I was pulling myself up and in from sheer habit though and I knew I couldn't look fat. I hadn't had the time or the stomach for food for at least twenty-four hours.

"Right."

I faced her again.

"Before you say anything to me, Elaine," she said - she sized up my face and neck, "it is to your advantage to be confident in here. Your career depends on it. If you sell yourself short, I may see you like that. It's up to you to convince me that you are worth taking on. What do you think are your best qualities?"

"As a...." My voice sounded high and small. I adjusted it down. " - a dancer?" Now I sounded breathy like Marilyn Monroe.

"As a person."

That was the last question I'd expected. As a person I didn't think I was up to much, nor did I see the connection. I said what I thought she expected to hear.

"I want very much to be a dancer."

Olivia glanced away. I was wasting her time.

"I suppose that makes me ambitious," I said quickly.

"Ambitious enough to overcome the physical difficulties of a late start? I see you didn't begin studying until you were - " She looked down at the form again.

"Thirteen," I prompted. "Yes."

"So do you always arrive late?"

"I'm really sorry about that." No point inventing any excuse, but lateness was beginning to look like a habit.

"Why this school?"

"It's the best."

She glowered. Flattery didn't appeal either.

"What else then?"

Don't sell yourself short.

"I work hard. I like to get things right."

"If I said to you not this term, but come back and audition again next year, what would you do?"

That was it, a way of fobbing me off. Next year, sometime, never.

"Next year's too late." No, don't give her another reason - "I'd come back! You won't put me off. I'd make sure you wouldn't be able to refuse me next time. And

30

I'd be out to prove you made the wrong decision today."

"There are other schools."

"I don't want other schools."

"Why ballet particularly? There are many forms of dance."

"Not for me."

"Variety may be the only way to get work. There are hundreds of dancers out there. Ballet takes only the cream."

"Then I'll be the cream."

"Your pirouettes are atrocious."

"Then I need your help, don't I? That's why I'm here, isn't it? How can I be a good dancer if I don't have the best teaching!"

I'd gone too far, I could tell. She wrote something on my form, passed it to the man and picked up another.

"Send in...Diana Meecham."

"No enchainments?"

"No," she said dismissively.

I turned to go. To hell with her then if she didn't want me. I left the room with my eyes dry and stinging bright and my head held high. A row of expectant faces turned as I emerged.

"Call Diana Meecham," I said, as if it was the Grand Inquisition and swept past them into the dressing room.

I made my escape quickly and instead of going into Leicester Square station, I walked all the way down to the river knowing I'd failed and feeling little, shrunk, and quite sick. I stood for a long time staring down into the churning depths of the grey water, then idly watching flotsam and jetsam being sucked out to sea on the retreating tide. The air was heavy with the sounds and fumes of traffic, the odour strangely intense, and sweet rather than sour, persuasively poisonous.

Ages later I went home on the District Line - now of course there was a train a minute. Only in the privacy of my bedroom did I let go and cry. How easily everything had gone wrong. How fragile were all my expectations. I didn't speak to my mother or Jonty. I didn't want anything to eat. I just went to bed.

I spent the next three weeks ignoring my studies and exam course work, and when it started, skipping the beginning of the new term at school. And agonizing over how I'd ever get through the rest of my life. I didn't bother to go to classes at Hammersmith either.

One day the phone rings. Rings and rings. Eventually my mother turns the television down and answers it. I hear her saying, 'She's ill, yes. Depressed. It must be flu', yes. I'll tell her...' She doesn't tell me but I know it's school. I don't care about that. I close my eyes again. There is no time. There is no space.

I hated our house with its lack of light and freezing draughts. My grandmother had perished in the room my mother slept in and no trace at all remained of my grandfather. My mother swore she had no recollection of him. The place was a prison from which there seemed to be no escape. But outside there was nowhere to go either. One day it occurred to me to ring in and tell Luigi I was ill. Though he had probably been pleased to save the wages, he sounded so sympathetic and accommodating that he made me feel quite guilty for forgetting completely about him, but it depressed me to think the cafe was all I had left. All the same I didn't go in.

Instead I lazed around doing absolutely nothing. I

32

suffered watching television a couple of times without making any effort to communicate with my mother, avoiding acknowledging her, leaving the room angrily if she so much as looked at me, but the screen might as well have been blank anyway. There was even a program on about ballet but I didn't watch it. I knew it would make me cry. After a while I did try to think about what I might do though. That was an absolute total blank! Future? There wasn't one. I was already pushing on age for ballet, and was convinced I was far too old to start anything else meaningful enough. I did see an opera program in passing on television as my mother flicked around the channels. Great love stories there too, but I had no voice. I sang like a cormorant. No, it was ballet. Or nothing. So nothing it would be.

Mostly I didn't emerge from my drab little bedroom, nor did I eat much. I just lay on my bed staring up at the dusty ceiling which I couldn't remember ever having been painted and listened disinterestedly to classical music on the radio, turned up so loud it had a numbing effect on my mind. And my mother's too no doubt, though she never once came and asked me what was going on, if I was all right. How dare she not come and ask me? I wanted to shout at someone, but no-one came. Well, Jonty did, but I threw him out. Talk to that kid? About ballet? He wouldn't have had the first clue. Days passed. I watched the trains come and go. Sometimes I just stared bleakly out of my window at the grimy brick walls and the bridge and my narrow view of grey river water.

Eventually I came up with one reasonable answer. I began planning how I could throw myself off the railway bridge into the river and end it all.... Yes. From the center, from the very center of the bridge. It was a way out at least. To celebrate I took a bath and lay for ages in the warm water feeling it lapping round me. Life seemed so tissue thin, so pointless... And there would be no pain, would there? Just falling, and river water lapping like this bath water, and then nothing. I would float with flowers in my hair like Ophelia.... Die. That would show that Olivia bloody Orlando, and make her wish she'd seen my startling capacity for playing the classic heroine. Yes, that would show her.

And my mother....

But before I had time to properly plan my dramatic exit, I received to my astonishment and utter joy, confirmation that Orlando's had accepted me. I truly believed my life had been saved for a reason. Fate is a strange thing, and I honestly believed that it had stepped in for the sake of art.

Chapter 5

In the dressing-room on the first day I discovered Diana Meecham had been chosen. And the elegant girl. She was leaning down tying the ribbons on her pointe shoes.

"What's her name?" I asked the exuberant Diana. Just for something to say. I was feeling as if I would expire from over-enthusiasm and for once I was prepared to make small talk with absolutely anyone who would respond. I needed assurances, even the smallest amount of friendly encouragement from any quarter, anything that might help me to survive the excitement of the first class.

"That's Beverley Soames," Diana whispered admiringly. "Her father, he's an advisor to the government. The family's really, really rich."

Beverley must have heard because as she straightened up she looked at me and a dazzling smile spread over her beautiful fairy-tale face. And it all happened in such slow motion somehow, my first sight of her. You know, like watching a film, when the heroine turns and you see her for the first time. And she fills the screen. She's it. Queen. Magic. Centre point. The reason for the story. The reason it started.

That was the moment when it began.

And I just stood there, staring, rooted to the spot, immediately in awe of this girl, aware of a physical confidence that absolutely appalled me. Her whole person, the way she moved, almost the air around her, was resonating with a wonderful kind of grace and tension, and I wanted to cry with rage and disappointment at the measure of it, that any one person could have been given so much. The rest of the room and the other people in it all seemed to be in her shadow, ordinary and unnecessary .

Is that what falling in love at first sight is? Instant attraction. Desire? Seeing the image of what you want. But can't jealousy hit you like that too? A deep unconscious sting of wanting that clots in you, right down deep inside your heart?

And right then a beat like a little drum beat started repeating inside me....beat, beat, beat....if only I could be like her, everything would be all right, and I could have anything I wanted, dancing, success, anything. And there she was, the extreme example, the real thing, smiling at me with madonna eyes, trusting me, willing me to ask her how - because apart from the beauty, there had to be some secret to that kind of aura.

There had to be a key.

Watch her, Elaine, urged the drum beat. Watch her. Follow her. Don't let her out of your sight. Her life must be wonderful. Yours could be too if you were like that. Want what she wants. Have what she has. Watch. Borrow. Stalk. Pursue. Copy. Copy until you get it right.

And I tell you, the only future for me then was to step forward, move right into her shadow, and like a thief, follow my prey. Maybe it was an unconscious decision. Maybe not.

"I'm absolutely shaking, aren't you?" Beverley said, and even her voice was like silver. "I feel as if I'm going to die of nervousness!"

She looked at me expectantly, willing me to answer. I hardly dared smile back. I'd almost stopped breathing. There had to be a way....there was some way....

And I thought, all I have to do, all I have to do to have all that, is to get in close enough.

At first though I stood back, in awe of her. Shy. And afraid, yes, afraid. I viewed her only from a distance - but I saw every move, every action. In class, and when she was dressing, what she wore. Hiding myself though. Not letting her see me, me dressing. She had none of my awkwardness, none of my physical shyness. She was my age, but somehow I felt like a child beside her. I watched the way she walked out of the studio each evening, shoulders straight, head held high. I spied on her constantly. Admired her. Most of all, far and away, I adored watching how she glittered and sparkled when she danced, like a jewel held up to the light. And I swear all I wanted then was for some of that light to rub off on me.

Making friends I thought would be reasonably simple. First you made polite overtures, offered a little thoughtfulness here and there. Nothing important, not to start with. Maybe you just picked up something dropped, smiled when you passed it back. Lent a hairclip. Mentioned the weather. And so my friendship with Beverley Soames began like that, with tentative looks, and shy verbal exchanges. Sometimes we talked about how hard the classes were - though of course in spite of her agreeing with me, they weren't for her. Even then. And I would take up a position at the barre next to her, not every evening to start with, but then more often, until it surprised her if I didn't.

Then slowly proper conversations came. We began trading opinions, shared amusement, talked about school rather than just dancing. Then came co-operation, compromise, and proceeding on, becoming real and special - but this needed time and real work - which would lead into a kind of mutual devotion, a shared response.

"Get off my things!"

I hadn't realized her precious practice clothes were on the floor. Quickly I stepped aside and gathering them up, held them out to her meekly. "Sorry."

Her smile as always was devastating in its brilliance.

Friendship.

But copying. Imitation. Becoming that other person. That isn't so easy.

Building. It's like building. Brick on brick. You have to take on new ways of doing, of being, and then make them into habits. Move after move. It's an exacting and painstaking process. Not an equal exchange but a following - but far more subtle than becoming the obedient and faithful disciple. It has to look exactly equal. Every action, every utterance has to fit in so as not arouse suspicion. It takes time, and intense application - and remember I was desperate for the whole Beverley Soames image, the dancing most of all, but the every day mannerisms too, the grace, the complete style. Then, I imagined, the confidence, her magnetism, her charisma would come too, quite naturally, as day follows night.

And for Beverley, I'm sure, when the sun rose each morning, it was doing so expressly for her.

I was absorbing every detail. Every detail. Such constant effort meant I had to give up trying to make friends with other people. I might have really liked Diana, any other time. But it was part of the bargain in a way, concentration. If you want something enough, you can only be completely, utterly loyal to that one idea. Anything else is confusing. You have to be totally single minded and narrow your gaze.

Sometimes I'd forget for a moment and return to my old ways, and end up back at square one. Habits are only ingrained by repetition, little by little. I knew I had to learn to remember in my sleep. Even sleep the same. And I was living my daily life one nano-second behind, concentrating, watching, watching, analyzing. How did she do that?

Beverley didn't notice. The truly confident don't. She accepted me as her friend generously and without question. And I did adore her, truly. But then that was only what she expected. And after all, isn't imitation the highest form of flattery? She basked in the attention. She liked people to defer to her. And if she saw her own familiar reactions reflected, well, isn't there mirroring in every relationship, in the body language: sitting the same, the same poses. laughing at the same things, discussing similarities? There's no threat in that.

But when I think of him kissing the tips of my fingers in the dark hallway. Of him pressing my body back against the wall, the fear and excitement of him slowly, silently opening the fastenings on my blouse, and his lips whispering against my breasts, when he was hers....but wait. I need to show you things as they were.

I'd had so-called friends before of course, at Hammersmith, and at school but - well, they were far more acquaintances than anything. Hardly even that. I didn't know them or like them. They were just girls I ate lunch with, sat next to, that they occasionally compared or copied homework with. But remember I was tolerated rather than liked myself, and I can't honestly say I made any effort to form lasting relationships. One girl I do remember, but only visually - an excellent swimmer. I never actually spoke to her but on sports afternoons at the swimming baths I loved to watch her gliding swiftly through the water like a fish. But that was just watching. That's all. No conversation or anything. I don't remember even knowing the 'fish's' name, or even what year she was in. Otherwise there wasn't anyone interesting, nobody I really cared about. Not until I saw Beverley did I ever imagine there was anything I wanted from other people. Needed.

It was with Beverley that I discovered the street market in Soho. It's Saturday, the dance class is finished. We are not yet on intimate terms. She is simply hungry, wants to walk to Berwick Street to buy some fruit, asks who wants to come.

"I will."

I should be considering Luigi. It's barely half an hour until I'm expected to start my shift.

The others, recognizing the kind of pending togetherness that we probably already display, back off, decline. Beverley smiles at me, perhaps, I suspect, a little disappointed that it is me, but it's as if I've agreed to some wonderful conspiracy. She's pleased to have someone who's so terribly eager to go with her. But she expected nothing less. We're last to leave the dressing-room, and there's no hurry as we dodge across the traffic in St. Martin's Lane and cut through the back streets of Soho. Through the bean shoot sweet and sour, peanut oil sleaze of Chinatown. Past the pseudo pagodas and the red faced lions and green dragons. Two girls together.

"Shall we?"

The flash in the photo booth makes us laugh. "Closer now," Beverley says. Flash! "One of us at a time now. Down!"

I duck. Flash! Then she ducks. Flash! We wait impatiently by the slot, smelling the fumes of us developing in the machine. Suddenly the four image strip lands. Upside down. Beverley snatches it up, shrieks in horror.

"Can I see?"

She throws them at me. "Have them!"

I shriek because she did and pocket them.

We run up Rupert Street past the hooded plastic of those stalls, and through the dark alley of erotic sparkles and shadows where the sex theatres are.

What was it that delighted me about the smell on the other side of that, the fruit and the vegetables and the noise of Berwick Street market that day? Was it because it was our first time out together? Or the late September sunlight? Or that essential readiness? Like the lush plumpness of shiny purple plums, the astringent ripe green smell of cooking apples, the clawing sweetness of yellow and zebra striped bananas. The shouts perhaps, the people milling through, the cabbage leaves cluttering the gutters, being stepped on, left bruised. Or was it just the freshness of what was on the barrows? The real thing when I'd always eaten frozen at home. Stuff out of packets, that's much more convenient. Doesn't need peeling, or any preparation. Cut the packet open, that's all.

Was it walking beside Beverley? Doing what she

would do? Being with her. Trying to be like her in this new setting.

She stops suddenly at a stall and points.

"Look! Watermelon."

"Fancy some, darling?" says the young barrow boy, reaching for it. He doesn't wait for her to say yes, he just carves off a slice. The knife runs easily through the flesh pushing the rows of black seeds aside. As he hands the crimson wedge to her, the juice dribbles back down his fingers. He wipes them on his apron and gazes admiringly at Beverley. He's not expecting to be paid. You can see he doesn't care about the money. He just wants her to smile at him.

Of course she does. She excited, though he's simply another admirer. Not that she really notices them, they notch themselves up. I, on the other hand, am crestfallen. I am not hungry, but I resent the fact he hasn't noticed me. He doesn't offer me watermelon. His eyes are fixed on Beverley.

To give her credit she realizes suddenly. "Cut it in half," she demands. He blinks, registers my presence and in an instant, obeys. He'd do anything for this beautiful girl.

Triumphantly she passes half to me, as if it is her gift. The barrow boy smiles at me now as she moves away, not in the same way though. He looks as if he's going to ask me to pay. I thank him and back away, and hurry after Beverley. We wander through more of the market, past more barrows, and dank little shops, costumiers, fabrics, antiquarian books, pungent cheese specialists. It's busy, but it's Beverley I'm concentrating on. She has such beautiful deportment - even in jeans and a simple jacket she looks chic. And it's astonishing the effect she has on people. Everyone notices her as she passes. She's laughing. I laugh too. She's slurping on the sweet flesh of the free melon, and flicking the seeds off her fingers. I try it, but my aim is nothing like hers. I follow her, one step behind her, in her shadow.

"We could drive you home sometimes." She casts the melon skin carelessly aside. It lands half-moon in the gutter beside me.

I would discard my melon into the gutter too only maybe someone's looking. Instead I stuff what's left of it into a box of waste paper and other junk by a shop door. The woman inside frowns at me as if I have contaminated her rubbish. I should have just done what Beverley did. Then no-one would have challenged me.

"My street's one way. Difficult to get to." It isn't, of course.

"Putney High Street, then? Daddy won't mind."

Eventually when we reach the buzz and traffic jams of Oxford Street, Beverley meets someone she knows, a sixth former from her school, who's wearing a fantastic wrap around dress. Italian shoes and butter gold earrings. Beverley's so busy talking she doesn't introduce me. She's completely forgotten I'm there, I think. She leaves me and goes off with this other girl. She doesn't even say she's going. She suddenly links arms with her and disappears off into the crowd and I see them catch a bus. And I think, I'll do that one day. Leave people filled with disappointment, wanting more.

I pull the strip of photos from my pocket. Beverley looks sensational. When I'd ducked the white of my blouse reflected the flash - the picture might have been taken in a studio, whereas mine! But the ones of us, laughing, leaning in. They're satisfyingly together. Close.

I had to find my way back through a maze of streets passing the watermelon man again, fast in case he saw me and wanted paying. And alone through sex alley and the sweet and sour dragons. But it was mad, I was elated, even though Beverley had left me standing. When eventually I got to the cafe I hardly noticed Luigi shouted at me for being late.

Chapter 6

It was definitely Beverley's dancing which was the hardest to copy because I wanted it the most. I had to teach myself new ways to move physically, a slightly different approach. And there's that moment when you can't do the step the old way, and you haven't quite grasped the new way and the movement doesn't work at all. That in-between time. You just have to be patient and try again and you could cry with the frustration of it all.

And have I mentioned what it feels like to dance?

Early morning. Evenings. Light slanting in through windows, mirrors, a piano. Dancers attached like icicles to the barre, vertical bare necks and horizontal shoulders shining, Beginning a slow and painstaking warm up. Extending the foot 'en croix', in the shape of a cross. Reflections, patterns, ritual. Sober black practice clothes over white. Genuflection with a reverence for physical perfection, a careful stretching and tuning and flexing of muscles to their limits, and then further. Limbs full of strength yet light as air. The scene seems almost spiritual.

Towards a life on stage, in performance, is what all this practice is for. Costumes, sets, lighting, and dancers. Put together they weave a kind of magic on the senses, a transformation, temporarily suspending reality. Think of Degas. It's another world, the theatre. And all the old romantic classical ballets are about love and death. Mythological. Modern dance might be more abstract, but the original movements are still there. And either way the soul is freed, and the body becomes intangible, apparently made of something less than solid flesh.

Imagine it. Sounds wonderful, don't you think, to feel like that? Magic?

Well, to get to that freedom is the hardest, cruel, most painful thing. Stinging tendons. Straining the muscles to raise the leg higher. Rejoicing when every nerve in your body is on red alert. In ballet the legs and feet must turn out which is really quite unnatural. And dancing on pointes? If God had meant us to do that he would have given us blocks instead of toes. I remember seeing a television program about Rudolf Nureyev and I've never seen toes like them - all knarled stumps, almost deformed, crunched up. Probably ruined by all that Georgian toe dancing he did early on.

Ballet's not a career anyway, more a magnificent obsession, like a religion, requiring extraordinary effort and clarity of purpose, and oh yes, most essential, the ability to suffer. Pushing nerves, sinews, muscles, bones to the extremes of endurance. Sometimes beyond that too. Crucifying yourself. I heard of someone who was prepared to have her feet broken just to get a better arch! Dance does have its moments of course, a kind of wild delirium, which I suspect is rather like taking drugs. Exercise does that, doesn't it? Releases a hormone into your system that gives you a high?

Yet there is more to it than that.

When you can do it, just sometimes when everything's working, you're performing and suddenly the balance is there, the control, and you feel the significance of what you're doing and you know you can't fail, it is as if you are tuned in to some extraordinary magical force. Dance is temporal art. You're up there with the gods. It's a heady place to be.

One Saturday by chance Beverley's walking through May's Court just when I'm emerging hot and bothered from a hard afternoon's waitressing. For the Beverleys of this world life doesn't involve having to work. I don't want to be seen here, but it's too late. I can't duck back inside however much I'd like to.

"Hello," she says, seeing me immediately. "You look hot."

I feel like ugly molten red lava now.

What is it about Beverley? No sooner has she stopped outside his cafe, than Luigi is in his doorway, ostensibly taking the air, but staring admiringly at her and nodding and smiling at me, willing me to explain who this beautiful girl is.

There's no way round, except by telling the truth to Beverley..

I try to carry it off with some panache. "Thees is the leetle place wherea I work." The Italian accent doesn't seem to impress Beverley, and Luigi looks faintly offended.

"Really?"

I cringe, wondering what she's thinking when she glances past me and sizes it all up. And then she looks at me. Now her image of me is Elaine Higham, waitress in a back street cafe.

Luigi saves the day. "You want to bring your friend for coffee?"

He wipes down a table with a flourish as if he is the waitress, and produces two steaming cappuccinos, and some individually wrapped bite-size almond biscuits and a vase with a carnation in it.

When reluctantly I have to offer to pay, "My

pleasure," he says.

"He's sweet," says Beverley, as he disappears behind the counter. He eyes her over the cups stacked above the Expresso machine with reverence, as if he thinks he has royal patronage.

Beverley sips her coffee and smiles at me. "It's rather exciting in here. Maybe we could meet here sometimes. When we want to talk. Better still, do you want to come over to my house tomorrow?"

A step closer.

Beverley, and that elusive shimmery quality of hers. The turn of her head, the grace of her movements. Her innate knowledge of when to flash that disarming smile. Her aura. She knew she had that, of course. And it was her birthright. No-one could take it away from her, could they?

You wouldn't think so.

But her exotic features might be copied with the right make-up, and with careful diet, the slender figure. She emphasized that perfectly with the simplicity of the clothes she chose. And she had beautiful underwear. Silk or stretch lace like that was what I wanted too. And her long legs - she had the most elegant ankles and arched feet I've ever seen on anyone. When she danced on pointe she hardly seemed to touch the floor. I set about cultivating a lightness which might give a similar illusion.

But her name, Beverley Soames - there's a ring to that, wouldn't you say?

Not like Elaine Higham.

"Do you think sex is important?"

Beverley and I were lying on the grass next to this

sort of mini beach thing they have in Bishop's Park, a pond with a sloping shallow end and edged with sand for kids to play in. It was a Sunday in late October and now I was spending all my spare time with Beverley as if I'd known her all my life. Friendship flourishes when you work at it. We'd taken a picnic out at the suggestion of her mother who looked bored to see me arriving at the house yet again. I was certain she considered me rather a dull friend for her daughter, and would have suggested anything to avoid having me in her home. But actually because the weather was surprisingly warm the picnic had been rather a good idea. Lazy and giggly and gossipy. Different anyway for a girl who was forever cooped up in school or at the ballet studio. Or having to work in a cafe.

"Well, do you?"

So there I was that autumn, lying back with the afternoon sun on my face, tongue-tied and suddenly utterly ashamed that at nearly eighteen I had not the first clue about whether I did or I didn't think sex or men were important. Or even how to answer her so as not to look stupid. I hated the way she made me feel sometimes, that if I could actually come up with an answer, whatever I said wouldn't be good enough anyway, she'd easily better it.

Perhaps being in Beverley's shadow was the last place I should have been, I felt so overwhelmed by it.

But back to the conversation. At that stage I had never seriously considered sex. Love, romance. Oh yes, that. But sex? I mean, you know about it, you couldn't miss it. They drum it into you before you leave primary school for goodness sake. Good thing they did because my mother never mentioned it. And some girls go off and do it and there are whispers, and out loud smirky chats about it all the time, innuendoes, and bragging. And though it's severely embarrassing, it's nice touching yourself suddenly, or stretching your nightie down through that crack. And you get periods and all that, and use tampons but actually it doesn't mean much. You don't have to take it particularly personally, do you? Not the actual intercourse side of it anyhow, but then if you ignore it for long enough, nor do you realize the strength of the threat, or how your own desire might suddenly overwhelm you.

Now I think about it, that picnic day was probably the moment when the idea of a man physically touching me became real in my mind, and I consciously considered what it might feel like, what he might do, and whether it would be different from the nightie, the sudden draw and heat and relief of that. That picnic was when it first occurred to me that this was something I really ought to be thinking more about. Late as usual!

"Who do you fancy then?"

"Sergei?" I offered, hopefully.

She screwed up her nose. "Sex with the invisible man?" Her eyes were shut. There was a little smile forming on her lips. "No. There must be better than that." she said.

There would be though, wouldn't there? For her. Someone with everything to offer, someone who men would fall over each other for. Well, I knew that at least. That sex would be easy for her, like everything else.

She's lying there on the grass. I could just reach out and touch her skin. Feel, maybe like a man would, what it's like. I tremble knowing instinctively how smooth, how sensational and soft, how faultless it would be, because this is Beverley Soames, the perfect woman, the ultimate experience. But is that what I want? Is it her I want to touch? Isn't it me I want touched? Aren't I lying on the grass too? Suddenly for an instant I'm inside Beverley. Right inside her image. I close my eyes and I'm being watched by Sergei because he's all I can think of, like I'm watching her. It's wildly embarrassing how much the thought of what's meant to happen suddenly physically excites me.

Wetness brings me back to reality and I press my legs together fearfully. I glance at Beverley. Thankfully she still has her eyes closed.

She's so close and her body is so beautiful it wears me out now just to look at it. I am exhausted by it, by its perfect shape, by the prettiness of her face, the darkness and shine of her hair, and the line and grace of her neck and shoulders. And I am worn out suddenly by wanting to be like her. Exhausted by the effort. She's the success. Why can't I just settle for second best?

But I can't.

And I'll never forget that day.

I remember thinking then - no, knowing, that things would never be easy for me - that I would always have to fight hard for what I wanted.

Chapter 7

Beverley's father, George Soames, was easy to be nervous of. He arrived back at their house from business in Paris just as Beverley was showing me inside the first time. Before this I'd only seen him in the front seat of his silver Mercedes. Simply a driver in the dark, while Beverley and I chattered in the back. Now as he climbed out of his car and walked up the steps towards us I recognized the resemblance. Beverley was so obviously his daughter. He had the aura too, that powerful physical presence. She had simply inherited it.

And now I was looking at him. There was something tall and threatening and thrillingly classy about the straightness of his back, and his well cut suit. Nothing creased the image. He seemed so immaculately pressed, so ready for anything. His handkerchief in his breast pocket arranged just so intrigued me. He looked more youthful than his wife though I decided, as I was introduced to him, and somehow too good for her. Forty something, was he? About my own father's age, I thought, with a sting of envy.

George was beautiful, you see, if you can say a man is beautiful; tall, trim, realized. I like a man to look established, don't you? Responsible. And nice trustworthy hands too. His eyebrows were fine, dark. And the face was strong, well-proportioned like Beverley's (though she had her mother's delicacy and Mrs Soames's more appropriate height).

I was surprised Beverley just said hello. She didn't hug her father or anything. Hadn't he been away?

"Call me George," he said to me, firmly shaking my

hand before going on past us into the house.

I was in very unfamiliar surroundings that afternoon. A family group. A wealthy home – huge, red brick, and draped with Virginia creeper, right by Wimbledon Common, facing it, but hidden behind gates and a high brick wall. In the lush garden, absolutely full of flowering bushes and plants, you would swear you were out in the middle of the country, it was so quiet. A Victorian conservatory on the side was dotted with lime-coloured maidenhair ferns and trails of heavily scented hot-house plants amongst blue verdigris wrought iron furniture and intricately woven cane chairs. Further indoors a daily cleaning lady kept constant apple-pie order amongst the paintings and the sofas and the pale carpets.

Here was a side of Beverley I didn't know. She was doing things I'd never seen her do, being the daughter I hadn't seen her be, and I wanted to absorb everything. And to fit in myself. For a few anxious minutes I was left alone in the sitting room while she went to help her mother bring in the afternoon tea. In spite of the cold outside, the room was too warm - central heating radiators, and a huge coal fire as well, which was in fact gas, but looked so real it completely fooled me to start with. I waited in the center of the pale moss-coloured carpet, afraid to sit in any of the off white and feather-soft armchairs. Table lamps, ornaments, were all placed as if by some magazine design. Adorning the walls were simple pencil drawings and gentle watercolours. It wasn't a room I could sit down alone in and relax.

George came in carrying a sheaf of papers, glanced at me, and fed a CD into an impressive hi-fi set up.

"Do you like Fauré ?"

I nodded, hoping he did mean a composer. Maybe he was referring to the paintings, but when after a second the gentle notes throbbed on the air all round me, it was obvious, and I began memorizing the melody immediately, concentrating, to be sure I would recognize it again.

"Do sit down," he said, settling easily into a chair himself and leafing through his papers. Now he'd changed into more casual clothes, softening the earlier formal edges. I perched tentatively on the arm of the sofa. Then I stood up again worrying that perching on the arms of sofas wasn't socially correct and moved across to the window.

George glanced up. "I don't bite," he said.

I swallowed. "No," I said feebly, staring out very intently at the view of Wimbledon Common.

Beverley appeared then to my great relief and George's attention returned to her. I noticed all that Sunday afternoon how his gaze followed her. Whenever Beverley was in his sight, his expression, a mixture of delight and intelligent concern for her made me ache with envy. I longed for a father who would look at me like that.

George had a funny attitude to dancing though.

"So you're another one, entranced by this ballet idea, are you? It's only a physical outlet for young girls, you know. A nice hobby, but not essential."

His wife glanced briefly at him and then began pouring tea out of a silver teapot into the delicate bone china cups and saucers. She added milk.

Beverley, gazing out the window now herself as if she wasn't really listening to what was being said, muttered: "Seven years of not essential." No-one else would have heard her.

"She's done her proper homework, I hope?" George went on. "It's only a few weeks to the exams now. These results are important."

No-one answered him. Mrs Soames seemed too engrossed in cutting neatly into the lemon cake. She had made it especially for my visit she said brightly, breaking the lengthy silence.

"She didn't actually make it herself," Beverley said under her breath, this time directly to me.

Was I supposed to answer that? Or ask about it? I shifted in the chair a little. Whoever had made the cake, I could smell its piquant flavor from my seat on the elegant sofa next to Beverley, and I contemplated the calories it contained with dismay. And the slices were enormous. Just one bite would burst me through my waistband. Beverley's waistband at that. Helping me to make a good impression she'd lent me her long blue skirt to wear with my blue china-silk blouse. Borrowing it had given me some confidence, but could I chance the cake? Beverley, with the assurance of the truly beautiful, dressed with utter simplicity and her clothes always looked classy on her. Today she had on a pale button-through long linen skirt and a stunning handknit and new suede shoes. We were both wearing her smudge-proof lash-building mascara and her new kohl eyeliner too, and crossing my legs like her, I was trying hard to look as thin and sophisticated as she did. Though she looked older, I wasn't so far off eighteen either, and we were both being passionately theatrical.

"But you have finished your work," Mrs Soames said, putting cake slices on plates. "Haven't you, dear?"

"Daddy fusses so much," said Beverley, smiling

demurely. "As if I wouldn't do every bit!"

"Best to be practical," her father said, catching me looking at him again. He smiled at me and I felt I was being asked to confirm his opinion. I wanted to. I was desperate for Beverley's parents to like me, him especially suddenly. I couldn't understand anyone thinking ballet was any less than the whole reason for being, but it was my first proper visit to this household. I nodded.

Beverley glared at me. Surely she understood I was only being polite? I shook my hair back a little as if that was what I had been doing all the time.

But now the piece of cake was on its way to me, and if I wanted to please Beverley's mother I would have to eat it.

"Where did you say your father works?" Mrs Soames asked, passing it to me.

"Bellacoora." Pure invention. No such place. I'd thought up the name years before as a kind of protection, an unrecognizable never-never land. I had no idea if my father was still in our same house, or even if he was alive. But he must be alive, I thought, because the allowance is still being paid. "It's near Cowra in New South Wales."

The slice of cake was even bigger than I'd anticipated. "Thank you, Mrs Soames."

"You've been to Australia, haven't you, Daddy?" said Beverley, indicating her solidarity, showing off, or testing me out, I wasn't sure which, and for a horrible irrational moment I imagined that with her father's connections I might be caught out in my little white lie. I held my breath.

"Perth," George said.

My confidence returned with a rush.

"My father runs a big cattle station," I added, for even better effect.

"That's a hard life, I expect," said Mrs Soames.

"Oh yes," I said. "Very isolated. My mother and I much prefer being in London."

"Beverley mentioned you have a brother. Wouldn't he have liked it?"

"He's not into that sort of thing," I said quickly.

"Do you see your father?"

"Holidays," I lied, trying desperately to keep up with their expectations. "He comes to England sometimes."

"There wouldn't have been any local ballet schools for you to have gone to there, I don't suppose," said Beverley's mother, passing me my cup of tea.

Well, I thought, maybe that's one thing I can thank my father for after all these years! I doubted the truth of her words though. Even with my few memories I knew people could have funny ideas about Australia. Everything I'd ever seen and read about it suggested that it was freer and much more modern than Britain. Not only that, people seemed to think nothing of travelling great distances when they wanted something.

"The young people there can concentrate on their exams in that case," said George Soames and winked at me. Had he detected the nervousness in my expression, or was he just amused at his wife's apparent ignorance? Or was he teasing Beverley? I cast my eyes down at the enormous slice of lemon cake on my plate as he bit enthusiastically into his.

"You don't think like that, do you?" I asked Beverley, when we were alone in her bedroom. She was letting me try on the expensive Aquascutum coat her mother had given her for Christmas.

"What?" she asked, stretching out on her bed.

I pulled the coat collar up higher. "That ballet's just a physical outlet?"

"Oh that. Daddy's so stupid. It's more important than...." she fought for some possible comparison... "than living!"

"That's just how I feel too."

I stepped back from the mirror to under the light so as to get the full effect, deeply satisfied with my new friend's analogy. Even though we'd only known each other properly a few weeks by then, I knew Beverley adored ballet as much as I did. She had definitely become my kindred spirit.

"And more important than men," I added, deciding it was possible to go one better.

Beverley looked sceptical. But her father wasn't about to let her down and she had always several boyfriends at her disposal at school who were keen to take her out. The current one wasn't her Dream Man, but it was very convenicnt to have someone Very Interested.

"My mother says it's best to humor them."

It seemed to me that was certainly what she did with her father.

But a good father deserves better than that.

From the moment Beverley had first instructed him that they would drop me in Putney High Street on their way home, I'd noticed how George Soames seemed prepared to do anything for his daughter even if she didn't humor him. Compensation perhaps for all the times his government business required all his time and attention.

Beverley's allowance for clothes, for instance, was an astonishing sum. Though my mother actually gave me a little to spend that winter, it was hardly sufficient now I was trying desperately to imitate my new friend's style. As if in response, and of course now she knew I had to work, Beverley offered to come shopping with me. It frightened the life out of me the first time, when she insisted on going to the Kings Road and entering all the expensive boutiques, but I soon saw why. A right little double act we were. She'd reach down really expensive designer clothes from the racks, and hold them up against herself and ask the assistants for help. What did they think? Were there other colours? Surely this price couldn't be right? How blissfully inexpensive! They buzzed eagerly round her, and she nonchalantly kept them busy, asking about smaller sizes, inquiring the price.

It wasn't shoplifting, what we were doing, it was idea stealing. My role was to memorize the new colours, the cut and styles, and then we would go out into the freezing streets and walk and walk, to Oxford Street, or Kensington High Street, searching the ordinary shops and the smart second hand shops for a cheaper version. Sometimes we found one. And just sometimes even the real thing might have a mark on it and she'd insist on it being reduced. Or she'd even bargain if it had no mark! Oh, the audacity of the rich! In the cheaper shops though she always seemed a little out of her depth - she much preferred shopping for what she called labels.

We weren't always successful, but it gave me more time in her company and sometimes, as she said one day, it was amazing how nice some down market things were, and how we achieved a much more fashionable look for me with very little outlay. I was surprised to find myself feeling slightly patronized by that remark, as much as I loved those excursions.

I was learning of course, but it was still a matter of how to wear as much as what to wear. And who to wear it for.

In the beginning Beverley was sweet enough not to buy anything expensive in front of me, and occasionally she even bought one of the cheaper garments for herself. These bargains she enjoyed showing off to George. I guessed that in this she was 'humoring him', but it was amusing to see his face glow with pride at the thought of his daughter handling the money he gave her with such care. The rich like to think they can be economical.

After our shopping expeditions and sometimes after class too Beverley and I would find a sultry Italian coffee house - when we wanted a change from Luigi's - and if I had no money left, she would buy two cups of dark expresso to warm us up and we'd sit for ages giggling and talking and planning for the future. And when I think I was nearly eighteen! God, how immature I was! Such a child! But she could be too. For me, though, making wild, romantic plans was a release I suppose, and that time wasn't wasted since I had no other social life - no opportunity, nor the money for it, and certainly no home life, and our coffee times were a way to lessen the tension of my claustrophobic little world. After all, the physical torture of ballet was eating me alive. For Beverley dancing, like everything else, came easily, and she'd been doing it so much longer too, so this was just a game for her I think, but I needed to know I was heading somewhere wonderful and that success wasn't too far off.

And it was only a game in a way. We would imagine it all - a famous ballet company, in Paris probably. At first we only discussed favourite solos. Then both of us were ballerinas, alternating in the leading roles. Sometimes we would be performing together. To her Aurora in Sleeping Beauty, my part would be dancing the Bluebird pas de deux. The next performance, she agreed she would take the Bluebird part and I, the princess. Then there was Swan Lake, and Nutcracker and Sylphide and.... a never ending list! We would be feted, applauded and treated like queens. We leaned on the table, and listened seriously to each other's ideas and sipped our coffees and imagined.

Beverley would be my friend forever, I knew. I thought about her every second of the day. I never invited her to my home, though. I didn't dare. That would strain the friendship far too far. I mean my house? My mother?

I was visiting her home though, as often as possible now, and though Mrs Soames often ignored me, she no longer seemed to mind my being there. And when he was at home, her father was so nice to me. I felt almost like his daughter, and began to experience a security I had never known before.

Another of the things we did - God, it's really embarrassing. I can hardly believe I'm remembering this! We would practice in front of the bedroom mirror how to get the best out of any pose, sometimes casting our eyelids down for full effect, or trying out how to flirt up to a theatre's back circle. A particular smile suited particularly flashy steps, the full classical ballerina bit -

but there was also drama to be explored. Beverley searched for and found 'Stories of the Ballets', an old book belonging to her mother, and we practiced how to be near death, or heartbroken, angry, forgiving, or entirely in love. Mostly when we did this Beverley ended up collapsed in hysterical fits of giggling saying how idiotic we were being. Such retards! One of her favourite words, that. But for me this time was a period of serious observation and learning, even if it did have its lighter side. I could study her from every angle, close in, and I was even beginning to understand exactly how she used the muscles in her face and neck.

One Sunday I can remember catching the bus to Wimbledon just to stand on the Common opposite her house and imagine being inside with her and her family. The house is along near the windmill, and though it was coming up for spring and bright, it was bitterly cold. Anyone going for a walk and noticing me, must have been surprised to see me still there braving the weather when they returned. It was like when I was a kid and people used to see me in the streets when I should have been at school. That same suspicious look. I didn't care. I hardly understood why I needed to be there myself, except that it made me feel happier. Perhaps it was the fresh air. Perhaps though I was standing a little nearer my goal.

Chapter 8

May ended hectic and hot, ballet classes and rehearsals for the student demonstrations crammed in with last minute exam revision and more revision. And my work at Luigi's. Exhausting, but I was actually living up to my side of that pact with my mother that I'd pass my exams, though she didn't have to push it particularly hard. It was Beverley's influence. No. More her father's influence. Him attaching such importance to the exams. That and being able to study with Beverley at her house instead of at home alone in my own dingy little room. Beverley and I had begun to use every moment of our spare time together spreading our work out all around us on her bedroom floor. Even though we were at different schools the subjects were the same, but there were fewer in each class at her school. That luxury was costing her father a fortune.

June and the A Levels. For Beverley just another success to come. For me the possibility of complete disaster because of a fearful last minute threat my mother suddenly made that I had to give up ballet and earn a proper living. And I wouldn't pass anything, would I? Because I was never at home. Accusing me, in the odd moments she spoke to me at all, of not studying and ignoring my course-work. She wouldn't be convinced that I was doing it at Beverley's.

"I warn you, if you fail - "

I don't know how she thought she'd stop me going to class.

In those three vital weeks Luigi would only give me two nights off from my job to study even when I told him about her threats. "You do this work for your mama, maybe one day you understand my till? And you will want more hours soon, yes?" Denying me time to study, but offering extra shifts. Knowing I would soon need more money to afford full-time classes.

So you can see the examinations loomed large. As did Beverley's school boyfriend - Mr Nightmare we were calling him by now. He was becoming increasingly over-anxious for experience she told me.

"Will you humor him?" I asked her.

My own experience was still severely limited - confined to a snog behind the school gym with a boy from the lower sixth form. I was grateful to him for even speaking to me, astonished and flattered when he said he fancied me. Maybe, I thought happily, as he took my hand, being with Beverley was really beginning to have some effect. But the encounter amounted to nothing but confusion, his disgusting body odour and my revulsion. And afterwards hiding from him, in case. I needn't have worried. Neither he nor any of his friends ever bothered me again. There were plenty of girls who were game.

Anyway it had to be better than that!

Beverley laughed. "What do you think? Do you think I will?"

It had been a silly question. Beverley Soames didn't waste herself on school boys. She had good looks and great connections. And confidence with a capital C. She was made for better things. Anyone could see that.

The image of Beverley, those photographs in the market, that one of her on her own? I took it to a print shop and had it photocopied and enlarged. And enlarged again. And copied again. And again. And I took them home, all those copies, and pinned them all up in the privacy of my room so that I had her everywhere. Wallpapered the walls with her. If you want to imitate someone you have to have the image you want fixed in your mind. Imprinted on your psyche. Last sight before you go to sleep. So that you wake up to it. And in that photo she was captured, the exact contours of her face, her eyes, her lips, the shape of her neck. I swallowed that image till it consumed me. I dreamed it at night so that I could live it every moment of every day.

The examinations came and went and with great relief I finished with High school. Beverley was expected to achieve excellent grades and had already been advised she'd have no difficulty getting a place at her first choice University. They'd be begging her. Though my results would be much less sparkling I knew I'd done reasonably well in English, and my mother, probably having forgotten her dire threat, seemed prepared to settle for that. Whatever, she never mentioned it again and I was exhilarated by my sudden freedom from school. Now it would be the real thing: ballet classes all day, every day. But I knew too that the next few months could be make or break for me as a dancer. Beverley demanded to keep her options open and take a year out. She really had to fight George on the issue, and it was an extraordinary thing to ask of him, but she won that year's grace easily when her parents saw her dance in Orlando's student demonstration. But I would have given her the chance too.

God, she was brilliant that night. Basically it was a kind of exhibition class for the benefit of the parents - with Beverley centre front row of course and Olivia, seeing future success for herself and the school, even put in this simple little solo just for Beverley. Actually my technique was stronger I decided, comparing myself favorably for once with her in the mirror - but the way Beverley moved....

I watched George Soames's reaction jealously. His opposition to her continuing melted away that evening, as Beverley and Olivia knew it would. I saw it happen in his expression. One minute he was resolute, the next he was quite overcome. But then Beverley could always make you cry, she was so beautiful.

I learned a lot at Orlando's that autumn term. Becoming a full-time student meant I had to put pretty dancing behind me and enter the world of semi-professional slog in an even tighter little environment than before and packed with more emotional tensions and physical trauma. Aches and pains too, sometimes natural, sometimes self-induced.

In the month since I'd started full-time classes I'd lost weight with the combination of summer heat and increased exercise, but for hypocritical Olivia, who was always on about the dangers of anorexia, you could actually never be thin enough! She suggested I bought myself a weighing machine and kept on at me until I did. It infuriated me spending the money on it though. I kept it in my bedroom and that streamlined square of white plastic became an instrument of torture. A single ounce gained would send me off into a week of violent dieting, which inevitably forced my weight to see-saw back. There were fifteen full-time students and that was one thing we all had in common: how not to eat. Only for Beverley was dieting unnecessary. I tell you, she could eat anything. The rest of us starved ourselves, with occasional wild escapes into mountains of chocolate which Beverley ate as well, and which with pangs of bitter remorse I would make myself throw up afterwards. One girl, Sandra, became completely anorexic and actually stopped menstruating, ending up in hospital. Her mother made her leave Orlando's.

"That will only make things so much worse," cried Diana angrily. I expect she was right but we never heard. Once people left, they left. The studio was like a closed religious order.

Though Olivia Orlando was the most inspired teacher about, she could also be an absolute bitch. Often she undermined you to the point of despair until you hated her so much you were determined to do the sequence she was criticizing even if it killed you. Just to get back at her. Clever? Brilliant! The system certainly hardened the will. To her the body was a physical instrument which could be finely tuned, and its limits constantly extended. Only there were no limits in fact. Just practice, practice, practice.

"Repeat! And again! Candice, you're putting on weight!"

Poor Candice. She was a lovely fluid dancer but she adored food and spent most of her days in tears because she couldn't allow herself to feel hungry.

Only a stick thin figure was revered. Anything else was a joke.

Take the pianist, Mrs Scobie, for instance - 'a fine Christian woman' Olivia called her when she wasn't swearing under her breath at her, who apparently gave up her one day off a week from the studio piano to play the organ in her local church, but who, because of her very odd inverted triangular shape, was considered by us to be a total misfit. Her muscular calves and padded hips led up to a top heavy and very fullsome bust, and wide bolster shoulders. Someone only had to whisper when they saw her coming: "The bells! The bells!" to send us all off into hysterics. And in spite of the fact that she managed all day, every day to follow each dancer sympathetically, which for me relieved a great deal of the awful stress, it was a constant joke of the dressing-room how she could possibly see enough notes over her ample bosom to play anything. Beverley reckoned she mustn't have sighted the full keyboard for years and was playing simply by touch.

"What can she weigh?"

"At least nobody expects her to be thin," moaned Candice.

I always joined in the laughter but somehow Mrs Scobie, though she might not move easily herself, understood all those dancers' timing instinctively. She knew just exactly when to get them out of trouble at the end of a muffed pirouette, and how to wait that split second extra if by some miracle the balance was proving secure enough to maintain an arabesque. Secretly I appreciated her talents even if the others didn't.

Mrs Scobie was never particularly punctual and always insisted on a cup of tea and a ten minute sit down immediately on arrival which absolutely infuriated Olivia.

"She comes to work and sits down, and then she sits down to work!" she complained, consulting her watch. Nevertheless she would always wave one of us off to make the required cup of tea.

"I'll go!" I never minded doing it since it was a way of showing Mrs Scobie some gratitude. Sometimes it cost me the first exercise though. In desperation Olivia often began the class without music, while Mrs Scobie sat and sipped and cooled off.

Mrs Scobie also drove Olivia mad with another uncanny talent - striking a wrong note at the most moving moment in any piece of music. I began to wonder whether Mrs S did it to keep herself awake, since it must have been infinitely boring playing the same piece over and over and over again while Olivia's screams of 'Repeat, repeat, this is appalling!' rang through the studio. Maybe she did have a blind spot. Or perhaps she did it just to keep us all on our toes. Perhaps it was a way of having her own little tease with Olivia who flinched every time it happened, and scowled over at the piano, while behind it Mrs Scobie, face pink and shiny with her efforts, fixed her eyes firmly on the dancers' tempo and never appeared to notice the ballet mistress's fury.

Once a week there were pas de deux classes. Boys, borrowed from other schools, or occasionally from touring companies. It was strange but at that time Olivia had no male students herself. Perhaps they wouldn't have put up with her intimidation techniques. Perhaps they were harder to find. They came just for the pas de deux classes and disappeared immediately afterwards. It was as if Olivia was deliberately keeping her girls away from male company - partnering had to be learnt, but mixing was out of the question. But there was a coldness about it anyway. It was just hands to catch and support. Shyness, amusement, embarrassment, never entered into it.

"How much?"

"Sorry, I'll add it up again."

I was still working at Luigi's, weekends, two evenings and three lunchtimes, but often after classes Beverley and I went there together as customers. It had become our absolutely favourite haunt now because it was only a short walk from the studio, and besides, when Beverley was with me, Luigi gave us free coffees. One day when we were in there playing the your part, my part game, Beverley nudged me.

"Don't look now," she whispered, "but there's Sergei Lesarte coming in."

I did look of course, but his dark eyes were on Beverley so he didn't notice my glance. Everyone always focused on Beverley, you could count on it.

"You fancy him, don't you?" Beverley giggled, making me nearly die in case he'd heard her.

"Ssh!"

She laughed at my red face.

Anything to shut her up.

"Is he anything to do with the scholarship, do you think?" I whispered, as he sat down at a table at the other end.

There'd been speculation in the dressing-room all week that the prestigious Ballet Meridienne Francais was contemplating setting up a scholarship competition for a year's study with their theatre school in Paris leading on to an eventual place in their company.

"He might be," Beverley said, casting her eyes down and straightening her back to show off her beautiful long neck. God, she knew how to make herself look good.

I straightened up myself and glanced back at Sergei. His eyes were still firmly fixed on Beverley of course.

Sergei was the invisible man, the one sitting behind

Olivia at the original entrance auditions. Rumors about him were always rife whenever he appeared. A producer looking for new talent? A spy using the studio as cover? Well, we were given to imaginative invention! Eventually we had decided he was simply Olivia Orlando's lover since he seemed to have no real connection otherwise. Now his more frequent presence in the corner of the studio I found profoundly disturbing, though he never looked at me. Somehow while I really wanted him to, I dreaded the thought that he would, but his eyes followed other people, and Beverley more than anyone.

Diana was convinced he was sitting in for a reason.

"Why would he be involved?" asked Candice. But I began to be careful in class after that, to stand (in my watching position behind Beverley of course) but bravely in a gap where Sergei might notice me too. Lately he had begun to sit in on even more classes and with a new kind of intense concentration that only a dancer could feel, surely. And I had begun to look at him in a different way, realizing even if Beverley didn't particularly find him attractive, how lean and muscular he was, and for the first time I really began considering the masculine frame as a sexual object, that it could be attractive, something to be desired.... lateness is such a habit with me. It was also the first independent thought I'd had for ages.

George, because of his change of heart over Beverley, seemed suddenly interested in my progress too, and I found that very cheering. By late July I knew my technique was really improving, and my confidence was building. I felt happier about my appearance and I was certain Olivia was taking more notice of me. Someone even asked me when Beverley and I were out together if I was Beverley's sister. That was real progress, surely, and I was pleased with myself.

It feels wonderful to be in tune with your body, to increase the power surging through your muscles, to have oxygen at its finest and purest in your blood stream. Like Beverley, there I am balancing on pointe in an arabesque and it's as if I'm being embraced by the air, supported. I have time to adjust the line of my arm so that it's exactly like hers. I look in the mirror, Beverley and I could be twins, couldn't we? I hope Sergei is watching me now. There's no way I actually have to go on with the next step. This balance could last all day, I'm as firm as a rock. But let's go on. Beverley is, so why not? The pirouette's next and with a bit of luck.... Place, relevé. Perfect. A double. Straight into the posé arabesque. Now....

"Beverley?"

The class stops dancing. Mrs Scobie stops playing and leans round the piano.

I remember this scene so well.

Every second of it.

Olivia steps forward and takes Beverley in her arms.

"This is wonderful. So promising. You others take note. None of you can ever hold a candle to this beautiful girl. One day she will be a star."

Sergei has risen to his feet. He is smiling at Beverley too. His hands are pressed together as if he is silently applauding.

I stand there, feeling the blood retreating inside me. Where to? Not to my brain certainly. Perhaps to my heart. That's where you feel genuine despair, isn't it? To my eyes? That's how jealousy stings, isn't it?

Olivia is not embracing me.

Sergei is not smiling at me.

Beverley still has everything. I have nothing.

Nothing.

In the dressing-room afterwards I hear myself being excessively congratulatory. The others show slight hostility. But I am her friend, only hers, aren't I?

And in that moment by demonstrating my support, I unwittingly step into a new and closer inner circle. Gain valuable new status.

The drum inside me begins beating with a kind of breathless anticipation.

Beverley and I leave together, arm in arm, and head for Luigi's. And still I am effusive in my praise.

Excessive.

And very close in.

Dangerously so.

Chapter 9

Below us in the red and gold splendour of the stalls there's the rustle of programs and sorting out and settling into seats, and the buzz and mutter of conversation. Hands reach out to try the opera glasses. The harpist and two members of the wind section in the orchestra have come in early and are already tuning up, their string notes tumbling over the discordant brass edges of sharp trumpet bursts. The fringe on the curtain is shifting forward slightly. There are muffled sounds of feet moving around behind it.

By this time I'd seen quite a few ballets on television, and I'd bought myself videos. I'd been to cinemas too once or twice, tiny screens or enormous decaying old places which must have been quite grand once, and I'd seen a small ballet company on stage at Hammersmith. But that particular night was Covent Garden before it closed. In that wonderful old theatre even the air itself was shining....

Dust particles catching the light sparkle under the central chandelier. A delicious smell of chocolates and peppermint fondant comes from somewhere. People are circulating in the stalls, finding their seats, opening their programmes, leaning out from the balcony stalls to see how full the dress circle is, who's in tonight.

That next layer up glitters. There are some good pieces of jewellery in there, a few diamonds. A little gold too, glinting. You can see the faces there, and the fashionable clothes. Above that, in the top tiers, they're climbing the steep steps to their rows and chattering. Up there they are really excited. They queued, are thrilled to have seats. It's all magic to them.

From a theatre box the view is different. There's a feeling of them and us. We're not part of the ordinary crowd. We don't have to excuse ourselves and climb past others into the row, or deal with the crush in the interval. We can arrange our red velvet armchairs for a better view and sit down, stay discreetly back or lean over the balustrade with its little scarlet lampshaded figurines and know we're in the limelight. People are looking up. Trying out their opera glasses on us. Looking at Beverley, at her mother and father. Even at me. This is a stage here too.

Who are they? See? Up in the box? Isn't that - ?

"Comfortable, darling?" Mrs Soames asks Beverley. Mrs Soames, Imogen Soames, is wearing an elegant figure hugging little-black-dress, off the shoulder. And pearl drop earrings, pale and shimmery against the perfection of her straight fair hair. She has quite a reasonable figure, the sort rich women have because they don't do their own cooking. They can order the best foods to be served up every night. Reasonable in my eyes means it is probably absolutely perfect. Dancers see even the slightest curve as excessive weight.

The orchestra is all in now and settled. The house lights are dimming. The audience has gone quiet. George Soames leans forward and says to me:

"Are you feeling better now, Elaine?"

My gushed reply is drowned out by applause for the conductor. I turn round and find George's face very close to mine.

"Yes," I say again, so touched by his concern that actually I do feel better. "Thanks."

He's a father who cares. Beverley is so lucky.

It was over-excitement very likely, fear of getting to their house on time, and worse still, what to wear tonight, how to appear, that made me feel queasy as we drove here in the hire car. My bed at home is littered with the clothes I tried, despaired of and discarded, and tried on again. I'm still terrified I am not dressed for the part, which has not been helped by the funny look Mrs Soames gave me when she saw what I was wearing: a longish black skirt and a clinging black grandpa top (new). It's the best I could come up with. At least I look thin. Hopefully I'm invisible. Beverley's lent me some silver earrings, I can be sure of those. Most people are in evening dress. Only George as far as I can see has the confidence to wear a simple dark suit, but then he doesn't have to dress up to look right. I don't know why I'm worrying though. Even Mrs Soames can't compete.

It's Beverley they're looking at. Beverley, in a stunning deep wine-red dress which clings to her dream figure. She's stealing the show. Her dark hair is drawn up and shining, her skin is flawless. It's impossible not to notice her.

"I've ordered Champagne for the interval," whispers George, still there, still concerned. "Nothing like it for nerves," and he leans back. A subtle scent of expensive cologne lingers on the air just behind me.

He's being so nice to me. Perhaps he really understands I am not used to such grand surroundings, and that empathy gives me a little confidence. I copy Beverley and sit back in my chair and try to look as if I've done this every night of my life.

The overture begins, Prokofiev at his most emotional, and the last of my nausea and fear dissolves away. I strain forward and concentrate. The curtain goes up. It's close, the stage, it's at a distorted angle. I'm not sure I wouldn't rather be in the stalls, or better yet, up at the back in the gods. Seeing the dancers in the wings waiting for their entrances reduces the magic somehow, and I want to feel the magic tonight. Forget how to do it, just immerse myself in it. I glance at Beverley. She is still aware of looking beautiful, still on show up here in her rarefied atmosphere. Those are just people on the stage, performing for her entertainment. I try to be detached too, like she is, but I can't. I'm drawn in, hypnotized by the dancing, transfixed, and by the time Romeo kisses Juliet in the balcony scene I'm crying for what must become of them, for the tragedy of their ill fortune.

I'm embarrassed that George notices my wet eyes when the curtain falls for intermission and the house lights come on. He smiles to himself as he stands up. Of course he thinks me silly. This is only a night at the theatre, for goodness sake. There must be a tissue in my purse. I know I put one in.

The champagne arrives, there's a discreet little table round behind a curtain, and George tips the waiter and dismisses him, and pours the frothing liquid out himself. He brings me mine first.

"Enjoying it?"

"Mmm." I nod, fiddling with the tissue in my spare hand trying to make out that earlier I had something my eye.

He passes out champagne to the others. Beverley and her mother have seen someone they recognize out in the circle and are discussing whether to go and say hello, and who else might be worth talking to, whether there's anyone influential in tonight. George though, the perfect host, stands by me. Beverley and Imogen talk and smile as if they're being observed, and sip elegantly from their glasses. The bubbles are exploding red off the surface of the gold liquid in mine like a show of miniature fireworks in the auditorium light.

"But you've been here before, surely," Mrs Soames says, when I say how beautiful the theatre is. She's astonished when I admit I haven't.

Now Beverley is talking to me saying, Mercutio is so good, isn't he? Such placing and line. And she hates Juliet's tense fingers, and Lady Capulet is over-acting.

But secretly I hate Tybalt because he will bait Romeo, and Mercutio because he intervenes, and Montague and Capulet.... Angry at every antagonistic force that serves to halt the star-cross'd lovers....

"Are you hungry?" asks Beverley. "Supper later at Elfino's will be wonderful."

The supper was wonderful. Pink linen napkins, smoked salmon and wedges of lemon, crystal glasses of crisp dry white wine. Cutlery sparkling under the pin spot lighting, and waiters hovering and then silently replacing the empty plates with tempting dishes of tender white chicken breasts in cream sauce with satin ribbons of orange carrots and deep sea green florets of broccoli.

It was the most beautiful meal I had ever seen.

I was nervous, of course, terrified of showing myself up. As much as possible I kept my hands in my lap. My back hardly touched the chair, my eyes darted from Beverley to her mother, on to George and then back to Beverley, watching, echoing all their manners. I dared not speak in case I lost my concentration.

They were discussing the performance. Unable to

share the emotional elation the story had stirred up in me, instead I applied myself carefully to eating, taking only miniature mouthfuls to avoid any possible slip.

"Didn't you enjoy it then, Elaine?" asked George, as I was finishing.

A sliver of chicken fell off my fork. In horror I watched it float down like a feather in a kind of awful slow motion and land in its cushion of cream sauce on the pink napkin on my lap.

My fork hand froze in mid air. A flame of embarrassment licked up my neck.

"I - "

A ping! A flash of crystal.

"H'ahh!" said Mrs Soames.

White wine began to spread out across the table linen from George's overturned glass. A waiter rushed over with a cloth.

"Whoops!" said George. "Silly me."

"Let me get you another glass, sir."

The replacement glass appeared instantly as if by magic. More wine was poured into it. A pink napkin was being laid over the dark wet patch.

Compared with that, the offending piece of chicken on my napkin was minuscule. Hardly moving my spare hand I folded the napkin over to conceal it and put down my fork.

Everything was as it had been, as if nothing had happened at all.

"What were you saying, Elaine?" asked George, picking up his new glass nonchalantly as if it were the original. His silver cuff link caught the light, glinted across the table.

I pushed my knife and fork together on the plate

exactly as Beverley had and took a deep breath. "I loved the ballet," I said. "And this supper. It's so kind of you to invite me, Mr Soames."

"George, please. I thought we'd discarded formality long ago. And anyway it was Beverley's idea," he said, regarding his daughter.

"Thank you, Daddy," Beverley said demurely, and smiled her fairy tale smile.

George turned to his wife.

"Dessert, Imogen?"

When it was time to go home George called two cars, not one, on his account. He waited outside by the front entrance with me for mine to arrive while Beverley and her mother stayed inside.

He was squinting quizzically at me in the darkness and I wondered whether he was seeing the delight in my eyes at the sheer pleasure of waiting there with him, or simply debating my suitability as his daughter's friend.

As usual, the concern for my welfare: "You're not cold, are you?"

"Not at all."

How could I feel cold waiting there with Beverley's father on such an evening? How could I feel cold with him beside me?

The car pulled in at that moment, disappointingly too soon. I would have gone on waiting. Wanted to. Why couldn't it have been late?

"So will you be all right?"

"Oh yes. I'll be fine, thank you."

George opened the car door.

"I hope you don't mind travelling alone. I thought for once you should go right to your house."

"I - " I looked at him. Had he guessed my secret?

Perhaps he knew the road, knew it wasn't a one-way. Much better away early and in a separate car, I thought, as I climbed in. Because imagine the alternative, us all going together? Them stopping outside my house! That back street. And Beverley's face. Imogen's! Perhaps even George's. And I was moving beyond all that. I wanted to be, and was being included in this new world.

"Straight home now," George said, and smiled at me as he closed the car door. As if I was going anywhere else! He stood on the restaurant steps as the car pulled away. I watched him out of the back window melting away into the distance.

The roads were quiet. It was late, well after midnight. The lights of London shimmered as I was driven along the embankment, the river was full of stylish reflections. I thought about the evening. Want what she wants, Elaine. Have what she has.

As I travelled home that night in such isolated splendour, it seemed to me the sound of the drum inside me had begun beating a little bit louder and its rhythm was a little bit faster. I wanted more.

Chapter 10

"No more rides home like that!"

Beverley glared at me.

Humiliation and then a secret flush of guilt - could Beverley read my mind? Could she register the slight change in my direction? Probably not, so where had I gone wrong? Every detail of the night before flashed before my eyes. The chicken? Had she and her mother seen and been appalled at me dropping that off my fork? Had George, who I thought was the only person to see it, mentioned it? Had they all seen it? Or had I made some even worse mistake? Some really glaring social error? Crying! If only I hadn't cried watching the ballet. I must have looked such a child!

"It was disgraceful Daddy sending you home in a separate car."

"I didn't mind."

"Never again!

"But - "

"Well, he's working in Brussels for a week. After that we'll be taking you home properly."

"Oh no!"

One week to work out some way to convince her to still let her father drop me in Putney without turning into my street. And a week to analyze my mistakes, and to rehearse trying to say more intelligent things in front of George. But how and what? One night out with them and suddenly now I was realizing how much Beverley's father - and Beverley too, seemed so far out of my league. I could never, ever hope to fit in. Fearful of rejection, I reverted to concentrating even harder on

Beverley's dancing, desperate to make myself more like her.

Sergei Lesarte had begun sitting in on classes that week, and he'd begun bringing a woman with him too, a rather beautiful blonde with very delicate features and physique.

"I wish she wouldn't come," Diana complained after the morning class. "Do you think she's looking for dancers for some new production? Who is she anyway, sitting there making Olivia impossible!"

"As if she wasn't already," I declared gloomily. Lately I was finding Olivia's continual criticism oppressive, like living under a dark cloud. Please God, one day she might find some step I did met with her satisfaction?

"Maybe it's just the high temperatures," suggested one of the other girls. Maybe. London had been overpoweringly humid for days. A summer heatwave. Oppressive indoors, and at lunchtimes the parks full of office workers stripping off, determined to roast themselves raw, behaving recklessly like the British do in glaring hot sunshine. Even the buildings seemed to be shimmering in a heat haze.

The morning class that day had been a total disaster, the barre work beyond all human limits, and the centre... Olivia, unaware of time and possessed by extra demons with them there, had singled me out for particular condemnation.

"Ronde de jambe en l'air, fouetté, rotate to the back, hold the arabesque, fondue. Deeper Elaine, much deeper!" Holding yet another arabesque was murder, muscles knotting, cramping, tendons tightening.

"And again. Hopeless, Elaine! Get that leg up higher!"

In the mirror I could see Diana's face screwing up in agony. Even Beverley didn't look too happy.

"Again!"

I gritted my teeth and continued, my legs screaming with pain. I glanced across at Mrs Scobie. She looked fed up with repeating the same bars for the umpteenth time but she sighed and pounded into the piece once more.

"Oh God, I'll never make it," gasped Diana under her breath.

"Keep up, Elaine! Have you no sense of rhythm?" The music thumped on and on. I was becoming less and less conscious of the steps, only able to feel the searing throb in my limbs, and a weird lightheadedness. It seemed as if I was calling up energy from the very depths of myself....and in an awful way...I thought....this is what ballet really is....dancing from within....from the soul's energy....like dying....a detachment from reality.... beyond the confines of the body....

"Dancers without stamina are nothing," Olivia snapped at me afterwards. "Candice? Is that a sweet you're eating?"

Diana peeped back round the dressing room door. "Olivia is well wound up about something today."

"What understatement!" muttered Candice, tearfully searching her bag for another of her packets of calorie free peppermints.

"Maybe that blonde woman's her rival for Sergei and Olivia's jealous," suggested Diana.

But if anyone was jealous, it was me. Utterly frightened now of my standing with Beverley's family, and desperate for approval, Sergei's attention had suddenly become vitally important. In this strange week of ups and downs, just once he had actually looked at me. Only for an instant, but it was enough for me to start imagining him taking the class, coming in close, paying me special attention, correcting me. The daydream allowed me to forget Olivia sometimes, and my problems with Beverley, and lighten up, try to work harder, and aim higher. Thinking like that I found I could suddenly dance for him. The idea of his silent masculine presence made me more aware of my body, of what practice clothes and eye make-up I was wearing. Even what bra. And even more determined to move as beautifully as Beverley so Sergei might stop watching her and look at me again. I cast my eyes down and did all those practiced facial expressions hoping that he might actually be noticing.

And when I wasn't dancing and copying Beverley I was watching him, the way he sat, leaning forward in those tight black jeans, his legs apart, the tips of his fingers pressed together, his dark eyes concentrating on the movements, following each step with intense interest. But in the last couple of days with that other woman there, dressed in her elegant pastel blue suit and gold jewelry and pale shoes, instead of watching he was leaning back and talking softly to her. I felt let down somehow.

"I've left my pointe shoes out there," Diana said suddenly. She grabbed up her cardigan and disappeared.

When she returned her eyes were wide.

"She's talking French!" she whispered.

"Olivia?"

"Yes, and the blonde."

"What of it?"

"Don't you see? Maybe that woman's from the

Meridienne!"

All of us stared round the door.

The woman and Olivia and Sergei were deeply engrossed in conversation at the far end of the studio

"What do you think?"

"It's possible," whispered Beverley, urgently pulling us back inside. "The scholarship's supposed to be at the beginning of October. What's the date?"

"17th August."

"So they must be looking. They'd have to allow time for people to learn solos and things."

"Two classical solos and a demi-character solo," said Diana.

"How do you know?"

"They offered a place five years ago. That's what they did then. The boy who won it ended up a soloist in the Canadian Ballet. Anthony Claire."

"I've seen pictures of him in Dance and Dancers," said one of the other girls.

Candice nodded eagerly in agreement.

"But don't they have auditions?"

Diana had no idea.

The relaxed attitude to Sergei and the woman sitting in on classes evaporated. Now we all were terrified as we filed in for the afternoon pointe class and our fears were well founded.

"This," announced Olivia, "is Irina Caillouet from Ballet Meridienne. She will be taking the pointe class."

Sergei dressed as usual in his favourite black, went to sit over on the side and Olivia went with him. Irina Caillouet waited in silence for us to find places at the barre. It took longer than normal as we jockeyed for favourite positions and pushed the limits of our personal space as far as we dared, fearful of how to begin with this different person. The voice was dove-soft with a lilting French accent which matched the pale colouring, but her eyes were like a hawk's, noticing every tiny detail, the slightest incorrect movement, and when I made a mistake as she walked past she swung round to see who it was faintly out of time.

Mrs Scobie held the following note a fraction. Just enough.

Of course Beverley was watched constantly and at one point Irina had her repeat a sequence of steps on her own.

"Excellent!" she said, when Beverley finished.

A sort of exhaustion began to flood through me. I drew back to the rear of the last group of girls waiting to start the next enchainment, and took a deep breath. Beverley began, skimming off across the studio on the diagonal with that extraordinary lightness - and then in the following group, Diana. The music was building to the next phrase. The others in my group were rising up onto demi-point, poised for take off, but my arches were refusing to obey me. I was near to tears. Oh God, Elaine Higham, where's your perseverance? What is it with you when the opportunity comes! Aren't you ever going to be capable of seizing the moment? I pulled myself up and stepped out and somehow the strength came. I didn't do it well.

A final port de bras.

Irina dismissed us with a curt nod and went to join Sergei and Olivia in discussion.

Olivia announced that we should wait please, names would be called out, an important selection was taking place. The room went absolutely quiet.

Beverley came over and stood beside me. She leaned down and untied the pink ribbons and removed her pointe shoes as she always did after class. For once I didn't copy her. We didn't speak. The sweat began to freeze on my shoulders. I shivered and flexed my feet nervously, and fiddled with the elastic band holding back my hair, unable to focus for more than a moment on any person or any part of the room.

Beverley had a place of course. She didn't even glance at me, just picked up her bag when they called her and moved away towards some pre-ordained high road she had been bound for all along.

"Diana?"

More discussion.

"Candice?"

Candice! I turned my back on them all, my eyes stinging. I couldn't look at Beverley or Diana and Candice or any of them anymore. The silence in the studio seemed less real than the roar of the traffic outside the window beside me. That's what I felt like, actually, exactly as if I'd been abandoned out on a motorway, like some unwanted kitten. I leaned down and picked at the pink satin knots at my ankles, watching my fingers working rather than feeling them. Eventually the ribbons untied and I removed my pointe shoes, and lifted my bag.

"Elaine?"

Was it Sergei's voice calling out across the room, or just a car braking suddenly? I turned and stared across the room at them.

"Elaine!" A surge of love for Sergei rushed through me. I couldn't help it. He had seen me, noticed me, just that one time, and I knew he had convinced them to take me. I hurried over and stood between him and Beverley, breathless with delight, willing him to look at me, and see my gratitude.

But his gaze was elsewhere; his eyes were feasting on Beverley, on the exquisite shape of her body beneath that sleek black leotard.

Chapter 11

Jasmine. The humid evening was alive with layers of the fragrance, humming almost. Perhaps it was my own excitement, but there's a bush that grows across there, spilling over the wall from the adjoining garden wall to trail beside the grimy station steps, and somehow tonight its scent was following me. The train I'd been on moved off rattling onwards towards Putney, roaring out over the bridge. I felt its vibrations retreating away along the girders of the footbridge. Below me, its music blaring out over the dark water, swished the riverboat Queen of the Thames, deck lit brightly enough to see the faces of the people on board, who were dancing or leaning over the rails. Close enough for me to share their party atmosphere, be elated by their chatter and absorb their energy, to peer into the glistening lap-lap-laps of the water with them, to laugh and tap my feet in time to their music. Because it should have been me down there. With Beverley. Us. Somewhere like that tonight. Celebrating.

But she had gone out. Been picked up by her father to go out somewhere. No lift home for me on this evening.

Coloured streamers fluttered back over the riverboat's wake, lifting, dancing on the updraught. The river water smelled enticingly of the heat of the city, of the sea itself. I leaned for a few minutes enjoying the coolness of the iron balustrade against my arms, watching the boat glide away into the twilight, downstream towards Battersea, and listening to the music drifting away with it.

I thought then I was getting it all under control, life. I

thought I'd cracked it, you know? I was convinced then I knew exactly what I wanted. That for once I hadn't lost everything. At last, at last, things were going my way. Well not quite. I might be in the scholarship along with Beverley but there was another problem. But when isn't there?

I was five minutes from home. I walked quickly up Merrivale Road, between the terraced houses with their diamond patterned flagstone paths, and out into the main road. It was fun ducking dangerously between the steady stream of cars heading back to the city, then I crossed and turned urgently into the narrow side street that led home. Maybe, somehow, that urgency fits in. Perhaps we know when we're going to be happy.

My mother glanced up only briefly from the television.

"The Ballet scholarship. I'm in. I'm in, Mum! So is Beverley."

"Shush!" she said, concentrating on the screen. "This is the most important bit. Tell me later, whatever it is. Get yourself some tea."

I tried to remember a time when I'd seen anything more than the side of her head. It was years since she'd looked me directly in the face. What colour were her eyes again?

I persevered. "There's an entrance fee, Mum."

"Mum?"

No answer.

"I have to have it."

Still no answer.

Why didn't the woman talk? Suddenly all I wanted to do was get away, remove myself from her silence.

"Where's Jonty?"

My mother shrugged. She seemed to have heard that.

"Playing football down in the park, I expect."

"Still?"

It seemed to me that from the time we arrived in this house, my mother was always falling back into that chair and telling me to switch on the television. She did the basics for us originally, more probably than I realized, but any conversation she ever had with either of us clashed with that bright twenty-two inch screen. It kept her amused. Filled the gaps in her life, I suppose. But I'm sure it made Jonty grow up wilder than he might have been. He used to sit dumbly in front of it with her, until he learnt he could escape out into the street for hours.

"Mum, I'm going to need the money."

She still ignored me.

"Mum? Why don't you ever listen?"

I went over and pressed the sound off. She simply raised it again with the remote control.

"Go away," she said. "Can't you see I'm watching this?"

Voices, actors' voices on the screen, not mine, not her own daughter's, commanded her attention.

Fuming, I went back out into the street looking for Jonty instead. I passed the burger bar on the corner which was full of kids just like him and walked along to the embankment. It was getting dark now and it was a bit scary down there by the river at night, the black water lapping against the slipway and the starlings all jostling around above the rim of lights on the pub. That's what Jonty and his friends liked about it, I expect, that spookiness. I could tell immediately where they were. There was this collection of little glows wavering about like fireflies in the darkness under one of the trees. I moved in on them silently.

"Home, Jonty!"

"Hey, Elaine, stop creeping up on us."

"Errrr! Not your fucking sister again!"

Amongst their trainered feet lay a few kicked-in polystyrene cartons and some chips smashed into blobs of tomato sauce, but that wasn't why they were there.

"You lot'll wreck your lungs," I said angrily. "Not to mention blowing your minds."

I made my brother come with me with whispered dire threats that I would tell on the others for smoking, and let on where they all met if he didn't, and was he sure it was just ordinary cigarettes? Because I wasn't. Not at all. Playing on his loyalties. I'll give Jonty credit for that. He was always loyal to that scanky lot. He always came with me if I threatened to tell on them, but maybe that was the fear of what they'd do to him if I did. But what was the matter with all those other kids' parents anyway, letting thirteen year olds out all hours to roam the streets?

On the way home I told Jonty about getting into the scholarship finals.

"Four from Orlando's. Me, Beverley, and Diana, and another girl. Olivia's really pleased. There were only ten places."

"Yeah."

Jonty wasn't really listening.

"I have to get three hundred pounds though, for the entry fee, and then there'll be pointe shoes and things."

"So?"

A starling swooped over our heads and across to a street lamp.

"So everything, stupid! It's only my whole life we're

talking about."

We turned into our road. Jonty ran ahead and up the three steps to our house, and began to dance around on the doorstep, shouting and waving his arms like a two-year-old loony.

"On-ly-her-whole-life...na na na na na."

I ran after him and grabbed him furiously, clapping my hand over his mouth to shut him up. He elbowed me in the ribs then sank his teeth deep into my fingers.

"Ow!" I snatched them away and struck him round the ear. "You little beast! You can die of whatever it was you were smoking next time. See if I care!"

He stared at me as if he would kill me, but there was an awful disappointment in his eyes too. He darted past me and inside. I chased him through to the kitchen.

"Jonty?"

He stood by the fridge just gazing insolently at me, and swallowing down a whole carton of milk. Which of course left none for any of us to have a cup of tea. Angrily I left him to it. Mum was still engrossed of course. If my brother and I had beaten each other up then and there in the kitchen she wouldn't have noticed.

I used to turn the television right off, and try to hold a reasonable conversation with her, but she got bored and listless so quickly that I stopped bothering. Like Jonty I'd learnt not to care - but when someone's bursting full of exciting news, and needs to discuss the difficulties of raising so much money quickly, such banal competition for attention really hurts.

I went to count what money I had saved of my own. It came to only thirty pounds. All that time - but it had been the classes themselves that had cost me. Now I would have to get more somehow. Meridienne would provide the costumes, but I'd still need money for the entry fee and loads of new pointe shoes and tights. I wondered how few I could manage with.

Before bed I sneaked in and searched my mother's room to see if I could find some evidence of a bank balance or maybe even a savings account. I was trying the drawers when Jonty appeared at the door and gave me a dreadful fright.

"What are you doing?"

"Ssh! Ssh. Nothing to do with you. Go away."

Suddenly my hand closed over something cold and hard. Hidden in amongst the clothes, a bottle of vodka. It clinked slightly against another lying next to it.

"I'll find it," Jonty whispered from the door.

I closed the drawer and went and pushed him out into the hall.

"I told you, it's nothing to do with you. Go to bed."

"My mates could organize something."

"Don't you dare! Don't you d - "

"Sod you," he said, and went to hog the bathroom. I glanced back into the bedroom. Best left alone, that drawer. A secret better kept secret. An expensive secret, all the same.

I wondered briefly if Jonty himself had any actual cash. Unlikely. Besides, he probably smoked his. Anyway he'd never give it to me now. It occurred to me I should hide from him what I did have. Maybe I should be hiding it from my mother too.

"Elaine? Are you still up?"

Her voice floated up the stairs. Her bedroom was over the living room. Maybe she'd heard me moving about. I ignored her and went to my own room. I had been at the point of giving up anyway. Pretty obviously now there was nothing to be found. But I was angry with myself. Why hadn't the need for money dawned on me? I'd been so busy dancing I hadn't considered any fee for this, and now there was no time, a few days, that's all. It wasn't so much, but even with the best will in the world I couldn't earn it in time. It would take a miracle to get it now.

There wasn't anyone I could ask. And I couldn't confide in Beverley. She was the last person I could consult, I'd pushed myself into such a corner trying to live up to her ideas, inventing a home life to suit. Much less than hers of course, she wouldn't have expected anything else, but an acceptable background all the same which had given me access into her world. And lose that? No, there was no way I could talk to her. Nor to any of the others, not even Diana, though her family weren't well off and she'd understand - they'd do it for her, they believed in her. Nor could I mention it to Candice - she was having enough trouble with her family over not eating enough. Nor could I consult Olivia herself - because what if she talked to people? What if Beverley's father.... what if either of Beverley's parents found out?

A moth was fretting at my window, tap-tap-tapping, dusting the glass with a fine powder. How horrible it is when you want something, you want it, you can see through to it like it's just the other side but you can't get there, and there's no-one to talk to and no way round. Panicky, it is. And money's the worst. Needing it, really needing it, and having none leaves such a sick gaping hole inside your gut it makes you feel your whole life will fall through. I opened the window and leaned disconsolately out into the night. There was no moon.

Between the buildings, my narrow view of the river, the water looked quite black.

Even Luigi was away. He'd left the coffee shop in a relief manager's hands and gone to Italy to see his relatives. All I could think of was to wait until he was back at the end of the week and see if he would consider lending me the money. He'd probably have spent all his in Milan, but he might lend me some. It was just possible. At least worth asking. If I won I could pay him back because part of the prize was money to live on. If I didn't, he might let me work it off with extra hours.

The moth, stupid thing, was still fighting the glass, unable to see the way out into the night.

Yes, I'd ask Luigi. I'd have to be patient though, and feign confidence in front of everyone because the money would come at the very last minute, but what other solution was there?

Chapter 12

Remember that lemon cake Mrs Soames said she'd cooked on my first visit to their house? She gave me the recipe for it for some reason. Maybe when I tasted it again I said how much I liked it. Trying to impress her. Maybe she thought all girls should collect recipes. It was a funny thing to do though. Dated. Who cooks cakes nowadays anyway? But it was something she probably regretted giving me later. I've baked it a few times. It's crazy. I'm no cook, am I? But I always think it might amuse me. What odd things we do at important moments in our lives. Four ounces of sugar, four ounces of butter, two eggs, milk, lemon rind, flour. And it does amuse me in a way. Beating it gives me some pleasure. I put violence into that cake, and triumph. I don't eat it. I only make it to remind myself, just to recapture a feeling.

So there I was in the Scholarship but with the urgent problem of how to raise the entrance fee. I asked one of the other waitresses at the cafe if Luigi ever gave subs.

"Don't ask!" she said ominously. "He can be difficult."

I frowned.

"Yes," she said. "That sort of difficult."

Oh God.

She was right too.

"What you do for this?" he said, running his beady little eyes down my body with a light in them I'd never seen before. In spite of my inexperience I knew exactly what he was getting at. The threat of it.

A greasy little finger reached out and stroked my neck. I recoiled. The finger withdrew, but the eyes continued their progress.

"Extra hours?" I said, wishing he would look away.

He stepped closer. "Maybe." His tongue ran along his lip leaving it shiny with saliva. "After hours, better."

Panicking, I glanced at my watch. "I'm expected home." I said, and darted for the door, grateful to find it open and tearfully dreading what might be suggested on my next shift in a couple of days time. Too much maybe to even consider returning.

I wished I'd never asked.

Another problem too. And money again. Beverley's birthday. Her eighteenth. And her father would be back in time, so Mrs Soames had organized a dinner party.

As Beverley's best friend I was invited.

"And Mummy says spend the night with us. You won't want to be going home so late."

The rest of the guests according to Beverley would be absolutely ancient. Relations, close friends, her parent's inner circle. People who would be sizing me up, assessing my value.

So I needed to spend some of my precious savings to buy my best friend a present, to arrive with. There was no way out. Beverley would expect it of me. Her parents would expect it too, but not only was I absolutely stuck for money, I was terrified of Beverley's taste. Clothes? It would have to be something small. Anything to do with fashion? Well, that selection was her prerogative, wasn't it? Jewellery, the same. Even perfume I wouldn't dare choose. Besides she was into the really expensive level there. I would have to find something ordinary that I could afford, and quickly. Like bath oil. Well, even that I couldn't afford, but what choice did I have? In desperation I ventured into the local second hand shop next door to the chemist and found this exquisite little wooden box with an inlaid geometric pattern of black and mother of pearl on the lid. Stupid because it cost me much more than I'd meant to spend. But it was beautiful, and it was her birthday and Beverley would love it as much as I did I was sure.

She had originally asked me to go to a pub restaurant the night before for a meal with a few of her school friends. Her father was paying, she said. But right at the last minute she rang me up.

"This pub evening, Elaine."

"Yes?"

"Look, I'm sorry. It's cancelled. A couple of people can't come."

"But it's your birthday - "

"We'll do it some other time. Okay?"

"What will you do instead?"

"Oh, nothing."

"Couldn't we - ?"

And that's when she suggested this family do the following evening and I was quite flattered to think she'd want me there. And excited at the thought of it. This was only a few days after she and I had just been chosen for the scholarship too - so it could be a celebration for us both in a way, she said. But what to wear? George and Imogen Soames moved in such sophisticated circles and apparently this was to be quite a formal party for their only daughter's birthday. The occasion definitely called for dressing up. I was determined to look good but I couldn't possibly afford anything new. Gloomily I sorted through the few things in my wardrobe. She misunderstood the reason, I know she did, thinking it was still a lack of suitable taste and style rather than severe financial limitations, but anyway Beverley came to my rescue. I got to her house early.

"Like my new mini hi-fi?"

Silver it was, the birthday present, glistening in the corner of her bedroom, and able to tell you what you were listening to, what disc jockey, what album, the time, the date, practically the air temperature. Tell it what you wanted to hear, it found it. It could almost cook dinner for two. We lay on the floor and listened for a while to some of her collection of CDs - in magnificent quadraphonic sound.

"Want some vodka?"

"What?"

"Vodka," said Beverley, reaching under her dressing-table and producing a small bottle.

"Why not?" I was tense and apprehensive at the thought of the evening ahead. Maybe this would relax me a little.

"Lemonade?" she asked, rolling that out too and two glasses.

"You're well equipped."

"It's my birthday."

"Many happy returns," I said, sipping the mixture tentatively. This was what my mother was on. It didn't taste strong. It didn't really taste at all disappointingly, and it was masked by sweet lemonade. Beer or wine was better.

"Let's make a start," Beverley said.

I began trying on clothes, the ones I'd brought with me. Nothing I had was right of course, none of it would be good enough, I knew that. At first Beverley watched, then she tried on one or two of the things herself. And wouldn't you know, they looked exquisite on her? The more she tried on, the more depressed I was. And what was worse, she began laughing - the effects of the vodka maybe - we were onto our second. But laughing. My clothes on her made her double up.

I wanted to cry, but I made myself laugh too, like she was laughing. And it was raw, cruel laughter and it hurt me deep inside, and still I had to stand there as if I was enjoying the joke. Eventually she peeled off the last thing and stood there, reflected in the mirror. Fine lace bra and flimsy knickers. And I found myself thinking if I reach out now and rasp my fingernail over your bare skin, Beverely, I'll discover what you feel like, down over that slim curve of your hips. Maybe grazing the sleek muscular shape of you will ease my anger. Then I trembled, wondering how I could even consider such a thing.

She took off her bra - and I thought she knows what I'm thinking. For a frightening split second she held the pose. God, Beverley Soames, you have timing.

But I kept myself in check. I reached for my drink and finished it. Maybe she was tempting me, seeing how far I'd go. Maybe she was just exercising her power over me.

"Another?"

"No thanks."

Wrapped in a towel now she chose one of her own dresses from her wardrobe for me, black, and quite elegant. I felt rescued, relieved to be offered something she would wear, confident that if she owned it I would look good in it, and suddenly very grateful to her for letting me be here and that she didn't mind my borrowing her dress.

Using her little bathroom made me feel better, all those spotlights, and the mirrors. I threw back my head and let the shower fall like warm rain on my face and hair. The white towel I wrapped myself in was feather soft. I wound another round my hair.

"Try this," said Beverley, when I emerged. "Present from Mr Nightmare."

I took the perfume bottle and sniffed a subtle mix of what I imagined was myriad bouquets, sophisticated theatres, expensive dinner parties and a thousand beautiful nights.

"I expect it cost him a fortune."

"Oh yes! I told him what to get. Try it."

I dabbed some of the perfume on my wrists and passed the bottle back.

"That's no good," said Beverley. She upended the bottle and let the scent splash over my shoulders and down my back, leaving me totally overpowered, heady with the aroma. Even I knew you could have too much of a good thing.

We spent a long time together on our make-up with her experimenting with new colors for me. She painted on my lipstick, outlining the edges of my mouth carefully, raising the center into two definite cupid points.

"Quite sensuous," she said, standing back to admire her handiwork. She handed me the face powder and puff. "Powder over it now to set it."

The new me was quite interesting. 'Sensuous' - well, a little bit. More unsure really.

While she set about doing her hair I took the borrowed dress down from its hanger. It was velvet, soft to the touch. I put it on carefully. It nearly fitted me very well. I looked in the mirror, pleased with myself.

Beverley put on her own dress. It was new and fitted her like a glove. Emerald green. With her dark hair drawn up into a jewelled comb she looked stunning.

"Are those the only shoes you have with you?"

I nodded.

"Oh well."

She blotted her second coat of lipstick and powdered it again.

"At least your legs are brown."

"Summer," I said.

"But what," she said, suddenly making a face, "can we do about your hair?"

I turned back to the mirror in despair. My hair was frizzing. I wished I hadn't washed it. Beverley lent me her hair dryer.

"We could try mousseing you," she suggested, "as a last resort."

So it was with defined curls glued into shape with mousse, and two vodkas inside me, and a distinctly insecure frame of mind that I shadowed Beverley down the staircase, through to the sitting room, and out into the foliage and the cane furniture of the Victorian conservatory. The other guests were already there. They all embraced Beverley, admired the way she looked and wished her happy birthday.

"And this is Elaine," Mrs Soames said, introducing me. They all looked at me. I tried to smile and look confident, even though I was painfully aware that my arrival had filled the room with excessive fragrance.

All rich, this gathering, you could tell - Uncle Cyril, Mrs Soames' balding brother who stared rather quizzically and long I thought at the tight moussed curls of my hair, George's cousin Dorothy, and her husband Alec. Melanie Powers and her husband Sir John Powers - Melanie was Beverley's godmother.

Sir John Powers seemed to have connections work-wise with Beverley's father. Later in the evening I discovered he was an MP.

"Better call me plain old John," he said, holding out his hand for me to shake.

"Call me Imogen," Mrs Soames said genially to me.

Introductions over, the attention quickly centered on Beverley again. I stood beside her, well, slightly behind really.

"I swear she gets prettier every day," said Melanie.

"George, shall we open the champagne?" Dorothy clapped her hands affectedly. The white stones on her several rings flashed in the light.

"Champagne! How very appropriate. Such a beautiful occasion, dear."

"Sweet eighteen."

"That's seventeen."

"So what goes with eighteen?"

"Life!"

And champagne - obviously for the Soames, the only thing to drink. The cork popped. The bottle frothed. Foaming glasses were handed out.

"Many happy returns, darling!"

We lifted our drinks.

"Have you heard she's a finalist in the Ballet Meridienne scholarship?"

"Entrant," Beverley corrected.

"When? When? How exciting. We'll have to come."

"Elaine is too," said George.

I shot him a grateful little smile.

"Really!"

"We found out this week, didn't we, darling?" Imogen Soames said, standing next to her daughter and smiling benignly at her. "It's to be held at the beginning of October. They're going down to Sussex to prepare."

"Where?" asked Melanie. "Near us?"

"Near Cuckfield."

"Not far then," said John, looking across at George.

"Elaine's Australian," George announced, as if it was important.

All eyes turned to me.

"Ages ago," I said nervously.

There was the slightest hesitation before Melanie said: "Hasn't the weather been glorious today, George?"

"How did the party go last night?" Cyril asked Beverley.

"Fine!" George put his arm round her. "My daughter and her friends certainly know how to spend my money! More fun with your own age group though, darling, isn't it?"

Beverley didn't look at me, or see my disappointment. Perhaps she'd forgotten she'd even asked me. It was her friends from her posh school of course so maybe she'd thought I wouldn't fit in. She was being considerate, wasn't she?

Mrs Soames, Imogen, excused herself and slipped away to oversee what the caterers were doing with the dinner. Apparently even the usual cook wasn't good enough for this gathering. Nor was I. Contenting myself with sipping my glass of champagne, letting the bubbles settle on my tongue, I contemplated the blue and cream design of the expensive looking Italian floor tiles. Only vaguely did I hear Alec and Cyril questioning John on the dealings in the House of Commons, and the extent of some disagreement there. And Beverley chatting to her relations, and her father talking quietly to Melanie. The evening was happening without me, so instead I started thinking ahead to rehearsing for the scholarship, ignoring my money worries and privately celebrating that like Beverley I had been chosen too.

"More?" asked Imogen.

Only Cyril took up her offer. He helped himself to extra salmon en croute.

I was beginning to regret what I had already eaten, let alone having more, but the champagne was worth it. Coming on top of the vodka it had given me a bit of confidence.

One of the women caterers entered and the salmon course was neatly cleared away to be replaced by a third course - huge dishes of luscious fresh strawberries with crushed raspberry sauce and jugs of thick cream. Imogen set about serving it.

"There's a difference," John was saying. "Some people are peasants by nature."

"Pour more wine, George."

"Come now, all men are equal," said George, picking up the wine bottle.

"Some are more equal than others," Melanie said, as he filled her glass.

"Was the South African trip productive, John?"

"Excellent!" said John, flashing a smile. "Hot!"

"Freedom from him then, eh, Melanie?" asked Cyril.

"Shopping," said Melanie quietly, running a finger round the rim of her glass. "I went shopping."

Dorothy shook her head. "Nightmare, parking nowadays."

"Yes," John took a sip of wine, "but without Mandela, it'll be the test. Too many bloody tribes, too many races."

"The supermarket, it's two hours there."

"Could still be a blood bath, Alec."

"Always."

"That's independence for you."

Looking at me suddenly, Alec said: "So what about the Aussies?"

"Good cricket team," John said warily, chasing a strawberry round his plate.

"You've started this," said Imogen accusingly, glancing at George.

"I started nothing!" said George.

"Pyjama players! Ruining the traditions."

"That's old argument! Played out!"

"Need we?"

Alec hadn't heard Imogen obviously. "Attractive country though."

"Well, they haven't got a race problem." Cyril spoke with his mouth full. .

Imogen glared at him.

"What did I say? Don't look at me!" he said innocently, and reached for his glass which was empty.

"Give my brother more wine, George."

George obediently leaned across and did so.

"They murdered the originals and kept it all out from then on," said Alec.

"We did that. Us," George said. "When you think about it."

"So who are they to criticize? Flags! Royalty! We

made them!" Alec was adamant.

"What do you think of the original white Australia policy, Elaine?" asked John.

I frowned, not quite following and nervous at my sudden inclusion. "I'm not really s-sure."

"Come now, John," George said in measured tones. "It's so long ago. Way before she was born. Just because you had that stupid argument about it in the Commons yesterday - "

"Difference of opinion," John said.

"Difference of opinion!" said Alec. "Uproar, you caused."

"So what does she think?"

"I - "

I had no idea what they expected me to say. I agreed? I disagreed? But with what? Republicanism obviously, but what aspect? And some early political idea I knew very little about? All I wished was I'd concentrated harder in history. What I'd learnt about Australia's past wouldn't cover the head of a pin, and was from a British point of view in a British school too. Not only that, what understanding would I have had? I'd hardly lived in Australia. How could a child of four be politically aware? Their policies weren't mine. Then, or years before then. I wondered how my father would answer.

"I - "

"Aren't the people responsible for the government they elect?" asked John, arrogantly holding his glass out too for George to top up.

"Are they here?" Beverley said.

There was a hoot of appreciative laughter, some of it though I suspected was at my expense.

The wine was being passed further down the table.

"Let's be specific. You think Australia should be a republic, Elaine?" asked George, leaning forward in his chair so he could see me.

It was different somehow, him asking. More serious, and flattering that he was interested in my ideas. I considered carefully. All I knew were opinions I'd read in newspapers.

"I don't know," I said truthfully. "Either way it seems a pity."

"Come now, don't you have a definite point of view?" said John.

"The child's mother is English, for goodness sake. She grew up here apparently." Imogen's emphasis was rather irritatingly on 'the child'. She sounded annoyed. "You can't expect her to feel strongly about it."

"It is a young country," I said, suddenly anxious to impress, and wanting to have my say. "And Britain's chosen Europe. It's a new millennium. Perhaps it's time for Australia to stand alone."

"Who wants coffee and lemon cake?"

"Platitudes," Alec sneered. "Correct speak."

Cyril swallowed the last of his strawberries. "Alone it will be, sweetheart."

I was angry, fed up entirely with their gibes. "I don't see a problem with dropping the union Jack off their flag when you've split things up yourselves," I said. "Or not wanting a monarchy."

"No royalty?" exclaimed Dorothy.

"Yes, but where does it lead?" John's voice was agitated. "Bloody iconoclasts!" He had a problem with it obviously.

"Australians," Dorothy sniffed, "seem to like working here!"

"Brash lot if you ask me," Alec muttered.

"Australians are themselves," I said haughtily.

George smiled.

"No class system out there then, eh?" Alec upended the bottle to get the last of the wine from it. "One might say no class at all. And they owe a fortune. Worse than all the Russias."

George stood up and went over to the sideboard for another bottle.

Beverley giggled. "Kangaroos hop down the Sydney streets, don't they?"

How dare she side with them?

And Imogen was smiling approvingly at her!

"Sydney is a beautiful sophisticated city!" I cried indignantly. My opinion was based on television and glossy photographs in magazines. I had been too young to really remember anything but an intensely sweet eucalyptussy kind of smell, and long, sweltering days, and out where we lived a feeling of vast space, far horizons and cobalt sky around and above, but I wasn't going to tell any of them that. "What do you know?"

The new wine bottle appeared right beside me, as if to silence me. I caught sight of enough of the label as it tilted very slowly, deliberately towards my glass. Produce of Australia, Orange Muscat and Fl...

George smiled down at me and filled my glass and for a brief moment I felt special, that it mattered what I was feeling. Then his attention was gone.

"Anyone else want more of this excellent wine?" he asked, offering around the table. "Home, this weekend, are you, John?"

Coffee and cake had been served.

Alec and John had abandoned their jackets. Cyril's nose was getting pinker.

"Bloody Americans keep paying the rest of us so they can keep up their emissions."

"Parking's becoming a tax in disguise."

"Wouldn't it be fun," said George wickedly, " if we all went on strike from our cars for a day – and everyone went out catching buses and trains, the whole lot of us."

"Chaos," agreed Alec.

"But I don't know how one will be expected to do one's shopping," Dorothy declared. "The cost of living will rise if we're forced to shop at corner shops."

Imogen nodded. "What corner shops?"

"What banks!" grunted Alec. "There ought to be a tax on creating pollution. It's jump in your car for everything now."

"Nothing's thought through," said George quietly. "Short term rescue always wins in the financial sector. And too often, quick government finance fix."

John frowned. "The country needs reforming."

"It's almost too big a project," George muttered.

"Wrong bloody government of course," said Alec.

"Always is," sighed Cyril.

"So, Beverley, said Dorothy, turning to her and smiling brightly, "when do you leave for Cuckfield?"

Melanie leaned forward. "Do you need accommodation, darling?"

"No, no," said Imogen. "It's all included. They're going to be staying in this wonderful concourse. Everything's provided. They'll work all day."

"Dancing all day? How long for?"

"Too long." George sounded depressed.

"This cake really is delicious, Imogen."

I nodded in agreement, carefully keeping my silence and picking at the huge slice on my own plate.

"It's George's favourite."

"We have three solos to learn," said Beverley.

"The big night's at Kings Theatre."

"In Wimbledon? How thoroughly convenient!" exclaimed Dorothy.

"Isn't it!"

"And if nothing comes of it, it's back to school directly after that, young lady."

"Don't be such a wet, Daddy."

"He's not going to stop her! George, I refuse to let you dictate to her – "

"She's got a perfectly good brain, Imogen. Really she should be going straight to university. "

"Daddy, you promised I could have a year out!"

"If our daughter wants a career in the theatre – "

"Imogen, you know," said George, getting to his feet for more brandy, "wanted to dance herself."

The blusher on Imogen's cheeks seemed to darken.

"Why didn't you?" asked Melanie, sounding really sympathetic.

"She'll tell you she gave it up for me."

"I wasn't good enough," replied Imogen crisply.

"Personally I'd like to see Beverley looking to do something more constructive with her life."

"Not politics, George, surely!" said John.

"Ballet is far more exciting than politics!"

Every person in the room turned to stare at me, even Beverley.

"Anyone want more liqueurs?" asked Imogen, rising sharply to her feet. "I fancy a comfortable chair. More coffee, Melanie?" She was speaking too fast somehow.

"Cyril, another brandy?"

"Why not? Wonderful dinner, Imogen. George, you're a lucky man."

"Yes," said George.

Beverley disappeared to the loo and I went after her, following her out into the thick carpeted hall, and up the staircase. The bathroom was bigger than my own bedroom at home, with pin spot lighting and gleaming tiles. The toilet was separate in there, like a hotel or something.

"Some people are absolutely determined to ruin my evening," Beverley said, when she emerged from it.

"Who?"

It seemed to me that everyone was trying to make the occasion special for her.

"I knew I shouldn't have invited you!"

"Me?"

"You!"

"What do you mean?"

"Ballet's more exciting than politics! You sounded so offensive."

"What? I – "

"And you mustn't argue with John on foreign affairs. He's a brilliant man. Questioning his views puts him in a difficult position."

"Excuse me?"

"Australia."

"But I didn't!" What on earth was she talking about? I'd only answered all their questions. "Beverley?"

She didn't elaborate. Instead she went on: "And Daddy's being such a nightmare! How old does he think I am?"

She renewed her lipstick and pressed her lips

together. She looked at least twenty-five and still absolutely perfectly groomed, like a fresh orchid.

I tried to think of something to placate her.

"Well, you'll win the scholarship anyway," I sighed, "and show him! So you don't have to worry."

Well, she would win, wouldn't she? It was inevitable. And in a strange way I suddenly found the prospect cheering because there was hardly much point concerning myself about the money.

"No, I don't have to worry, do I?" she said, looking in the mirror at me and smiling, a glorious smile full of friendliness and forgiveness and intimacy again. Of course she would win.

I glanced at my own reflection, the collapsed moussed curls and faded make-up, at the creases where the dress she'd lent me didn't quite fit. I realized how idiotic I must be appearing, and gave up on myself entirely.

Beverley, Beverley, how your self confidence appalled me. And how easily and how often you ripped away my own.

Chapter 13

The guests all stayed until well after midnight, chatting. I went on drinking rather too much wine, even though George did not always offer it in my direction. He forgot Beverley sometimes too.

"At least it's Saturday night. The girls can sleep in," said Imogen. The wine seemed to have mellowed her, now the subject of ballet had been dropped, I had been effectively silenced, and the dinner was finished - or perhaps the caterers were gone and her responsibilities as hostess and mistress of the house were over and she could relax. She leaned back in her chair, crossed her slim aristocratic legs and watched George closely as he did the rounds of the glasses again, Melanie's, his cousin's, Cyril's, Alec's.

Her high heeled shoe tapped the air, and her chin was tucked in above the elegantly draped neckline of her silk jersey dress. Rather a good shaped face for the stage she had, defined jawline, high cheekbones. Memorable. But in her expression tonight with the people in this room, did I detect some slight distrust? Sometimes I hated the way she looked at me with such a measure of disapproval, but not any more tonight, she wasn't concentrating on me now. Well, not since I decided to keep quiet for fear of saying the wrong thing again. But earlier I had been aware of her tucking her chin in slightly like that at me. I wasn't a suitable friend for her daughter, and tonight I'd proved it - not bright enough, tactless, not nearly stylish enough, not even very interesting. Beverley deserved so much better.

How odd you can tell Imogen's sort of woman from

the pageboy cut of her blonde hair. She was certain to have a tailored navy coat and a patterned silk scarf in her wardrobe to go with the mid heeled navy court shoes she often wore. Classic, dependable and - did I dare think it? Slightly dull. There was me, judging a woman like that, when my own mother was sitting at home in her crumpled skirt and cardigan with her feet up, forever watching tele!

Imogen began talking to Dorothy so I shifted my gaze onto Beverley's father, onto George. What I like about some men is they don't have to wear suits. The women can dress up, but a man like George, with a figure like his, could even get away with jeans and not look out of place. So he wasn't wearing a suit, just a nice pair of comfortable olive green trousers, and a soft white cotton shirt tucked in loosely at the waist. Somehow sitting there, one leg crossed casually over the other, he appeared dressed up, more interesting than anyone else in the room, bar his daughter of course. But that same aura. It was nothing to do with his clothes or the fashionable silver watch and the very classy pair of leather shoes he had on, nor the way his dark hair wasn't quite straight but curled. Undulated. Nor the strong facial features, and the intelligent expression in his brown eyes. But more, there was sort of tenderness about him. A deep understanding somehow. A knowledge perhaps of how to be alive. It made me feel warm watching him, slightly excited, oddly excited, ache almost. I remembered his concern for me at the ballet, and him waiting outside Elfino's with me for the car, and him pouring that wine into my glass earlier and I began to wonder what it might be like to be in really close to him, idly considering the shape of his mouth, and the little vertical lines near it which showed just before he smiled, or appeared on their own if the conversation was amusing. It interested me too how he noticed what the women were doing more than the men. When Alec or John or Cyril spoke to him it was as if they interrupted his train of thought. Twice I saw him glancing over at Melanie but she was concentrating on her wine glass. The second time he caught me watching him.

"All right, Elaine? Can I get you anything?"

I shook my head, embarrassed. He regarded me for a moment - he couldn't be reading my thoughts, could he? Imogen glanced at me. I took a quick self-conscious sip of my wine.

George looked away. Imogen too, and the general conversation, which neatly excluded me, continued. Investments. Thousands of 'K'. Government expenditure. Suggestions. Backhanders. Denials. Talk of open government, of principles.

I turned my attention back to Beverley who was beside me on the sofa. Even though it was so late she still looked fresh, leaning back, relaxed, smiling, chatting to her aunt and Cyril, interjecting occasionally in the other talk and managing to say just the right thing all the time, so totally at ease. I leaned back too and made a conscious effort to release some of the tension that was locked into my shoulders.

At one point when there was another toast because Cyril had said, 'Eighteen, eh? A voter now,' George shook his head slightly and looked at Beverley with a that's-my-beautiful-daughter expression as if he could hardly believe it, and the little smiley lines appeared again. I eyed her enviously, then settled my gaze on her father again. An established man. Such a confident man.

Nice, his wide shoulders were, leaning against the chair.

But that was something I'd begun to notice too - that he seemed to have quite broad shoulders. Maybe it showed he was capable of carrying responsibility. Perhaps older men develop somewhere for a woman to cry on.

Beverley's mother put her head round the door to say goodnight.

"Don't be long now," she said.

"Goodnight."

The exotic scent of the mock orange growing outside floated up as the fine muslin curtains lifted a little. Near them was a door into the tiny private bathroom. I could hear water running, and Beverley cleaning her teeth. Without her in it, I considered the bedroom itself. Much as I knew it well, tonight the lamp light seemed to make it especially beautiful. A rectangular Persian rug, blues, purples and luminous ruby red, lay as usual like a mosaic of precious stones in the center of the pale carpet; the walls were white. The desk and a dressing table were light oak; a cane chair, cushions, multicolored like the rug, and a poster under glass of mosaic figures which picked up the same bright jewel colors. In the corner the mini hi-fi gleamed. The bed I was in seemed an unnecessary extra, an expensive new addition, a convertible armchair which I was sure had been purchased for my exclusive use. Except when I was there Beverley did not have to share her space with anyone. She didn't have to now really. There were other bedrooms. I thought of my own room. Small, plain, and mostly untidy. Comfortable only because I was used to its confines. It was my private place, but it contained nothing of the grace of this room.

Our dresses were draped over hangers on the side of the wardrobe. On my skin I could still smell the gorgeous perfume Beverley had anointed me with. I had, I decided, survived the second half of the evening better. George had been nice to me. Melanie had even kissed me goodnight as she left. Imogen had presented me with the lemon cake recipe. Perhaps I still had a foot in the Soames's door, even if I'd made some serious conversational errors. And in here, in this bedroom, was a private world, Beverley's, and mine tonight too, and more familiar than the rest of the house, easier to contend with. Under the bedcovers I felt warm and comfortable and relaxed. I reached above my head, and pointed my toes hard, stretching my body out like a contented cat.

"It's wonderful being here," I said, when Beverley emerged.

She beamed at me. "Want the bathroom?"

Our differences were forgotten. Good.

"The entry fee for the scholarship," she said though, as soon as the light was out. "How ever will you manage?"

"I'll cope," I said, furious suddenly that she could question my ability to pay. That she'd guessed. But I would cope. And I remembered she still hadn't unwrapped the little box. It was over on her dressing table and had cost me so much. It was all right for her. Her doting father would pay for whatever she needed. I blinked angrily into the darkness. I was surrounded by rich people but with no access to any finance myself. What a fearful difficulty money was suddenly becoming.

Luigi might let me work off a loan but at what cost? Maybe I could convince the Meridienne to allow me time to pay? If I could get my mother to listen for long enough maybe she did have something put aside, though having seen those vodka bottles I seriously doubted it.

"I expect my father will pay," I said grandly. "The worst way I'll do a few extra hours at Luigi's."

As if it was as easy as that.

Beverley fell silent. Where I had thought we might talk long and confidentially into the night the room was hushed and still.

Hushed and very still.

I wished I had been as silent earlier, and not spoken up at the dinner table about Australia, not argued as Beverley had insisted I had. I wished I'd known the clever answers they wanted, the well-informed replies they expected to all their questions, that I'd been able to keep up with their amusing anecdotal conversation. And then I thought about the label on the wine bottle, and the little lines beside George's mouth deepening as he filled my glass....

The wine and the silence began to wrap around me like a warm dark blanket.

A bell. Ringing, ringing.

Ringing, ringing. A muffled voice.

I turn over.

More voices. Then silence. The darkness closes in around me again.

And sleep.

"Elaine?"

An urgent whisper from the door. I open my eyes, and blink. Is it my dream? A narrow shaft of light paints a dazzling white line across my pillow.

"Elaine?" hisses a shadowed figure at the door.

"Yes?"

"I need to speak to you. Can you get up?"

It's Beverley's father. It's George.

George.

Suddenly I am wide awake and sitting up, excited, that strange aching excitement that I felt earlier when I was watching him. And anxious. Anxious that Beverley should not hear his voice, that it is only me he is calling, that he wants to speak to me, and it's still dark and everyone else is asleep. It's the middle of the night.

"Ssh," I whisper.

I climb eagerly out of bed, tidy my hair with my hands as best I can and, wrapping my gown around me, creep to the door. George is waiting on the landing. The house is very, very quiet. There's just us. He's wearing a dressing gown too, tartan, and under it, black pajama trousers. His hair is ruffled, endearingly out of place. He signals for me to close the bedroom door and to follow him downstairs to the sitting room. I have to stop myself walking a little too fast on his heels.

He closes that door there behind us too and switches on just one lamp. Our shadows play up the wall. Why do I feel so excited suddenly? So alive?

"Sit down, Elaine."

I smile at his invitation and do as he says.

He sits down too. On the sofa right beside me. Close.

I am very aware of his nearness. Of those broad shoulders and the fact that I'm so much smaller than he is. Of the dark hairs on his bare chest I can see under the tartan robe, and that my own gown has fallen open a little. I make no attempt to adjust it. It surprises me to

122

feel no modesty, that there's even some pleasure at not feeling it. His breathing. I'm up close to his breathing, it's so close I can almost feel it on my hair. I have a little warm pain way down in my abdomen. No, lower. Lower. An urgent tingling.

"That phone call."

I concentrate harder. He is pale. Now I can see the colour has drained from his face. I realize something is the matter for him. The little lines beside his mouth have disappeared. He's frightened I think of what he's going to say. I want to help him. I want him to know I want to hear whatever it is. I put my hand on his, then I know I've gone miles too far and draw it back quickly into my own space again. This is the night, the half light is playing tricks with my confidence. I blush. Why did I touch his hand? This is Beverley's father, for goodness sake. For a moment I'm so ashamed I can't look at him.

"The phone," he tries again. I've never seen him lost for words before. Tongue-tied like this.

There is something wrong.

"The phone," I say, to steady him.

"The phone," he says, then he hesitates.

I'm instantly frozen. Frightened. What's happened? What's the matter with George? Why can't he say what he wants to say? I glance beyond him to the clock on the mantelpiece. It's 4 a.m. Who on earth uses a phone at this time of night? Who...?

"Your mother...."

"Jonty? Is it Jonty?"

"Jonty? Oh, your brother. No, no. Nothing's the matter with him. It's..."

"My mother?" Now I'm indignant. She's ringing to check on me. Suddenly she's playing interested because

I'm out overnight.

"Yes. No - " He's thrown by my anger.

"What then?"

"She's asked me to - this is so difficult - "

I'm looking at him, puzzled. Is it really my mother we're talking about? Asking people to do things at this mad hour?

"She wouldn't have rung but..."

"What?" Why can't I just let him finish, stop interrupting?

"A phone call from Australia."

Now I'm confused. The time difference. There is, isn't there? Hours. What's so important that her ringing here in the middle of the night is necessary...

"This is madness. I should have waited till the morning. Elaine, your father - "

Suddenly I've started listening because the room is trembling. Bright with anticipation. I'm as still as still, and the whole room is trembling. George too. He's staring at me, trembling. He can see I'm hearing now.

"He's coming?" The lamp is shimmering. It's as if there's a note of music zinging on the air, high, high up, strumming off the walls. "He's coming here?"

"Elaine, listen to me. Your father's died. He's taken his own life."

The imaginary music explodes, shatters like glass into silence. Dead silence. Dead calm the room is. Dark.

Hollow.

I want to ask: Excuse me? What did you say? But my lips won't move. My mouth is too dry to open. I can't even control swallowing.

"Elaine?"

Silence.

I thought I had forgotten what it feels like to be that child. When he wasn't coming back. That awful sense of loss. I wanted....hoped that my dream was only a dream. I thought I had forgotten. I always hoped.... I wanted him to.... One day I wanted him to come up the stairs carrying the suitcase, the one I thought he went back for. In a sea of faces I have always been searching for his....

He won't come.... he won't ever come....

Not now....

And I let the plane leave without him.....

George clasps my hand sympathetically. The sensation takes time to register. It's as if my circulation has stopped, my hand has gone to sleep, the life has drained out of it. I know George is holding it but the feeling isn't there.

I can't remember... I panic that there's no outline, no shape, no memory of the face.

"There were fearful financial problems apparently. They found a note."

George is squeezing my hand. I know that because I can see he's doing it.

"H-how?" The word leaves me suddenly like a puff of wind. It's all I can say. It's all I want to say.

"In his car. A hose pipe from the exhaust."

For a moment I can't breathe at all. I know my eyes are wide and frightened. George is staring at me helplessly. Time stands dreadfully still. Even the clock seems to have stopped ticking. Then George does what I need him to do, the only thing that will save me from this awful moment. He puts his arms around me and presses my head close to his broad shoulders. Close. My tears are crushed against the sweet musk smell of that masculine bare skin where those dark hairs are, and suddenly all I can think of is I want this closeness to go on forever. I cling to him, dig my fingers into his chest as if I am drowning and only he can save me, and I feel his breath on my hair, and he's whispering: "Ssh, ssh, Elaine, I'm here."

"Ssh, ssh."

Hands clasping and unclasping. Dust rising in moonlight. A car travelling through the night, through the night towards a new life. In a car. A car.

Hands. His hands.

No, George's hands.

Strange. His hands now are all I can think of, all I want. The rest is all too long ago. I don't want that past. It's too far away. Way out of my reach.

"Ssh, Elaine darling."

George is holding me close. His breath is warm on my hair. On the wall our shadows have become one.

And inside me suddenly the blood thins, reverses, turns and breaks past what ever was blocking it and begins to rush through me now like a tidal wave, streaming right to the tips of my fingers, spreading down through my groin, burning me so I'm hot with the speed of it, with the sudden passionate force of it, with the danger of feeling like this. As if I'm travelling at two hundred miles an hour without a seatbelt.

And this isn't my father I'm clinging to, nor a substitute for him. And I don't want it to be. But it isn't. It isn't.

No.

There are too many physical tensions. Far too many taut nerve endings in all the wrong places, I know it, for just grief, and George is feeling it too. I am as certain of that as I have ever been of anything in my life. His consoling hands are not quite still as a father's would be, but responsive, moving. Only slightly, minimally, but enough for the woman somewhere inside me to recognize, though I have no experience, that this man's hands are exploring my surface, and I know that this feeling deep in me might be what I've been stumbling through my life towards.

And it will come out, it's like a fireball starting to roll, and there's a magnet in it pulling me into the future, I hear an echoing somewhere out ahead, some cataclysmic augury of the choices I shall make, a gun on the wall warning of winning and losing. Tonight something more powerful than I am is taking control.

When eventually George places me back at arm's length I can see my astonishment mirrored in his face. And then a shadow of guilt as he remembers who I am and why he embraced me....

He rises now and stands back, tells me I must try to get some sleep and suggests I go back to bed. We go back upstairs. He opens Beverley's bedroom door very quietly so as not to wake her.

"Try to sleep," he whispers.

I do try to do what he says. Obediently. I want to do anything he says.

My head is resting on the pillow, but I'm awake. All my senses are awake and throbbing, and parts of me, inside me that I never knew before have sprung to life. But am I just deceived by the darkness? By the enormity of this night? After a while I hear the dawn chorus and light steals in round the edge of the curtains. How quickly the sun is rising.

Beverley is asleep, as beautiful unconscious as she is

when she's awake. But I'm not watching her. Not now.

It's a new day.

Things are different. It's light now and everything is completely different. I have no father, and it's as if that makes me suddenly older. Suddenly I am my own woman. And in a single night the drum beat inside me has taken on a very vigorous new rhythm, a different sound, louder, much, much louder. Impulsive, reckless, and far more insistent than it was before.

Chapter 14

So it was that the following morning before he drove me home, George Soames, Beverley's father, who didn't really believe in the idea of dancing as a career, gave me the money I needed for the scholarship entrance fee and more, because he thought it was what my father should have done for me, it's what a father ought to do for a daughter, and perhaps George imagined it might serve to restore the proper balance between him and his daughter's best friend.

I find it strange it was my father's ending his own financial nightmare that prompted that gift of money. But then influences in life are strange, aren't they?

I think George kept the money a secret. In fact I'm sure he did, for he gave it to me in private and in cash. More than twice as much as I needed because he said there were bound to be extra expenses I hadn't thought of. When I told him I'd pay him back he said it was a gift, and to take the money because things would be difficult now and please not to mention it to anyone, anyone, (and I took that to mean Imogen and Beverley) because there was no need, and to stop worrying because I had enough problems. And then he said he was sorry, he hadn't meant to remind me, and was I sure I would be all right?

We were alone in the sitting room, and I started to cry because I wanted to feel his arms around me again. But it was daylight now and he didn't seem so tall and he was shifting from one foot to the other, looking very unsure and rather embarrassed about how to deal with what he thought was my grief, and I suppose some of it was grief, or perhaps a sudden, violent release of tension. I must be brave for my mother's sake, George was saying, and work hard at the scholarship because it would help. The best thing to do in his experience he said, was to concentrate on something. I wondered if he would mind if he knew that I was concentrating on him.

And then he stepped in close and kissed me, quite quickly, quite unexpectedly, on the forehead, like a little blessing, and said:

"Will you work hard for me?"

And I suddenly wondered if George had ever actually been happy either, because he understood so instinctively what counted when you weren't. Only I was. In a crazy kind of way I was.

But perhaps he just thought that kiss was what my father would do.

"Imogen's told Beverley," he said, "so you don't need to talk about it. We all understand how you must be feeling," and he took my hand.

He took my hand and led me through to breakfast. His hand was warm. And I went with him because I wanted him to take care of me. And at the table, in front of the others, I sat down like an obedient child.

Imogen fussed about pouring out coffee for me and asking did I want to eat anything? And when I said no thank you, insisting on making me toast.

Beverley sat opposite me, looking sort of sympathetic but wary of what she should say, and not too sure of someone who had a relative who might do themselves in. Then she suddenly stood up from the table and left the room and returned with the little box still in its wrapping paper. When she opened it and saw what it was, she oohed and aahed over it, and Imogen admired it and turned it over and over until I thought I would go insane. It was only a little box, for goodness sake, and now it was in her hands I knew it wasn't nearly as nice as I'd originally thought it was.

George drank his coffee and pretended to read the paper, but every so often his eyes strayed to my side of the table. Not directly onto me, that would have been too obvious, but enough to make me certain though that he was concentrating on me.

And that made me feel whole somehow, as if his concern was holding me together, supporting me like he'd wrapped some invisible safety net around me.

After Beverley and Imogen stopped over-reacting, for a few minutes no-one said anything. There was just the smell of toast and fresh coffee, and the chink of cup on saucer. Then Beverley stood up and came and put her arm around me, but in a funny, pretty kind of way as if she knew how good it would look.

And Imogen said: "I sure there must be something I can do for your mother." And I wondered what on earth she thought that might be, since it seemed to me she'd have trouble even bringing herself to park in a street like ours.

And then George told them he would drive me home.

"I'll come with you," said Beverley.

"No!"

"I don't think so, Beverley," George said.

When we stopped right outside the house, he didn't seem to notice the kind of street it was, the kind of house.

He asked again: "Will you be all right?"

"Yes."

But I didn't know whether he meant me to climb

straight out of the car, or whether I was waiting for something. He didn't move for a moment either.

Then he gave me a business card with his telephone number at his Westminster offices, the private line, in case I needed anything, even if it was only to talk.

"Anything, Elaine. Any time."

And he made me give him my phone number. He wrote it on a leather note pad with a silver pen, and I watched how his hand held the pen, how the fingers pointed down it, and the elegant shape of them. He put the note pad and the pen away in his inside pocket again and smiled at me. I felt nervously for the door handle and extricated myself from the car then, effusively thanking him for driving me back as he lifted my bag out of the car.

"I'll carry this in for you."

"No, no."

"Are you sure you're all right?"

"Yes."

"You've got everything? You've got the money?"

"Yes. But it's so much. Are you certain - " Asking! Asking that! God, don't let him change his mind.... I held my breath.

"And tell me if you need more. Promise?"

"Yes." But I wouldn't need to ask for more.

He took me at my word and didn't carry my bag up the steps to the door. I wouldn't have let him. He might have wanted to come inside. And into our house? I mean, what if my mother had been sitting watching television?

She was, of course, but for once it wasn't switched on. She was staring at the blank screen. Now it was my turn not to know what to say. I sat down beside her and we both just concentrated on the twenty-two inch gray square in a strange shared silence. After a while I went to the kitchen and made her a cup of tea. I decided not to tell her about the money George had given me. I didn't need to ask for her help anymore and now there was plenty for her to think about. Why bother her at all? Besides I thought suddenly, what if she needed it? No, better to keep it secret.

"Jonty's still asleep," she said eventually.

"Does he know?"

"No." She turned to me in panic. "You'll have to tell him, Elaine."

"Mum!"

"He'll listen to you."

I turned away from her, appalled that she should ask so much of me. "You have to do it, Mum."

"Please!"

I wished in the end I had, she made such a rotten job of it. She didn't hug him or anything. She just said it. No explanation. No tenderness. God, I was grateful I'd had George to tell me. I tried to soften the blow by putting my arm round him but Jonty just shrugged me away and went off down the street to search out his friends. No reaction. It was as if he'd been told an out of date weather report.

But then afterwards I thought, why would he really care? He'd been a baby when we left. Why should he worry about some man he'd never known dying in a far off country he couldn't remember. I relaxed a little. Of all of us Jonty was the least involved.

Even to me though my father was nothing but a shadow. I had no real memory of him. For a while I sat on my bed trying to picture him but nothing came. I wondered if I was trying too hard, that if I relaxed I might more easily conjure the image up. I tried to let go, release the tension inside me, but then what came instead was the feeling of George's hands, his hands on the surface of my back, holding me, moving oh so slightly. And the sensation, just the remembered sensation, travelled down inside me, down so deep, burning, burning into me with its heat. Extraordinary, the pleasure of it. The excitement of it. It made my stomach, no lower, lower, it made me churn down there, the heat of it.

I stood up, and forced myself to ignore such feelings, to stop thinking about George. Anyway I was being nonsensical, wasn't I? He wasn't feeling anything. People didn't feel like that about someone less than half their age. About a friend of their daughter's. It was my imagination. And what was it I was feeling anyway? Calm down, I told myself. George was being sympathetic, fatherly, and no more. It was me, my stupid romanticism, turning that embrace into something it wasn't and never would be. But I still felt excited, slightly sick, tender, and sort of bruised emotionally. I unpacked the clothes I'd taken to Beverley's, those clothes she'd laughed at, and I'd laughed at. I put them back in my cupboard. I could never expect to impress anyone in them, least of all George. But I would live with them. I wasn't going to buy anything new now. Anyway, impress George Soames? Dream on, Elaine Higham. The scholarship had to be what counted now and I had the money for it. He'd given me the money. And it was with kindness, concern. Sympathy. Nothing more. Poor Elaine, her father's died, what can I do to make her feel better? That was all. Even so I copied his phone number onto the plastic surface inside of my make-up purse, and into my address book in a way that made it look like a bank account number or something. I hid the actual card and the money under the lining paper in the drawer beside my bed. And I piled clothes on top of it.

George rang the very next night and talked to my mother, asked her how she was. Then he said that as he was driving Beverley down to Cuckfield the following weekend, would it make sense to take me as well?

"You'd better ask her," my mother said, passing me the phone. "Cuckfield?"

"Cuckfield, Mum, I told you."

"His voice sounds familiar."

Go away, I wanted to say, leave me with the phone. For goodness sake!

"You've spoken to him before, that's why."

"Oh."

She wandered back into the other room.

"Is that all right with you then?"

"That would be wonderful, George. Thanks."

"Your mother sounds as if she's coping?"

Television voices droned in the other room. I wanted her to be listening to them. To be concentrating elsewhere.

"Is she coping?"

Who could tell? Who could tell what she was ever feeling? But the picture was back on, had been for hours - perhaps that was an improvement.

"I think she is."

"What about your brother?"

"He doesn't even remem-....." How easily lies can be

caught out. "He's okay."

"Your mother says the funeral is next week."

"Yes, but - " And none of us going. How shameful. In spite of the distance, how dreadful, how callous we were, not even making any pretence at an attempt. But the funeral would be like Christmas and birthdays in our family. Just another day. "We can't go. It's too far, too sudden. Even for Mum."

"Well, I can understand her not wanting to leave you two right now."

"Mmm."

"So I wondered, Imogen and Beverley have gone back with Cyril to stay in Cambridge tonight - "

I outlined my lips and powdered them to set the colour. I pulled my hair back off my face into a low pony tail - several times to make sure it was just right. Beverley's skirt I put on, one she'd passed on to me, and a pretty embroidered blouse she had chosen and insisted I should buy in the Kings Road. It was the only concession I made to reality, for his sake, to make myself look as much like his daughter as I could. I mean, it was unreal, this, wasn't it? Me going out with an adviser to the government, a man more than twice my age. But I wanted to see him, I was aching with excitement to see him, and I didn't care if it was going to be a crowded restaurant or where we were going. if I ate, or what I ate, what wine the waiter would bring, nor that it was the day after my father's death. As far as I was concerned the rest of the world didn't exist.

"Where are you going?" called my mother.

Why would she ask suddenly? "Out!" I said.

"With Beverley?"

"Just out, Mum!"

I closed the front door behind me without a second thought. Not reason nor sense nor any other wisdom guided me to the street corner where he'd said he would meet me.

I was going to have dinner with my best friend's father. With George. So close in, I was. But you have to be close in if you want to steal.

It was dangerous what we were doing.

It should have been innocent, a father taking his daughter's friend out to cheer her up, shouldn't it? I mean a father ought to be able to do that, if the friend needs it. Even if his wife and daughter are away.

But it wasn't innocent. Surely George knew as well as I did as we sat at that small round candlelit table, in that tiny back street bistro that only a razor edge divided us? Surely he'd recognized the shine in my eyes for what it was, and understood I saw him as no formal father, but as a man, a man with sexual heat radiating out in great waves to the young woman beside him. I'm sure he saw it. He had to have seen it.

Dangerous.

"Have you sorted out the entrance fee with Orlando's?"

"Tomorrow morning and I - "

"Didn't we agree not to mention paying it back, Elaine? Besides it's satisfying to be able to do something that counts. My time is usually spent twisting figures and manipulating statistics according to how they need to be read." He smiled. "Pity we're not all 'ourselves', as you put it the other night."

I cringed, and held my breath. If he remembered one

remark, then what else? Beverley had admonished me for arguing. Maybe George was going to as well. But then the waiter arrived to take the order and that night was supplanted by this one.

"So what would you like?" George asked. "The pasta's good here."

"You choose," I said, happy to let him take over.

What little anxiety I felt was dissolved away by his gentle questioning - how was I feeling now? Would I prefer white wine or red? Did I know what to expect at Cuckfield? Such a nice country sort of area. Had I been down to Sussex before? No further mention was made of the other dinner night. Nor was there any demanding political brilliance I was secretly dreading - nor was anything said that was uncomfortably clever, but he wasn't talking down to me either. He seemed so interested in what I thought, even if our conversation was just ordinary small talk about me, about school, about Orlando's, did I like London? But I knew there was nothing I couldn't say to him if I wanted to, apart from pointedly not mentioning Beverley and Imogen. And that was pretty important. Presumably like me, he didn't want their names at that table either because he never mentioned them once himself. And you'd think he would - I was his daughter's best friend, and doesn't a man speak of his wife?

But really the talking was unnecessary and meant nothing. Sometimes it was the moments when we were saying nothing, just eating, him passing the bread to me, him pouring more wine, the pasta sauce glistening red in the light. And all the time that physical tension like electricity buzzing through me, as if I had a heightened awareness of the slightest reaction, each movement of the lips, mine and his, every blink of our eyes within the separate circle of candlelight we occupied. The sound of wine as it surged into the glass, the sparkle of it. The colour. The flickering flame of the candle, the heat of it almost singing into the air. The exquisite taste of the food that he had chosen for me. And after dinner sitting there, seeing those little lines beside his mouth, the depth of the warm brown tones in his eyes, the concerned expression, the minute criss-cross pattern on the skin of his fingers as his hand lay on the table just an inch from my own. And the distance between them. The expanse of red tablecloth in that inch, and the extraordinary aching necessity to cross it.

Dangerous.

His hand moved first.

Away.

I caught my breath.

Was it that?

Was it that acknowledgment of my disappointment that made him smile and take my hand, and say: "It's all right Elaine, I know what you must be feeling."

"Do you?"

"I think so."

Could he understand how much I wanted him to touch me? Not my hand. Touch me!

"I - "

"You don't need to tell me, Elaine," he said, as if he was reading my thoughts.

I frowned. Did he know?

Someone opened the restaurant door then. Only a stranger. But in that moment I knew, for George let go of my hand and turned so quickly to see who it was that the candle blew out, like the flick of a silver fish.

Guilt.

Wicked wonderful guilt!

And at the waxy smell of the extinguished flame, and the fine wisp of smoke rising up from it, I could only smile, anticipating suddenly with excitement now what I imagined might become of us.

....what love can do....that dares love attempt....

George! My best friend's father.

Would he dare? I wanted him to.

But the sounds of the restaurant had intruded for the moment. The present magic evaporated. Not tonight then. George signaled to the waiter and pulled his chair back and stood up and put a safe distance between us again.

"It's time you were going home," he said. "It's very late and your mother won't thank me for keeping you out past midnight."

Chapter 15

It must still be somewhere in my make-up case....I search suddenly excited by the thought that it is there. Among the things I've wrapped up as treasures and put away to keep. Like dry leaves disturbed the tissue paper rustles. The edges unfold and a forgotten breath of Jasmine escapes....

It's another little card. 'Good luck,' it says.

'Elaine, from George

- and Imogen'.

The 'and Imogen' is written lower than it should be. There's an unnecessary distance between the two names. It leaves room for me to read between the lines.

I trace with my finger the way my name is written, the shape of the letters. How idiotic to get so much pleasure from such a simple thing. That card came with a tiny bottle of perfume, the really expensive sort Beverley used, and was given to me on the day we went to Cuckfield.

There are things I should remember about the few days before that. Apart from my thinking of George all the time of course - thinking what it would be like walking round Covent Garden with him, or shopping in a supermarket, or drinking coffee together in Luigi's. What energy those daydreams, that thinking about him used up. I spent time too fingering the rest of the money he'd given me as if it was part of him, and read and re-read his business card: his name in print, the phone number, where his offices were. Back and forth in the West End on my way to class I searched eagerly for his face in every crowd as if by chance I might see him, as if by chance he might be where I was, even though Beverley had mentioned he was currently working long hours at the House. As if he might have told her that just so he could be walking somewhere near me without being noticed. At night I went to sleep remembering his hand on that red tablecloth. Dreamed of him touching me. And woke up with my nightie tight in the crack. Woke up visualizing his face.

Other things.

The day of my father's funeral. I thought that would matter but it passed without me noticing, only acknowledged in a sudden guilty realization before I went to sleep that night. Except that I dreamt my dream. The classes of course - confined to the mornings so that we would have more time to get organized. And the excited dressing-room chatter. And Mrs Scobie wishing me good luck and, quite out of the blue, giving me a hug. The anger and frustration in Luigi's voice at me phoning him to say I was suddenly leaving.

"Waitresses! I have them up to here!"

But it's the anticipation I remember best. The shimmery feeling, the brightness, the colour of the waiting. The time it used up. The intensity of it. The longing. The craving for the day to arrive when George would drive me to Cuckfield and I would see him again, be near him. Even though Beverley would be there too. I counted the hours down, worrying if I had the time right. Was it two o'clock? Perhaps it was three? No two, surely. I thought about the distance. Yes, two. Why hadn't I written it down? Yes, two, I was sure. I could ask Beverley of course, but I didn't want to. I rang George on his private line on the pretext of checking.

He answered. "Hold on a moment." He sounded anxious.

Then after a click: "Is everything all right?"

"Oh, yes," I said. Because it was once I had heard his voice. "I - I wanted to know, is it, is it two o'clock?" Why couldn't I speak without hesitating?

"Sorry?"

"Saturday."

"Yes."

"Yes. Two o'clock."

"Two o'clock. I'll see you then."

"Yes."

"Take care of yourself."

I held onto the receiver for several minutes as if I could prolong the connection. But he was gone. Two o'clock. Nothing could be clearer. There was no reason to ring him again.

Hardly bearing to eat or sleep after that, I gathered my clothes and practice clothes and pointe shoes together, and for once, bravely shopping on my own without Beverley's precious advice, I bought the rest of what I needed, suddenly endlessly trying on, daringly, time and time again, before choosing, changing my mind, and choosing again, carefully considering what made me look and feel really feminine, because suddenly I did. The remainder of the time passed without any other thought. I was only concerned for....well, him and the actual journey.

And three things I remember about that.

Beverley's face as I emerged and she sat waiting in the car and I realized with some concern she was staring disdainfully at my home, and the slight reticence in her greeting now she'd seen for the first time where I lived.

And George's hand brushing against mine as he took my bags from me and stashed them into the boot of his silver car, the thrill it gave me just standing beside him; and a feeling that inside the houses people were aware of this man and his beautiful car in the street, beside the house I lived in.

And George's eyes not quite daring to meet mine while Beverley went to find the loo in the restaurant where we stopped en route for a coffee, because a couple of people at another table had recognized him. The conversation there was bland. Nothing unusual was said. But for me nothing needed to be said.

When Beverley returned she dug in her bag and produced the gift of perfume.

"I chose it," she said, finishing her coffee as I unwrapped it.

"Beverley knows what you like," said George.

"Thank you."

I read the card. "Thank you," I said, looking directly at him as Beverley was glancing at the expensive marcasite watch on her delicate wrist.

"I don't want to be late. Shall we go?"

It was the last thing I wanted to do, but we returned to the car and drove on. I wished George would slow down. We were covering the miles too quickly. I didn't want to arrive. I wanted to stay in that car forever, even with Beverley there too if that was all I could have. Just George's presence in the front seat - Beverley and I were sitting together in the back, was enough, and the opportunity for furtive glances at his profile, his eyes in the rear view mirror, concentrating carefully on the road. But now we had passed through Cuckfield village and out into the rolling Sussex countryside again and the

Rosehill Concourse sign appeared at the roundabout and we turned and then turned again between two fields into a long drive. At the end of it was a low red brick building, a purpose-built study centre and attached accommodation block.

We drew up beside other cars, other people arriving. I could see Sergei standing inside the glass doors which led to reception. Irina too. Now there would be four weeks here to learn solos and rehearse them, one week home and then the actual performance night, and in all that time I wouldn't see George.

"Will you ring?" Beverley asked him, as we unloaded the bags from the car.

"I'm in Paris on Monday," he said, "and then Milan for a few days."

So far away. He looked so strong, so protective, as he lifted out my suitcase. I felt little and insecure, and in chaos suddenly at the thought of him leaving. Almost a blind panic.

"Rather like boarding school, this," he said, as if he could read my thoughts.

"Is there a porter?" asked Beverley.

George helped us in with our cases.

I walked behind him and Beverley, frightened George might set the luggage down and leave without saying goodbye.

I saw Sergei notice Beverley immediately she came in the door, of course. He smiled at her as she passed. He smiled at George too, but not the same way, just in vague recognition and awe of a public figure face. But for my smile there was no acknowledgment.

The reception area seemed full of waifs, just like us

I suppose, with large doe eyes, overloaded with belongings, and waiting to be given instructions.

Diana appeared with Candice trailing behind her

"Hi! You two are sharing like we are. Your room's down that corridor, I think. There's list over there."

"I have to get back," said George briskly. "Work hard."

He hugged Beverley and over her shoulder his eyes met mine, and he smiled briefly. Then he disappeared quickly out through the doors.

As he walked towards his car I fingered the little box with the perfume bottle in it in my pocket, and the card. George climbed into the silver car and drove slowly up to the main road. The two fields seemed to divide before him.

"Elaine? Elaine! Come on!"

"Not many dancers are given a chance like this at the start of their careers," Irina was saying to the assembled group. "And I expect you to make intelligent use of it. In the end there can only be one Meridienne winner, but for the rest of you this intensive training, and the experience you will gain here, will be invaluable for the future. It will be hard work but you may never have another chance like it and you will probably remember these few weeks for the rest of your lives."

"I'll bet we do," muttered Diana under her breath. "This is a terrible way to choose someone they might eventually make a company member. And only a month to learn everything."

The tiny box in my pocket was smooth against my fingers. Four weeks seemed an eternity.

"There is a general dance class this evening, and then

we will begin in earnest in the morning. Have you all settled in to your rooms?"

We had. The rooms were big and comfortable with twin beds. Beverley took the one nearest the ensuite bathroom. I didn't care. That didn't seem very important. There was a nice full-length mirror, a television, kettle and all that, and a door out to the garden, and two study desks. Although the centre was equipped with three wonderful dance studios it was used for all sorts of other activities and studies.

"There's a swimming pool somewhere," Beverley said, as we unpacked. I saw her counting the available coathangers in dismay. She'd brought more clothes than she could possibly expect to wear. Surely our days would be spent in practice gear.

"Will there be a chance? By the look of the program we'll be running to keep up without going swimming."
Actually the crowded schedule was something I was really grateful to see. I needed to concentrate now if I could, and not on George, and if I had no time to think it would be easier, and the time would go faster. Maybe.

To introduce us to each other there was coffee served in a small lounge. Black coffee of course. Which of us would dare to add milk to it here? As Olivia's girls we stood together, Beverley, shining with confidence, Diana and Candice - and me feeling particularly insecure and more in awe of Beverley's assurance and looks than ever. Beverley and Diana began sizing up the opposition with comments under their breath.

"She's ultra thin."

"Look, there's the boy."
"Not very tall, is he?"

One of the five other girls was talking to him.

"Christopher.. something.."

"Delaney."

"Well, no-one will fancy him!"

"Poor thing, imagine being the only male," Candice whispered to me.

According to the list in reception the others were all from separate theatre schools scattered around the country. Olivia had done really well to get four of us in and that gave us status. Together we must have presented a rather smug front.

One girl introduced herself. To Beverley of course. Lillian Ingram she said she was, from Winchester.

"You have to be the group from Orlando's."

Then a couple of the others came over, and Beverley was smiling her fairy tale smile and then they were all clammering to speak to her, Christopher Delaney included. And Diana and Candice and I stood back a little and watched.

"Are you Beverley's sister?" the girl called Meg asked me. I shook my head but secretly I was pleased. Maybe that was a propitious beginning.

In the promised first class that evening everybody was watching everyone else, wondering who amongst us all had the best chance of winning in the end. It seemed to me it was pretty generally decided to be Beverley. Irina concentrated on her, and had her stand centre front row, but even if she hadn't, that's where Beverley would have ended up. The others all let her take centre stage.

I placed myself where I could see her well and pushed myself harder, strained a little more.

Overall the standard was very high but as Olivia's

girls we were quite capable of keeping up. Of the others Lillian Ingram had stunning deportment but not enough turn out, red-headed (an unattractive pale red making me glad mine was auburn) - pale red-headed Wendy Pearman's hips were very slightly out of proportion with her narrow shoulders. I hated the way Tanya Fields's neck seemed faintly loose in its socket as if she normally did advertisements for hair products, Meg Ryan had a lovely figure but kept falling behind in the sequences, and why Christopher had been chosen at all beat me. Nice elevation but he had fearful arches. Don't get me wrong, they were all excellent, but ballet demands absolute perfection, doesn't it? Chloe Tremain, the ultra thin one, was the best of them, but we weren't bad either. As always Diana showed her exuberance, Candice was lyrical, I was technically proficient and working really hard, and Beverley....well, of course Beverley just shone.

"Isn't it wonderful?" she said, as she bent down to remove her pointe shoes as usual before we left the studio.

"It's wonderfully hard," I said.

The next day began early with a warm up class, and then mid morning we were divided into two groups to begin learning the set solos, one adage and one allegro. There was no time for thinking. I was surprised and delighted to find Sergei was my instructor, and how good he was at teaching. It was the first session for months I completed without the vicious correction I always expected. But there was one big problem. I was out on my own. Beverley had been put with Irina.

After the lunch break we returned to continue in

those groups and then eventually came back together for a final class. What a relief it was to stand in Beverley's shadow again. I relaxed and danced confidently for the first time that day.

In between all this we were each given a private lesson to make a start on our short individual pieces. These were taken from ballets, not demi-character but classics, solos lifted directly from the grand pas de deux, and they were designed not only to test us but to end the evening of the competition performance on a spectacular note. At lunch while everyone was only picking self-consciously at the food, afraid to be seen being hungry, we discussed the list. Sugar Plum and Bluebird for Tanya and Chloe. The Waltz from Sylphide for Wendy, Prayer from Coppelia for Meg, Lise from Fille Mal Gardee for Lillian, and Christopher got the Prince's solo from Nutcracker. Lilac Fairy from Sleeping Beauty was chosen for Candice.

"That will really suit you," said Diana.

"I'd rather have Aurora. You're so lucky."

"I know," said Diana, her eyes sparkling.

Beverley had the showy Black Swan solo from Swan Lake, Act III, and Sergei to teach it.

And me? It was awful. I was given Kitri from Don Quixote - and Irina. Now I would have to cope with flicking a fan open and closed, and Irina herself. Not only that, there was no Beverley to imitate. I would have to work out for myself how to do it.

George rang Beverley up from Paris on Monday evening. I knew he would ring. A good father makes inquiries, doesn't he? He cares about those who matter to him.

"He asked how you were enjoying it," Beverley

mentioned.

If you had seen me moving around the bedroom after that preparing for bed, you could not possibly have guessed the pleasure I was feeling inside, only recognized the scent of a little jasmine on the air.

Chapter 16

I was being irrational of course, but when someone follows you around you do begin to wonder why, don't you? You think, maybe he's interested in me, maybe he wants to talk to me. And maybe.... Well, it's possible. And after that night at the restaurant with George, things were different. If one man finds me attractive, I thought, why not another? And it makes you feel prettier, and gives you a bit of a lift, doesn't it? It makes life seem nicer all round, even if it isn't the right person, even if you couldn't fancy them in a million years. You preen just a little, toss your head slightly, set your lips into a prettier position. Well, that's what Beverley usually did anyway, so that's what I did, those first few days at Rosehill.

But of course inevitably the revelation came and it wasn't like that at all.

"How can I get to talk to her?"

"Just go and say hello," I said, suddenly bored out of my mind with the opposite sex. Except George. I couldn't be bored with him, even though he hadn't rung in a couple of days. No, just this immature idiot of a boy, and anybody his stupid age.

"Introduce me," Christopher pleaded. "Tell her I want to talk to her."

"You know her. Stop asking me."

"Please?"

"Oh God!"

Beverley wasn't the slightest bit interested in Christopher anyhow, when he did eventually pluck up courage to go and speak to her when she was on her own, though she smiled and flirted slightly, enough to make him want to do anything for her. To start with he fetched us both coffee (but of course he soon forgot mine) and anything else she needed, and hung around mooning over her instead of concentrating on his work until I thought I would go insane if we met him round another corner. When finally he settled his affections on Chloe instead, I was the one mightily relieved. He gazed at Beverley from afar though, as if she was some goddess on a pedestal, out of his reach but still to be coveted and admired. He'd never even considered me. Of course I didn't want him, but it's demeaning when you're just a stepping stone. There were other men there too among the staff, the administrator, the boys in the kitchen, a garden man, enough of them to make any girl look around occasionally. The other girls. Not me.

Apart from the private lessons which I dreaded, and in spite of revelling in Sergei's teaching, one class melted into the next, one exhausting day into another, with barely time to think about what was really in my mind. I was right about spending our time in leotards and tights, and legwarmers and woollies. Even for dinner nobody bothered to change into ordinary clothes, and mostly we just fell into bed at night to be up early for fruit and yogurt breakfast before the warm up. The only variation was an occasional costume fitting, and Saturday and Sunday nights when some of us sat for a while chatting as if to mark the end of another week.

We passed harsh judgment on anyone who happened not to join our gossipy little weekend circle, even if they had other things to do or had simply gone to bed tired out, while between ourselves we buoyed each other up by trading mutual admiration. There was endless interest in the solos and in Irina and Sergei, the Meridienne Ballet, and what the night would be like. You might think us a closeted little lot, but don't gardeners discuss flowers, don't shopkeepers rattle on about trade, don't nuns talk religion?

Besides I was actually thinking of other things, not to mention listening in case the phone along in the hall rang.

The second Saturday Christopher redeemed himself a little by smuggling in some wine and Diana stole some cups and on this rare occasion we talked on a different level. I was in a good mood. George had phoned in the afternoon and even though it was only Beverley he had spoken to, he had asked after me.

"What should I do?" Lillian was saying. "There's my father writing to me saying he'd love me to come into the business with him."

"Do you want to?"

"What business?"

She told us.

"No!"

Being an estate agent seemed so ordinary. We all set about trying to convince her to think independently.

"You could easily get into a ballet company."

Lillian pulled a face. "Back row, corps de ballet, I know."

"Never! But anyway tied to a dull old office all day. You'd hate it!"

"My boyfriend works in an office," said Wendy, in Lillian's defense. "We're planning to get married as soon as we can."

We all turned and stared at her and she blushed as

154

pinky-orange as her hair.

"What and give up?"

"Well!" she asked. "What's wrong with that?"

"Don't you want to have a career first?" asked Diana. "What about all your training?"

"And I suppose you want loads of children," said Chloe.

Wendy looked rather pleased at that suggestion.

"What's your perfect kind of man?" Diana asked us all.

"My kind," said Christopher. He was braver now he'd taken up with Chloe, and actually rather conceited.

She grinned at him. The rest of us howled him down.

"Seriously."

"Meg?"

Meg looked as if she'd been caught napping. "I haven't any idea," she said blankly. "I never thought about it." I think she was surprised to be asked. Usually we avoided her inane opinions.

"And Candice? A restaurateur?"

We all laughed. Poor Candice was in bed, no doubt dreaming of food.

"I wouldn't mind snogging Yogurt boy."

"Who?"

Diana giggled. "You know, the one who puts out the fruit and stuff in the dining room."

"Errh!"

"What about you, Beverley?"

We waited for her to speak, for a gem of information, Christopher looking as if he was about to find out the secret of the universe. After all Beverley could have her choice, but what was she looking for?

"Someone I can trust," she said. "And I don't care if

he's not rich."

Was she right? Trust, not money? But rich people can afford to say things like that. They don't have to worry, do they?

"But handsome," said Diana.

Oh yes, that would matter. Appearances were very important to Beverley, and come to think of it she was being far from honest. Her sort of appearances needed financing. She would never manage without money. In a way though even what she was saying was for the sake of appearance.

"I've seen your father on television," said Christopher, looking at her in awe. "On the financial programs."

Beverley shrugged. "Money isn't everything," she said.

There was moment's silence. Perhaps everyone had just realized that with her connections Beverley could go to Paris anytime she liked. She had no need of a scholarship.

But Beverley always knew what she was doing. To the untrained ear it might have seemed she was trying to be one of us. In reality that statement had set her apart, lifted her onto a higher plane.

Diana laughed nervously.

"What about you, Elaine?"

I answered so truthfully it even surprised me. Perhaps it was the wine. Besides I had always imagined that as Beverley had suggested, trust was important, and that anyway I would, as always, agree entirely with her that it was dependability I was after.

"Someone dangerous," I said.

And they all laughed thinking I was being stupid.

We were interrupted then. Irina hurried by followed a

minute later by Sergei.

"What's going on?" muttered Christopher.

"Something's up," said Chloe.

In the morning we found out what. Tanya had slipped in the shower and injured the muscles in her ankle. She would have to rest for several days. It was touch and go if she would make the competition.

Of course to start with I was secretly looking forward to leaving Rosehill. Madness, of course. I mean, it was stupid, wasn't it? That wonderful opportunity and all I could think of was George, how once it was all over, he would be coming back in his silver car to collect us, and I would be in London again, near him, and that even if Beverley went to France I might still have some contact with the Soames family. Beverley would come home for holidays sometimes. Even dancers have time off. And we would keep in touch. I could write to her absolutely all the time. Make sure. After a while though, and perhaps it was the lack of phonecalls or just the constant exercise and concentration required to master the solos, I began to realize that when Beverley went to Paris, that would be that. All connections would cease. She would meet new people, and a busy man like George wouldn't think twice about his daughter's former friends. And I was kidding myself that he had any interest in me at all, wasn't I? Imagining it.

It severely depressed me to think things through so honestly. But after all - I considered it rationally - me and Beverley's father? Even Sergei was a more sensible choice.

Suddenly perseverance was all that was driving me forward. Well, the result was a foregone conclusion, wasn't it? But I tried to convince myself it would be a performance, and that somebody important might be watching. I'd learnt the two set pieces by heart and Beverley and I practiced those together when we could. I almost knew the Don Quixote solo, and I had all but mastered the flick and flutter of the fan but the final turns still bothered me.

"There's one comfort," Beverley said, "at least you're only doing Kitri's solo. You don't have to cope with the fouettés in the coda. Or the posé pirouettes in mine."

Her solo finished with a circle of twenty-eight of them. Which of course she could do perfectly. Need you ask?

There was no doubt Beverley was dancing divinely. I longed to watch and pick up new ideas but since we were in separate groups I was seeing less and less of her. Every minute of her spare time too she devoted to rehearsing Black Swan with Sergei while between classes I needed time to sit down and recuperate. I was envious of her unending vitality and energy.

I only saw her dance the Black Swan solo once at Rosehill, towards the end of the time we were there. By then once was all I could bear.

It was a single costumed rehearsal designed to give us a feel of what was coming. When it was Beverley's turn we all stood and stared in awe at her technique, at her presentation, and a kind of brittle sparkle she gave to the dance, an electricity which not one of the rest of us could hope to match. The ecstatic burst of applause from everyone in the room at the end confirmed what we all knew.

On the night of the Meridienne Scholarship Beverley Soames would be unstoppable.

"You never ring your mother," said Beverley one evening, as she came back from using the phone herself.

I shrugged. "She's got Jonty."

"How old is he?"

"Thirteen."

"Fun?"

"Nightmare! Luckily I hardly see him."

"School? Does he board or something?"

It amused me, her view of my world.

"He's into drugs," I said wickedly, and then seeing her face, wished I hadn't.

"I always knew where to get hard drugs at school if I wanted them," she said rather grandly, while she loosened her hair. It fell around her shoulders, dark and glossy. "Of course I turned them down."

I frowned, not sure how she was expecting me to react. Was she being disapproving or trying to impress me?

"I was kidding," I said. "My morbid imagination!"

She looked almost disappointed.

"Jonty sometimes smokes pot with his friends. I'm always catching them out down there by the river."

"Near where you live?"

I nodded.

"On the slipway. They sit there in the dark like a load of gnomes, him and his friends, puffing away."

She laughed.

"Perhaps I will ring my mother," I said.

I could hear in my mother's voice I was disturbing some television program, so that was the only time in that whole four weeks that I rang home. Beverley rang her mother every two or three days. George rang

Beverley whenever he had a chance, which wasn't often.

He came back from Milan and went almost immediately to Geneva and then on to New York from where he sent a postcard.

Because it had a picture of Broadway on it, Beverley handed it to me. I turned it over on the pretext of identifying the place.

'I hope you girls are working hard,' I read.

Girls. I was included. I felt the brush of his lips on my forehead. Will you work hard for me? The remembrance of it was so exhilarating I resolved to stop giving in and try harder.

Melanie Powers rang one evening and said if we had any time off to come and see her and John.

"John's up in the House most evenings. One Sunday perhaps?"

She seemed miffed when Beverly explained that Sundays were workdays too. She couldn't believe it. "Don't miss your father on Question Time tonight," she said.

Beverley, though she told me, didn't seem interested herself.

But the thought of it! George. On television. In an hour. I watched the minutes disappear one by one as the hands moved forward on the bedside clock.

I don't know where Beverley was when the program came on. Perhaps she had seen her father so often on television it didn't matter, but I couldn't imagine how she could miss him. I was mesmerized. This was the man who had put his arms round me, who had touched my hand. I found myself smiling with pride every time he spoke. At that discussion table he seemed so responsible, so charmingly intelligent, so practiced in the way he dealt with the questions and other panelists' responses, so deserving of the approval of the audience.

And far away. So far away. Why would he care about me?

The next day was exceptionally hot, and my eighteenth birthday, though not one person noticed. I didn't even get a card from home.

And Beverley said: "I've told Daddy to stop ringing up. Honestly anyone would think I was a child!"

The day's rehearsal was full of disastrous mistakes and Irina, her constitution deeply rooted in the snows of Northern Europe had been, because of the heat, in a particularly evil mood. Even with her quiet voice, she could be worse than Olivia. The morning class was one of her fearful tests of stamina, and my private lesson followed on in much the same vein. My lungs felt as if they would burst. With only seven days at Cuckfield to go all I wanted to do was cry. Why couldn't I get the steps under control? Why didn't my balances balance? I flicked the fan, and sent it spinning across the room. Irina remained silent and rewound the tape while I rescued it.

We were allowed to use the studios on our own in the evenings but that night it was no use going back to practice again. The muscles in my limbs were so used up I could hardly feel them. Somebody said it was extra oxygen in the blood stream, and a wonderful thing. It gave me a strange, languorous, floating sensation, whatever. Back in the bedroom there was no sign of Beverley. I pulled on a cool blue cotton shift and some sandals and went out and sat quietly on the lawns and picked angrily at the grass with my fingers. The evening air was particularly humid and there were regular bursts of high pitched humming from mosquitoes, a hallelujah chorus of them.

Away to my right the reception doors opened and Sergei emerged. He just stood there for a while and then he noticed me. He hesitated before he wandered over. Maybe things were about to improve.

"For a moment I thought you were Beverley."

I felt too exhausted and fed up to be pleased about that!

"Where is she?"

"How should I know?" I said crossly.

"It's just you two are normally together."

"Not always."

"She's such a beautiful girl."

Why did people always say that? Why, why did I have to be reminded all the time?

"Yes," I said, finding it especially hard to disguise my jealousy.

"It's cooler out here."

"Yes."

"I didn't see you at dinner."

"I wasn't hungry."

He was about to suggest that wasn't very bright, I could tell. Then he changed his mind and asked me instead how the Don Quixote was coming.

I shrugged. "It isn't."

"No?" He sat down on the grass beside me. "I thought it would suit you well."

"It's lightweight."

"Lightweight?"

"Compared with Black Swan."

"Or Aurora," I added quickly.

"That's strange. I've never thought so." He tugged at a blade of grass. "Ever seen it performed?"

"Only on video."

"Shame. It can be a real show stopper, all that scarlet and black. Have you worked out how to do your hair?"

"No."

Typical. He was critical of my appearance, like everyone else.

He concentrated on a new piece of grass. "I've got a book with me. I'm sure there are photographs of Don Quixote in it. I'll lend it to you."

I looked at him. He did seem to be trying to be genuinely helpful.

"Thanks."

"The important thing is to look sexy. Kitri is a flashy little flirt. You have to give all of yourself to your audience. Concentrate on the phrasing and balance. And there's a lot of stillness in it."

"Stillness?"

"Hanging on sometimes for a split second extra. Gives it that fiery quality. And you want an absolutely static finish after those final turns."

I sighed.

"We'll go through it tomorrow if you like."

The prospect thrilled me. I beamed at him. "Do you mind if I ask you something?"

"What?"

"Why don't you dance?"

He stared out across the garden. "I injured my knee fourteen months ago. It was a nightmare. I had to stop completely until just recently or risk my mobility. Teaching for Meridienne now may give me the chance to come back." He still had time. He couldn't be more than twenty-five or twenty-six.

"Are you French?"

"My father was from Provence but I grew up here in England."

"My father was Australian but I grew up here too," I said.

"We have something in common then," he said, looking at me unusually carefully.

As always he was dressed in black. His face was that olive colour that goes so well with very dark hair and brows. Nice jawline. Interesting eyes, almost black too. And a kind of maturity, but much too young for Olivia, that was for sure, though I was convinced there had been something going on between them.

"Ouch!" He slapped his arm and got to his feet. "Little bugs! You shouldn't sit out here, Elaine. You'll get eaten. That grass is damp too. Bad for the muscles. Come on." He pulled me to my feet. "Now go and have a relaxing bath and an early night. I'll find that book for you tomorrow."

"Thanks," I said, and we walked back to the front doors. I could have gone in through the garden door, but it cheered me up going back with him the other way, as if I'd been out with him, and escaped somehow. Not only that, Beverley saw us coming.

She wasn't there though when we reached the entrance which surprised me.

"You should be eating plenty of protein," Sergei said, holding the door open and standing back to let me through. "Will you do that for me?"

I nodded enthusiastically. The words were delightfully familiar, and when he left me I hurried back to the bedroom inspired to have the recommended warm bath. In the steamy, soapy, milky liquid the tiredness soaked completely out of me as the ripples washed over my skin.

I was in bed when Beverley came in an hour later. I noticed she was carrying a book.

"Sergei lent it to me," she said. "He says I've got to make my solo sexy, and there's some photos in here might help."

I watched her for a few minutes as she moved round the room, tall and arrogantly beautiful, and totally unaware of me. She brushed her hair, undressed. I closed my eyes, wanting to forget her, and Sergei, and that stupid book too. How dare he lend it to her? I heard her go into the bathroom. I lay there, eyes shut, pinned down under the warmth of my bedclothes, thinking, trying desperately to picture George, to find comfort in that look of concern that I longed to see in his eyes again, to remember the feel of his hand clasping mine in that restaurant, and wishing he would ring up in spite of Beverley's orders. And I pretended he was my father instead of hers.

He would understand my frustration.

You would have, George, wouldn't you?

A good man understands his child, doesn't he?

And that's what I was, wasn't I? A child.

But perseverant, George. Covetous. A child wanting, craving, no, voracious for love and attention, and longing to be thought of as a woman.

There was sudden smash from the bathroom, a splintering of glass. I opened my eyes as the smell of Jasmine swamped my nostrils.

"Why on earth did you leave that perfume I gave you near the basin?" called Beverley angrily.

I bit into my lips, wanting to cry. I could hear her in there and the scrape of the glass over the surfaces as she gathered it together and binned it.

When she came back into the bedroom she just said: "You'd nearly used it all anyway."

"No, I hadn't!"

My anger seemed to surprise her. She shrugged. "What's it matter? You can get another one when we get back to London."

She had no idea what that tiny bottle had meant to me, the delight I'd got from just touching it every night. And almost certainly she wouldn't bother to replace it. Anyhow it wasn't a gift from her. And another one wouldn't be the same, would it?

Chapter 17

In the morning I stopped Sergei outside the studio. "You said you might run through my solo with me today?"

He glanced at his watch. "Fine," he said. "Ask me later on."

I took some change and my make-up purse and went to the public telephone.

"I'm sorry, George Soames is not available." The voice was snooty, excessively cultured. "May I tell him who called?"

I didn't leave my name. I said I'd ring again. I needed to hear his voice, and the television program had given me an excuse to ring.

I tackled Sergei again after lunch.

"Not now, Elaine."

He strode away down the hall after Irina.

"There's so little time left and he promised," I complained to Diana.

"The studios are usually empty in the evenings. Why don't you suggest tonight? He and Irina are always so busy in the day, aren't they?"

George still wasn't available either. The woman sounded slightly annoyed this time when I wouldn't leave my name. But what was it to do with her?

When Beverley wasn't in the bedroom I took the opportunity to leaf through Sergei's book. There were pictures of Don Quixote and I could see what he meant about the hairstyle. I called into the wardrobe mistress's room to ask about my headdress. She dug around in a hat box and produced a large velvet flower.

"Can I borrow it?"

"Why?" Dotty demanded. She was a skinny little woman with narrow boney fingers, always two of them with metal thimbled ends which were presently poking and pressing the poor scarlet bloom into submission.

"I want to experiment."

Dotty glanced up at my hair. I could tell she was thinking, Poor girl, I can see why. Auburn and bright red too. What a mix. "Bring it back immediately."

"Can't I have it until tomorrow morning?"

She frowned. "Must you? Oh, all right, but take care of it."

I had twenty minutes to spare if I gave up the chance for an afternoon cup of tea. In front of the bedroom mirror I fiddled about with hairpins but the thing wouldn't sit properly. Not only that, I couldn't get it to feel secure. It was all the flower's fault. There was something rather odd about the shape. Oh God, yet another difficulty to cope with. Was I to be constantly frustrated? There was no more time just then. I left it lying there and went back to the studios.

In the first one Sergei had just finished with Meg.

"Practice it," he was saying to her. "Don't let it defeat you."

Meg picked up her things and wandered vaguely out. Sergei was gathering up his tapes.

"Would the evening be best?" I asked him. "Tonight perhaps?"

"What for?"

"My solo."

"Look, Elaine, we'll do it in the next a couple of days. All right?"

"All right," I said submissively. It had been his suggestion last night, not mine. Now he didn't seem remotely interested. Irina appeared at the door. Her diaphanous smock made her look slight, its pale blue colour and the matching leggings showing off her fine skin and groomed blonde hair to perfection.

"Why aren't you in the other studio, Elaine? We're waiting for you." As always her voice was soft, but its acid tone made me feel like an outcast.

I crept past her. This is my future you're jeopardizing, I thought. I want to improve and you're both belittling me.

"I hate them," I whispered to Beverley during the class. She looked at me, quite shocked.

But she only sees Sergei smiling at her, and when Irina corrects her, she bends in to her solicitously, reverently, it's if she is frightened of Beverley, of her confidence. Of her ravishing good looks.

I wouldn't have known if I'd shared with Diana or Candice.

I wouldn't have seen Beverley come back late that evening flushed and excited, her dark hair still wet. Or smelled the faint scent of chlorine. I wouldn't have guessed that Sergei had suggested that since he had nothing else to do they should go swimming together.

"How could you?" I cried angrily.

"What?"

"Go swimming with him?"

Beverley looked at me in astonishment. "Why shouldn't I?"

"You knew I was trying to get him to run through my solo with me."

"Come off it, Elaine, he'd been working all day."

"He promised me!"

"Don't you have enough of it with Irina? How much time do you need?"

"Unlike some people," I said, "I have to work at it."

Beverley looked genuinely hurt. "Sergei wants me to go out with him," she said, justifying herself, "after the scholarship is over. He says when I get to Paris - " She stopped. It was obvious what she was saying.

Obvious.

I was shaking inside. Of course the prize was hers for the taking. Everything was. Everything. Stop it, Elaine, stop it. You need her, and more than ever when she wins. Don't burn your bridges now. There's far too much at stake. There won't be any reason to see George if you lose her.... Keep control. Shh.... I forced myself to calm down. I even managed a wan smile.

"Where's my headdress?"

She looked at me blankly.

"The red flower."

"It's in the bathroom. I was trying it on."

"Oh."

I couldn't stay in the room anymore. I went into the bathroom and closed the door, carefully so as not to give away how angry I was. The scarlet flower lay damp and discarded among some black hairpins, its dye bleeding away into some water near the sink. I bet it had worked perfectly for her. When I eventually emerged Beverley was in bed with her eyes shut, only feigning sleep though.

"I understand," she whispered, after I'd turned out the light. "You don't have to apologize. You're having to work so hard I expect you're overwrought."

The following day was Sunday. Out of the blue Irina had

announced it was to be a day of rest, and she allowed us all to sleep in to catch up on our depleted energy levels.

"You are all falling apart," she complained. "You have only a few more days. How you expect to survive the rigors of any ballet company I have no idea."

Beverley and most of the others had gone off because of the warm weather to have a picnic near some reservoir, and they'd taken Tanya with them to cheer her up. Beverley tried to convince me to go too but I said I wanted to practice.

"Of course you must if you need to," she nodded

A couple of the girls went to church instead, Meg and Diana, driven there by Candice's visiting parents who, much to Candice's relief, offered to take all three girls out to a slap up lunch afterwards. It was obvious poor Candice was starving hungry. She literally fell on her mother and father when they came. I don't think she would have lasted the final week without that extra meal.

Irina left to catch a train to London. "In search of some sophistication, for goodness sake."

Sergei was nowhere to be seen, probably gone with Irina.

So to my deep satisfaction the centre was deserted. All mine. Even the phone. But George wasn't. An answerphone informed me the office was closed and in an emergency George Soames could be contacted at..... it was the Wimbledon number.

Her voice I hear, something I hadn't expected. For some reason I hadn't imagined I would have the barrier of Imogen.

"Hello?"

I am tongue-tied.

"Who is this?"

I regain a little composure. "Imogen? It's Elaine."

"What's wrong? Is there something the matter with Beverley?"

"No...." But she would jump to that conclusion, wouldn't she? Why would I ring otherwise? "Um....I saw the television program.... On Friday night?"

"Oh." She sounds mystified. What am I talking about? One program that George is on is the same as another to her, I suppose. "Is Beverley there?"

"She's gone out....um.....there's a picnic. Some of the girls...."

"How nice." She's lost interest. I'm not Beverley so this is boring, this telephone call.

"I wanted to say....how well it went....the night before last.... George, I mean."

I'm not controlling this conversation at all.

"George? George! It's Elaine."

"Hello, how are you?" He sounds so far away. So distant. I could be anyone. His grandmother. An acquaintance. His worst enemy. There's no tone in the voice, except that far away official quality.

"I rang to say....um....the TV program.."

"You saw it then?"

Is she still there in the room? Yes, she's there. I know it. I can hear it in his voice. I'm talking to the man in the presence of his wife. They're a couple.

"I just thought it was good. You were."

"How kind of you, Elaine."

I hear Imogen say something in the background.

"Beverley's gone to a picnic then?"

"Yes."

"Well, give her our love, won't you?"

When I've hung up I'm in tears. Why did I ring? The television program was no reason. And I sounded like an idiot child when I spoke to him. Where's the adult woman he took out to dinner?

But it's not that that hurts. No, it's not that. What I heard in his voice was an ending. That distant quality. Before we've even begun, I heard the ending.

With everyone out the studios at least were all mine. I chose the largest one. The wall of mirrors, the barre, the whole floor, mine. And the air space too. No crying in there. No despair. No more feeling. Just cold hard work.

I would have worn my gorgeous purple leotard, and the matching woolen tights that I'd bought with George's money, my favorite things, but I'd found them amongst Beverley's stuff she'd worn, borrowed and screwed up and damp on the bathroom floor, so I'd ended up in simple black. Still I could plié and stretch, watch each movement critically in the mirrors, or leap and spin across the room with total abandon. No crowding, no competition.

The windows were open, letting in the unusual September heat and the consequent dry scent of the fields outside, so it didn't take me long to warm up. The reflected port de bras was flowing, even quite stylish I decided. A triple pirouette came off easily. I tried a few fouettés. I got to thirty two without the slightest hitch. Why couldn't I do that in class? I dug around in my bag for the recorded music of the solos, but suddenly I put those tapes aside in favour of my own Giselle one. I'd had it ages and I loved Adam's music, the richness, the drama of it. With no-one around I couldn't resist the temptation of putting it on. It always gave me the same thrill. In my mind's eye the curtain goes up, the hunting horn calls, the prince knocks at the cottage door, and Giselle shyly emerges....

I'd seen the ballet performed on video and I'd played that again and again until I knew all the steps, every one. Now for nearly an hour I was engrossed in my performance, village and ghostly forest, both acts. Who needs a partner, when transported by the imagination.... Finally the music draws me back to my grave as dawn breaks....but I have saved Albrect from disaster....love has triumphed over evil....the curtain falls....applause.

Like glass breaking around my created world, the sound came. Harsh. Repetitive. Real.

I blinked.

Hands? Real hands? Clapping. Smacking together.

I swung round. Sergei was leaning against the door. I blushed from head to foot with horror. How long had he been there? I couldn't ask him, I couldn't speak, I was too embarrassed. I darted for my cardigan, as if covering myself up would help. He just went on standing there though, smiling.

"I th-thought you'd gone out."

"It would have been a pity. I might have missed that."

"I was mucking around," I muttered, hugging my cardigan closer.

"Run the tape back to the second act pas de deux."

"What?"

"Run the tape back."

I looked at him stupidly.

"Go on."

I moved to do it and he knelt down in the centre, hand on brow. This was Giselle's entrance. He meant to dance the duet with me. I hesitated.

"Play it."

Would he write me off if I didn't dance with him? I wanted to, but I was terrified as well. Nervously I discarded my cardigan, pressed play, and balanced in an half-hearted arabesque behind him as the music began. He rose and held my waist, his hands, his hands round my waist, and I began the slow deliberate rond de jambe. It wasn't what I expected, the sensuousness of his support, our fingers entwined, but more, somehow he carried me through; he was Albrect, grieving and exhausted, enlightened and enchanted by the spirit of his lost love as the dance progressed to its climax. As I whirled by in the final pirouettes he caught my hand and pulled me close. He was breathing hard. He stared down into my face as if indeed, like his character, he'd seen a ghost.

But the kiss was real enough. I tilted my head back into the strength of his hand, short of breath myself, and intoxicated by the hunger and sweetness of his lips, of the urgency of his body pressing against mine. It was Albrect's kiss for Giselle, and Romeo's for Juliet, the kind I'd imagined in every love story. What I'd longed to experience. It took all my remaining breath away. Was it only the heat of the day that began to make me wilt?

He let me go and stared at me.

I wanted him to take my hand and lead me to his room. I wanted him to surprise me, to bring me to life, to let me find out if my nakedness could make a man want to cry. Like every love story. First, desire they say in books, and then possession.

But he drew back, stepped away, his shoulders stiffening, as if he'd come to his senses, as if he had recognized me suddenly.

"I'm sorry," he said, his voice loud and real, brusque. "I shouldn't be dancing. I - I'm sorry."

He walked out and there was the click of the studio door as he shut it after him.

Silence.

Silence.

Just the tingle left of his lips on my lips.

Why didn't he take me to his room?

I go alone to mine and strip naked in front of the mirror. Am I so unattractive? I must be. Through the tears I still need him to touch me. I'll have to make it up. Imagine if I can't have real. I lie down on the bed.

Am I dreaming?

At my bidding he speaks softly of early morning river mists twisting round the spires of Notre Dame, of the fountains of Rome, of the pigeon gray Thames running deep and fast through the very heart of London....It's as if he's there guiding my fingers, teaching me not to be afraid of my feelings. I'm crying but I still ask him to tell me more. The Paris Opera, La Scala, he has seen them all....and then I want more.

One day, Elaine, you will see it all, he whispers.

"Soon, Sergei," I correct him, my back arching responsively to my fingers and the thought of him next to me. "I am at Rosehill because I want to win."

I could teach you how to stop wanting to win.

"Teach me then," I say indignantly. "But why do you want to stop me?"

No-one can stop you! Except....

"Who? Beverley? You don't think I can win, is that it?"

"You're not Beverley."

I am angry with myself now. I'm letting him say things I don't want him to say. But he goes on.

There's a kind of power comes, Elaine, when the desperation disappears. Stop wanting.

I don't understand this idea. Ambition is essential for success. How can not wanting do any good? Right now what I'm thinking makes no sense at all. Instead I go back.... pick up the earlier threads of my dream....and let Sergei tell me I'm beautiful, though it's not something I can believe. He is though. Deliciously foreign looking, dangerous. I love the way he sits and watches us, the sound of his voice. I want him to touch me, to kiss me.

I make it start all over again. "Teach me."

The net curtains filter in the afternoon light. Above the incessant song of the air conditioning, voices, passing the window, laughter. The picnickers returning.

I wish, I wish I could turn in fear to Sergei and whisper: "Will they notice we are missing?"

Imagine it. The excitement of it, if he were here.

Ssh, he says softly, keeping his eyes closed. I so want him to be here. I keep my mind's eye centred on the beads of sweat on his chest, not daring to breathe in case the image of him disappears, a strange carved marblesque art form remembered from some art book, a body lying naked on the bed beside me, all cool damp skin, and curling marble hair, penis lying softly to one side.

The voices pass, and fade right away.

Silence again. This is stolen time, time when I should be practicing. Won't they expect to see me in the studio, all sweaty and loosened up? And those steps I had insisted on rehearsing. Just as bad they will be, no improvement. Irina will know.

And, I catch my breath remembering, my bag is still in there.

They'll suspect something.

But that pleases me. I stroke myself again, imagining, dreaming. These hands might belong to a scarlet woman. Kitri.

Then the most terrifying thought strikes me. What if they did suspect something, something that isn't true? What if someone saw Sergei kiss me and I get taken out of the competition?

Sergei opens his dark eyes and turns his cheek against the pillow to look at me. It's so real, the way I have conjured up his face. The curtains billow a little at the window, the first stirring of the forecast storm.

You are such an ambitious child, he says.

"I'm eighteen!"

That makes him smile. So old? Do you want me because Beverley looks at me?

"No!"

Do you think if I were here it would help your career?

It hasn't occurred to me. Now I wonder.

"Would it?"

The image is fading. I can't hold on to it. I lie back on the pillow and run my fingers over the new roundness of my breast. I know what happens, I've read it in books now, ever since that day at Bishop's Park with Beverley, I've read.... His eyes would follow my hand down, hypnotized by its advance, a kind of power. I try to bring him back and make him lean across to kiss the smoothness of my breast and I feel the sexual tides within me gathering again, like the wind rousing the leaves of the beech trees outside. His finger traces the outline of my lips. He puts his hands around my shoulders and raises my eager mouth again to his....

The door made a little click.

"Why are you lying down?"

Beverley's eyes were wide. She was shocked at my nakedness, I suppose.

"Don't you feel well?"

I sat up and gathered the bed cover around me, hating Sergei, hating him for not being there. Hating him for not being there to shock Beverley more.

But....

She glances into the bathroom at the pile of her practice clothes on the floor. "I think you might have done our washing."

Better still.

Oh, better better still.

Why hadn't I thought of it?

Forget Sergei. What if it had been George?

That made me feel wild and warm just to imagine. George. The real thing, not books, nor some trick of my imagination. A real man. But not the father she knew. George, as the man.

I unwrapped the bedcover and stood up brazenly.

"I was just going for a shower," I said.

There was a rumble of thunder as the storm drew nearer.

The real Sergei took no notice of me in the class the next morning. Though he stood nearby, it was as if I didn't exist at all. The studio itself seemed crowded and claustrophobic, the barre exercises unnecessarily painful. Sergei's apparent disregard made me feel empty and directionless. Except when he walked past. Then a wave of humiliation washed over me, I lost my timing, fell off balance.

"Elaine!" Irina was sitting in on the class. Her voice thundered across the room. "Concentrate!"

Sergei stopped beside Beverley and corrected her shoulder line. I watched the way his fingers held her collar bone. He moved round behind her. Now I couldn't see her, only recognize the tension in his own shoulders, how close in he was to her. Easy it would have been, yesterday's kiss. He would have stayed. It would have led on, wouldn't it? If I had been Beverley.

My body tightened up. Technique, technique. Protection in muscular strength. When Sergei passed me by again I was a fortress. A defiant queen. A brilliance I had never had before surged through me, a searing heat that lasted nearly to the end of class. Until Irina sent Beverley with Sergei to the smaller studio to perfect her pirouette placing.

Then my fortress fell in ruins. My energy was suddenly ripped away from me and my muscles collapsed in, leaving me quite incapable of finishing the steps.

Back to square one. The brilliance was gone. Everywhere Beverley was in the way, clouding my path forward in every direction. No-one can stop you winning, Elaine, except...

Chapter 18

Two days to go before we had to return to London, two days till he would arrive, till George would come to take us back. And then only six days after that until the competition, but I wasn't thinking beyond the travelling back....

George has been in Washington attending a world banking convention. An article in the newspaper mentions him by name, says that though he's one of the government's financial advisers, he's among only a few people at the conference talking sense. And is the Minister listening? Beverley throws the newspaper away but before the bin gets emptied I retrieve it and tear out that part of the piece. I want to keep it. It's good to read about a man being so well established in his career, admired. And to see George's name written in black and white. Besides it's easy to hide, a little keepsake for me that no-one will notice.

Beverley and I are on really good terms again. We've separated away from the others, and now in spite of her spending lots of time with Sergei, we have all our meals together, just us, and talk all confidentially in corners like we used to. She tells me Sergei kisses her, that the night they went swimming that they went too far, and sex with him is wonderful. (I knew it would happen like that for her.) Just what she'd always imagined, she says. Will it be for me I wonder? I wonder briefly too if it's actually Beverley's first time, she's so starry eyed, because she'd always implied to me she knew what she was talking about. Is that what I'll feel like? But she's saying that of course if they're seen together it might compromise her chances in the competition, and he says her career's too important, he respects her talent too much to take the slightest risk. She likes that, so even her ambition shows sometimes. But of course he's looking to the future, isn't he? After all she'll be in Paris, won't she?

Well, she will.

But I've been working on the theory that if I make myself absolutely indispensable she won't be able to just leave me behind. I'm helping her with her costumes. Darning her pointe shoes. Washing her tights for her. Telling her how wonderfully she's dancing. This timing's important. She'll have to keep in touch, she'll send me letters, maybe she'll even get George to ring to make arrangements for me to go over to Paris to see her. And I can ring him, there'll be a reason every so often. I'm trying to make her need me so that there'll be excuses to phone. There will be. I'm calmer, more centered.

This day has been useful, concentrated, dedicated to improvement, quietly industrious. Now it is evening and I am sitting on my bed diligently darning the tops of my own pointe shoes with thick pink thread so that they will grip the stage better and thinking about the pleasures of that car journey back when Beverley appears in the bedroom doorway looking flustered.

"He's having an affair!"

"Who?"

"How could he?"

"Who?"

Is she talking about Sergei? I know she likes him, she talks non stop about him, but this is Beverley Soames. I'm quite certain he's not too important. Not really. As with everything else Beverley could take him or leave him if it suited her. Why then is she so angry?

"My father."

My needle misses its target and pierces sharply into my thumb. "Who?"

"My father," she says again, as if she's trying to convince herself as well as me. She staggers a little in the doorway under the weight of the shock.

But it's me who feels knocked out.

Winded.... more.

Betrayed? A little drop of blood bubbles up on my thumb where the needle pierced the skin. Dark red blood. And fear too. Has he given us away? Our little night when nothing happened? Has he told Imogen he took me out?

I am almost too afraid to look over at Beverley. I don't know why I should feel guilty, nothing's happened. But as with Sergei, if she thought George had taken me out when she wasn't there, if she knew what I've been thinking, dreaming...

She must know about the meal out. But there isn't any accusation in her gaze. There's no anger directed at me there. For a moment I don't understand, then.....

Oh God.... An affair! A woman. He has someone.... What I thought he wanted.... he doesn't need me. What I thought.... what I wanted.... he hasn't been thinking of me at all!

Beverley?

But how can I ask her? She has no idea of the momentousness of what's she's saying. What she's just done to me.

"How could he? How could he?"

My diaphragm muscles feel as if they're being torn apart; there's no breath there, and my blood seems to be draining away from my face, down, down, down to my feet. Being like Beverley hardly seems to count suddenly. I have never felt as appalled as this. As empty. The obsessive need to see George that's been building up inside me is being sucked down and out of me. There's nothing left inside me except my heart which seems to have broken open. I can hear its rate increasing, as if it's trying in vain to pump the blood back up. Thank God I am sitting down so Beverley can't see this violent and sudden disintegration.

"How could he?" Her voice is so shrill. She just keeps repeating: "How could he?"

And I can't ask who with... or why.... or is she sure? I feel suddenly quite physically sick. Dizzy. Incapable. There's nothing I can do except sit here and hold on tight to the bed clothes. Beverley's feet are thudding across the floor, there's a squeak of the bed as she sinks onto it. I hear the angry weight of her hand as she strikes the pillow and says again, "How could he! Shit! He's my father!"

We both sit in our own stunned silences for a few minutes, facing each other, bed to bed.

"He's forty-two!" Beverley says suddenly, as if that counts. Her eyes begin to fill with tears. "How can he do this to me? Now, with the scholarship coming! It's too dreadful. How dare he? What will people say? And poor Mummy. She's sure there's something going on."

Wait. Wait!

You heard it too, didn't you?

Tell me you heard it. That element of uncertainty. I'm right, aren't I? It was there, wasn't it?

I cling tightly to that tiny thread of hope and catch my breath and return it carefully to a steadier, more controlled rhythm. Maybe. Maybe all this is hearsay. Gossip. Some invented media scandal. Of course it is. Successful people are prime targets. Poor George, what kind of daughter am I - because maybe that's all that's left to me, I don't feel sure.... what kind of a daughter am I if I can give up on you so easily?

But I need to know more. I need to know details. Right now. Exactly what is it George is supposed to be doing? And who with? Who is it Imogen suspects? What proof has she? I need to know. But I'm sure there's no proof. There is none, is there? I know there isn't. George isn't that kind of man. It will all be some silly story surely. Pure media invention. He has enemies like all people in high places have. But be rational, Elaine. Get Beverley talking. I need - I'm desperate - to find out for myself what Imogen said. So I know it's not true. So I know it's all just some story, some wicked invention. I'm Beverley's friend, her confidante. She'll tell me, won't she?

"What did your mother say? What did she say?"

"It's so awful," says Beverley, and falls weeping into her pillow.

I go in very close, kneel by her bed, put a comforting hand on her beautiful alabaster shoulder. "So what did Imogen say? I bet it's not true. How can it be true?"

"He's been meeting her. She rings him all the time."

I draw back. He goes to so many places. He knows so many people. Real and sickening doubts from deep down inside me begin to creep up again to the surface. He works long hours. All those times away from home. He could meet anyone he wants to. Men like that do. You read about them all the time. There's a nasty taste suddenly in my mouth, bitter. I think back to the dinner party, how it occurred to me then that George's eyes followed the women in the room. And then him talking quietly to Melanie, how I caught him looking at her, not once but several times.

Of course. That's who it is. It is Melanie Powers. It has to be. Rich and pretty she is. Well, pretty-ish. Beautifully dressed, amusing. What was it she said looking up at him as he poured her drink? Some men are better than others...

"He's taken the keys to the flat. He doesn't want to let it anymore. Why would he want to use the flat except...?"

What's she talking about?

"What flat?"

She doesn't answer, she's far too upset to be explaining unnecessary details. I can understand that. Whatever it is, I'll find that part out later.

"But Beverley, people like him have affairs all the time."

I heard myself, but I can't believe I just said that. I know now it's Melanie, that George has betrayed me. Well, I feel betrayed. Why, why am I still defending him?

"Daddy? Daddy isn't people like that! And think of the scandal, Elaine. Think of the kind of things the press will print. What they might say about him. Worse, what about the scholarship. What about me!" Beverley's voice burns into the situation now like acid. Her tone is suddenly vicious. She doesn't want this. Doesn't want it at all. Why should her father be allowed to interrupt her life now, threaten her future, when everything's going so well? There's the threat of retribution in her voice when she says: "Think of what they could print."

"What did your mother say exactly?"

"She's afraid it's... Melanie."

With the name said my fear is made flesh. I sink back on my heels, defeated. Imogen would know.

Melanie.

And I should have known too, because why would he look at me? If he was looking at all, if I wasn't kidding myself, it was only playing. Just a game. His eyes had been on Melanie all through that evening dinner. I should have seen. There I was touching his hand later, letting him put his arms round me, making a complete fool of myself, convincing myself he cared for me. Accepting his help. Then imagining he wanted to take me out to dinner, that it was me he wanted to be with that night, that he was pleased Imogen and Beverley were away so that an opportunity existed for us. But of course, now I think back, John Powers, I remember him saying he was home that weekend.

Melanie.

Melanie Powers.

Beverley's anger can now be mine too. We are sisters. United in pain. Suddenly I share all of her indignation. All of it. How could he do it? How could he?

Where's the good father now?

"Oh, Beverley."

"He took her out the night after my party. When Mummy and I were in Cambridge with Cyril."

Her? When they were in Cambridge? Her?

Her!

The room around me dissolves away, disappears... It's as if someone lights a candle. And in a crowded restaurant, God pours wine into my glass, fills it to overflowing. Oh, the brightness of that circle of light, two hands laid innocently together on a red tablecloth.

"I hate him. How could he do this to us? To me! How could Melanie...."

There is no Melanie suddenly, is there? But now Beverley has to believe her mother. I want her to.

"It must be Melanie. Who else?"

Now I am poor Melanie's accuser. What an actress and a liar I am.

But Beverley hardly needs encouragement. She believes the worst of her Godmother already. And her father.

"How dare he do it!"

She's right of course, George.

The irony is that we have yet to dare.

But soon Beverley will be in Paris, and Imogen will go there sometimes. There'll be moments when you'll be alone.

Close beside your door, I am lying in wait, lying in wait like a thief. In two days time I will see you again and then.....

I suddenly feel very adult.

"Oh, poor Beverley...."

Beverley's shadow has faltered, is not so dark. So close, so close in I am. It's almost like being in the eye of the storm.

"Oh Beverley," I say, "how awful for you. How simply awful."

Chapter 19

I sit on the front steps apprehensively. I packed hours ago, my thoughts sidetracked only briefly by the last class and Irina's final instructions. Unlike the others I am not distraught to be leaving. Not for me the tears and promises and hugs as if we will never see each other again, when the truth is only a few hours separate us from tomorrow's continuing rehearsals in the theatre. Instead I am squinting up to the main road, dazzled by the bright September sunshine. I have hardly stepped outside into the light in weeks.

By the time Lillian's family's car reaches the top of the drive he'll come....

When Diana and Candice turn halfway and stop to wave back before they walk on up, he'll be here... As soon as Irina gets into her car...

Soon.....

Soon he will enter the gates and glide in between the two fields and find me here waiting for him.

Alone.

Beverley has sworn not to give him the satisfaction of being ready, nor to show any interest in his arrival. She is in fact planning to drive back to London with Sergei instead, something she will tell George when he arrives so as to put him at a greater disadvantage than if she had him told not to come at all.

"Will you mind terribly, Elaine darling?" she begs me, "having to go back with him? Sergei's car is only a sports."

We're in the reception area and Sergei is hovering apologetically behind her. I doubt he even remembers kissing me, so besotted is he with Beverley. "Would you rather I went on the train?" A close friend should attempt to show some solidarity.

"No, no, no," she says. "That's too expensive. Besides he might as well do something useful."

"Not only that," she adds grimly, "Melanie lives nearby. I don't want him taking any unnecessary detours."

For Beverley's sake I shall go with George then, when he comes.

I sit staring out into the distance, waiting.

See, now, at the gate?

In what shining silver he arrives, amid the harvest, between fields of ripe wheat.

He smiles to see me waiting.

I wish I could spare him Beverley's cruel indifference when she eventually emerges from the building, and the disappointment and frustration I see in his eyes when she announces she would far rather travel with Sergei.

"Elaine needs a lift though," she says imperiously.
George hesitates and then turns obediently and picks up my bags and takes them out to his car. He stands watching as Beverley climbs into Sergei's red sports and they drive away. She doesn't say goodbye, or even she'll see him later.

"I am definitely not the flavor of the month," he says.

"Are you nervous of me?" he asks, when I'm beside him in the car.

"No. I wouldn't be here if you made me nervous."
It is a lie of course. It's why I'm here. It's that nervousness that is so exciting. I'm on the brink of danger and it's exhilarating. And I can't wait for things to get more dangerous. At any moment now we'll be caught out, someone will find out about us. At any

moment now George might kiss me and then.... then it will start.

But right now he is just driving.

Once out of the village, through the old High Street, past the quaint old cottages and the church, we head north through leafy Sussex countryside. I open the window and let the wind blow on my face. The air is dry, but this Indian summer is ebbing away, it can't last. George likes driving on B-roads he says, he likes England as it was. I think maybe he's going to stop, that he'll pull in somewhere, by a field gate or something. Somewhere just off the road. And we'll sit quietly and...

"It's still there if you search for it." He changes gear.

"Hmm?"

"England," he says, "along these old country roads."

Then he goes quiet again, just drives. I like the way he drives, as if he's in total control somehow. But I'm still nervous. My nervousness makes me begin to chatter. About the scholarship, that there's hardly any doubt now that Beverley will win. Then I say I'm sorry, that will mean she leaves home and goes to Paris.

He says he doesn't mind. He's in Paris quite often. It's not as if he won't see her. It was bound to happen one day, her leaving home. And he would have to be proud if she won. "Go on," he says. "It's interesting, hearing what you've all been doing in the last month, the preparations."

So I go on. I tell him Tanya may not make it, her ankle's still swollen. How Candice thinks she'll die of starvation before Friday. How hard it has been for us all learning everything, getting it right.

"And you?" he says. "What about you?"

I say the fan is difficult, and –

"What fan?"

I explain about the fan, demonstrating as we drive the flicks and flutters involved in the dance. Then how temperamental Irina has been. How the flower I have to wear for my Kitri solo is awful, and what Sergei said about it being such a flirty dance....

George interrupts me to suggest we stop off for coffee.

"What about Croydon?"

"If you like."

I think maybe he just wants me to be quiet for a few minutes and so I am.

There's heavy local traffic. It's Saturday and it's hard to find a car park in Croydon that isn't full, but eventually we do and we walk into the noise and clatter of the shopping mall and up an escalator past the splashing of an ornamental waterfall, to the first floor where there's a shop George knows. It turns out it sells silk flowers as well as real, and he says:

"Find what you need, Elaine. It doesn't matter how much."

I can have anything I want and there's so much to choose from I don't know where to start. The sales assistant starts unpacking more, things that aren't even on display. After taking absolutely ages to look at nearly everything on offer I find three really expensive red velvet camellias that are absolutely perfect and the woman boxes them up just as if they're a corsage or something, and smiles warmly at George as he signs the account for her.

And then we go into a jewellery shop next door just to browse George says, and he buys me these delicate sparkly little diamond (not real - diamanté) earrings to wear with the flowers.

"Since Kitri's such a flirt," he says, and laughs at my

astonished delight.

Then we find a cafe and he buys me a coffee, the best I've ever tasted. I'm thirsty and I drink it too quickly, so instead of sitting over it as I hoped we might, he drinks his down too and we go back to the car and continue on our way.

I stay quiet now. George doesn't talk either. Somehow we don't need to. The roads are busy anyhow. He just drives through the traffic. The wind is blowing on my face. I can see myself in the wing mirror. I look different. Older. And I feel alive. Somehow, and I hardly noticed when, somewhere in the last hour I know the real danger has begun.

When we reach my street I don't want to turn into it. I don't want this journey to end.

All the curtains in the street are twitching so there's no way George and I could sit and talk in the car for a few minutes. We climb out, but before my bags have touched the pavement my mother's running down the front steps towards us.

"Elaine, Elaine!" she's crying.

Can she have actually missed me?

She flings herself at me sobbing.

"Jonty, Jonty - "

"For goodness sake," I'm embarrassed at this sudden show of affection going on in front of George. "What's wrong?"

"It's Jonty, Elaine. Come quickly!"

Who but a father can restrain a protesting loutish boy of thirteen who's got blood streaming from his wrist, and lift him bodily out of his tantrum, off the floor and onto the table and grip him firmly? The kitchen's an absolute shambles, glass, china, cornflakes, crunching underfoot.

"He's trashed the place," screams my mother.

"He's -"

The gash is deep and pulsating blood.

"Jonty!" I stare at the cut. Is it deliberate? It's too high though, I think. If it was meant, he missed!

"Quick, Elaine," George says, "find some cloth, clean linen or something to tie round this. Stop the bleeding."

I race up the stairs to the linen cupboard for an old sheet. If there's one thing my mother has a lot of, it's those, hers, grandmother's. I grab the first one and start ripping it up as I run back down. In the hall there are broken pictures, the mirror's smashed.

My mother's trying to explain. "He suddenly starts throwing things. Do something for once he yells at me!"

"Fuck off. Just tell her to fuck off!" George ignores the violent protests and snatches Jonty's arm and winds the first strip of linen round and round the gash tightly. I keep tearing, the fearful hollow sound of it fills the kitchen, and even as George winds the next, the blood is seeping red through the white layers of the first bandage. I can smell the sticky sweetness of it.

"More!" George says, breathing hard. I pass another strip. My brother is swaying and suddenly silent, maybe he'll faint. He's horribly pale. Blue, almost as blue as the formica surface he's sitting on. Is he high on something? Slices of bread on the floor are spattered with his blood. George's shoes crunch as he moves to get a better position to work faster.

"He's smashed up my television!"

Of course, the television. He would. But that's not all. Look at the place. I'm appalled Jonty's capable of doing so much damage. He's staring defiantly at Mum.

There's so much anger in his expression, I never realized it was there before. Why did I ever think he didn't care?

"Elaine, call an ambulance," orders George.

My mother has been standing there watching George and paralyzed to the spot. Now she has another fit of shrieking. It's frightening how loud she can scream.

I run to the phone. My hand is shaking so much I have difficulty pressing the number. When it answers I can hardly get the address out. I have to repeat and repeat it.

"On its way," I report back breathlessly.

George nods. "Good. Now get a blanket."

A few minutes later Jonty is carried out on a stretcher and George is helping my mother into her coat to go too. Then there's a frantic search while she takes off her slippers and tries to remember where she left her shoes. In the end she wears a pair of mine which are tight on her.

"Wait here," George says to me, and supports my mother as she stumbles down the steps and into the waiting ambulance.

I am left standing shocked and trembling in the hall. The siren starts up and George comes back inside as the ambulance pulls out of the street.

"Elaine?" He sees my terror.

"Why didn't I think about Jonty? Not once in four whole weeks..." Until I stop crying and can breathe and the shadows flee George holds me, just standing there, he holds me close and strokes my hair. The hall is secret and dark, hiding us from prying eyes.

"Kiss me, George?"

"Kiss you?"

"Please," I beg. "Please!"

He hesitates, but then he does. And when he kisses me everything goes absolutely dangerously silent, there's just the achingly sweet taste of him that somehow I knew would be there, and the simple pressure of his embrace, the nearness of him, and then increasing passion from him suddenly, as if he's being drawn in to my lips. He's taller than I am, protective, but my body fits his precisely, all the way down. His hand begins to move down from my hair and presses me closer to him. It's almost unreal, what's happening. Some speechless language is moving between us, he's holding me so close, we're communicating our desire to each other like electricity. I am holding him too now, feeling the muscles low down in his back flexing. His tongue is fluttering over my own, as if he's tasting me, and one of his hands slips down to find how perfectly my breast fits into it, and then moves lower. No lower, lower, to where I'm on fire. There's a layer of clothing in between but it doesn't stop him. His fingers feel for the fire, and I don't want to stop him. He finds it and holds it tight and his lips are on my lips and there isn't anything else in the world except him. And I can feel his breath in my hair.

"Elaine," he sighs, as if it is the most beautiful name in the world and I think suddenly how far we can go, how very far I want to go because it's George, and more than just dreaming. Real. Real. But somehow the moment passes. His sense returns. He relinquishes his hold. Cold suddenly I am, naked somehow, as if it was his hand that held me together there, and without its support I'll crumble away now.

"I have to go," he says, taking my face in his hands instead. The smell of me is on his fingers.

I cling to him. I don't want to let go. I can't. He prises my arms open.

"Someone will recognize the car." His voice has changed, lost all its warmth. "I have to go. I had to give them my name before too. Don't ring me this week, Elaine, for God's sake."

Chapter 20

"There's a point where the person gives up wanting to win and just starts dancing," Beverley whispered.

True. And now I knew what I wanted to win more than anything.

Already it was the evening before the scholarship. The days had whizzed past. Only at night could I be still enough to enjoy the deep ache I had now for George's touch. Now I'd felt it. Now it was no longer just imagination. I wished I could ring him, just to hear his voice. I couldn't sleep much. Instead I lay wanting the power of his arms around me again, to plumb the new depths of myself that he had suddenly sprung into life. Aching like that is exquisite, a rhythmical electrical pulsing that is stronger even than any heartbeat, so strong you can't bear it to stop. Exercise dulls it, but otherwise all you can do is live alongside it, discipline yourself to acknowledge it only when you're quiet, when you're alone and everything is still. That way you think you can keep it under control.

Beverley and me. Waiting in the front stalls of the theatre for our turn. Watching the others in the final dress rehearsal. Listening to a panic-stricken Irina trying to sort us out yet again into our order of appearance. It was hot in the theatre, eighty degrees backstage under all the lights. There was a heady smell, a mixture of greasepaint and those sophisticated perfumes that some dancers wear trying to mask sweat and nervous tension, all wafting across the footlights and down into the auditorium.

Candice was in the middle of her Lilac Fairy, and not

a minute before she had tripped out of a badly placed pirouette and fallen right on her bum. She ended up in such an awkward position that Beverley and several other people giggled, but the sound man hadn't noticed and poor Candice was required to struggle up and continue.

"If that happens tomorrow night," Irina raised her voice. The comment was meant for us all, " - the music won't stop, will it? You must gather your wits and keep going. That's it, Candice. Spot, this time."

Candice's fall had embarrassed her beyond belief. You could tell the Lilac Fairy didn't care now whether the sodding Princess Aurora pricked her finger and slept for a hundred years or not - but Candice was suddenly dancing. Everything was coming off, pirouettes, balances, beats, everything. It was throwaway. Confidence born out of disaster. If this had been the performance Candice knew her chance would be already ruined, and so at last it didn't matter, and now there was no preconceived fear to hold her back. I watched her intently, wondering if, even at this last minute, there was a way I could grab that abandonment for myself without the ignominy of a fall.

But what Beverley had just said was right. There is a point where no more can be done. No more preparation. It's only a matter of time before what happens happens.

And that's true.

Jonty for instance. It had only been a matter of time before he broke out, a small bomb waiting to explode. I could see that he'd wanted to make something happen in his life. He was fed up with wandering the streets while my mother buried herself in that lounge room. Once I wasn't there, it must have finally got to him what a stupid isolated existence we had. He'd got away with his outburst - no-one had mentioned drugs and everyone seemed to believe he had accidentally injured himself, but my mother was still panicking. But for the moment I was home again and she could sink back into the confines and oblivion of her small screen world - she'd bought a new television immediately of course. And gone out for it, no less, being unable to survive without it! And thanks to George I could concentrate on my own escape because my brother was repaired and being stroppy again, and back out on the streets with his awful friends, no doubt parading his stitches.

I hadn't rung George, so I didn't know how he'd explained to Imogen where he had been, or why it had taken so long to drive me home, or if he might have had to bribe someone to keep his name out of the press - nothing about Jonty seemed to have been mentioned, which was surprising with George being involved. You'd think somebody would have noticed. He hadn't kissed me again that evening, though he wasn't out of the house until after midnight in fact, by which time we'd cleared up the mess, I'd made us some coffee, and the other two had returned and he could see for himself that Jonty was all right. I was sure he hadn't told anyone the truth because Beverley didn't ask about Jonty's injury. I didn't mention it either. I let her think George had dropped me off and gone on somewhere else. I remembered the expression on her face when she saw where I lived. To have a brother who could so violently smash things up wasn't something I wanted to broadcast.

But nor did I know what George thought. Maybe while he was helping me straighten the house, sweep up and wash the blood off the kitchen floor, he'd taken one look and decided the last thing he wanted to do was get caught up with any member of a family like mine. And forbidden to contact him, my fears were increasing hour by hour. I analyzed everything he'd said, searching for deeper, darker meanings. If you look for trouble you can find it. If only I could just see him, I thought. Speak to him.

But tonight a pale remembrance of that electric charge passing between us in the darkened hallway was renewing my belief in him. And he would be there to see Beverley's success, wouldn't he?

Twenty-four hours to go then. And I was almost resigned to Beverley winning because I knew how much it would please George. Better for Jonty too perhaps. Besides Beverley would go, and I would stay, and because of George I would survive. He would contact me himself now, I was certain. There was really nothing more to do but to wait and let it all happen.

Except I didn't. I couldn't. Because by the pass door to the auditorium I overheard Beverley talking to Sergei. She was still going on about the affair.

"How could he? How could he? At the most important moment of my life - "

Sergei's voice was low and soothing. Beverley giggled at whatever it was he said.

"Mummy and I will get an apartment in Paris."

"Meridienne can help you organize it. I will."

"Good, I don't want Daddy involved. I have a right to expect some decency from my father, don't I? He knows if Mummy took it up with the Minister there'd be a terrible scandal. Imagine if the papers got hold of it." There was such righteous indignation in her voice, and then such innocence when she said: "I could do that, you know. Tell them. Sell the story. And I would. Even from Paris. I've told him if he sees her again I'll do it and he'd better forget he has a daughter."

"He'd be ruined."

"Of course."

"Concentrate on the scholarship, darling. On winning."

"Why? Who's so dangerous?

"Chloe maybe, if she can get herself together. Elaine. Who knows?"

"Elaine? Elaine?"

The way she said it, the amusement in her tone - and then her sudden shriek of derisive laughter, dismissing the possibility out of hand.

"You can't be serious surely! Elaine?"

I'm at the back of the stalls trying to control my fury when George appears beside me and in spite of my anger my knees go weak, I'm so thrilled to see him. Jonty's outburst hasn't put him off then. Nor my mother's hysterics. He's here, here, standing right beside me and in spite of Beverley's warning too. He's here showing her he won't be dictated to, I know it. Clearly demonstrating he's her father but he'll stand next to any woman he wants to. He's not afraid of her stupid threats. Nor am I. And maybe all this scholarship business has only been a means to an end anyway - George will be the greater prize. And since Imogen's going to spend time in Paris with Beverley....

He hasn't said anything but he's standing so near I can feel the heat of his body. And my own. There's hardly an inch between us. He's here to collect Beverley, he says suddenly, and me too if I want a lift home. I would give anything to go with him, but it's only seven o'clock and we're still in costume, nowhere near ready, the rehearsal's still in full swing and anyway Beverley's up on stage talking to Irina. I smile at him. "We'll be a long while yet." There's no-one else here at the back, in the half darkness. He could take my hand and no-one would even know. I move it nearer, hoping he'll notice.

"Jonty all right?"

"Mmn."

"That night – "

He knows, he remembers how beautiful it was.

"Look, Elaine," George whispers. "I - "

"No!"

I can see immediately, immediately, what he's going to say. I can see it his eyes, even in this light. So Beverley's threats have got to him. She has made him afraid.

He says there'll be a scandal, that a story in the papers now could ruin him. He doesn't want to lose his career of course. It's important, he says, his work. Influence in the corridors of power matters. Nor does he want to lose his beautiful daughter. Even if she will be based in Paris. She's important to him. I can understand that. He is her father after all. I am only his daughter's friend, I am easily expendable. And he says John Powers doesn't deserve to be hurt.

"John Powers?"

There's a hesitation before he says quietly: "Well, they think it's Melanie, don't they?"

Is there something else he's afraid of? He seems surprised I have to ask him.

"I have a past, Elaine, of course I have, and there's Imogen to consider."

Imogen? John Powers?

"What about me?"

"Where's Elaine?" Irina's calling.

"What about me, George?"

Beverley has come off the stage and is walking up the aisle. In a few moments she will be here.

"There's nothing between us yet though, Elaine, is there? I only kissed you," he says. "We ought to leave it like that before things get out of hand." He moves, just enough, so that he's clearly out of my reach. Like he's made his decision.

"Elaine?"

But why should I speak to her, the way she talked about me earlier. Laughed. I sweep past her and on down to the stage and leave them both standing there.

"Elaine?" .

If that's the way they both want it....

In the wings the spotlights pick up the dust rising where the dancers are scraping their pointe shoes in the resin box, arching their feet and adjusting the pink ribbons around their ankles. The stage lights shine through their white tulle costumes.

"Elaine?" A voice, not Beverley's, echoes from the far side of the stage.

With stinging eyes I look across through the maze of mothers who are fussing around us all in preparation for the big night. There seem to be more of them every time I see them. They're nothing but trouble, getting in the way, tripping over wires, arguing with each other. This is one moment I am grateful that my mother is incapable. I couldn't stand anyone hovering around behind the scenes for me.

Olivia Orlando fights her way through them.

"Hello, Elaine. Nearly there, then?"

There's something different about the way she's speaking to me, she's not so stand-offish. She seems at last to have some respect for me. "You're dancing really well," she says, "I watched the Don Quixote earlier. I honestly think if it wasn't for Beverley - " She doesn't finish what she was going to say. She's seen Beverley, she says, and wants to wish her luck too.

"Elaine?"

This voice belongs to Diana. She's coming towards me smiling. Whenever she does a stage make-up she gets lipstick on her teeth. I won't tell her. Why should I? I want every advantage I can get. I intend to win. I want what Beverley wants. It's understandable, surely? What else is important to me now? This is a fight to the death, an end game now between me and this girl I have worshipped, who tonight laughed at the thought I might be remotely capable of taking what she wants. Oh, and I want it. I might have stood back, but not now. I want the scholarship to the Meridienne Ballet Conservatoire, and life in the fast lane on the other side of the Channel. And if I can snatch it away I shall leave Beverley and everything here behind me without a second thought.

"Well, tomorrow's the big night," says Diana. "Did you see Olivia?"

"Yes, she went over to say good luck to - "

"She's in an absolute fury with Sergei - "

"Merte, darling," Beverley says, appearing right beside me. Her eyes are sparkling. She looks triumphant, as if she's already won the prize. Sergei is hovering beside her. Behind him from a safe distance Olivia is watching us. She looks deflated, defeated.

The tall figure at the back of the stalls walks along to the exit doors and disappears through them.

I turn to Beverley and kiss her, and wish her good luck. We both say we want the other to win. Like hell we do, we both sound so insincere, but it would be bad luck to say anything else, wouldn't it?

So now we must wait and see what tomorrow brings....

Chapter 21

The face in the mirror then on that competition day, who was she? I don't think I had a clear idea anymore of my own image - sometimes I thought I looked more like Beverley than she did herself. It was almost impossible to tell the original me from the borrowed. The mannerisms, the style. The kohl pencil drawn carefully round my eyes, was that me? That colour lipstick, the way I outlined my lips, was it my choice? It had never been a question of beauty - but at that moment who was the real Elaine Higham?

My bedroom mirror was no help. I gazed out of the window instead. The church clock further up the river struck eleven notes. The sound travelled away under the bridge with the retreating tide. In my narrow view of it, and even on such a bright autumn day, the Thames was the irresolute colour of shadows, and full of oily reflections.

Behind me were clothes flung on the bed, tried, questioned and discarded. It wasn't important what I arrived at the theatre in, but it would matter later. Afterwards. In the end I chose what she would wear. It was easier. And safer. I knew myself better that way.

So I went to the Kings Theatre on the day of the Meridienne Scholarship dressed like Beverley, dressed as my rival, and Beverley, standing just inside the stage door, smiled to see me looking so familiar.

The performance would begin at 7.45 p.m. but before that there were costumes to collect from Dotty and take to our dressing-rooms, and a class, and any last minute run throughs we wanted, and plenty of time for nerves.

But as Diana said, being all together in the theatre helped. Everyone else was nervous too.

The program would start with each of us in turn doing one set solo, then again in turn, the other. Intermission.

Then the individual dances, followed by a period of time for the judges to make their decision. And finally the announcement of the winner. Way back on the first day at Rose Hill we had drawn our places. Wendy had number one, then came Christopher, Meg, and Candice. Diana was number five, then Chloe, and Lillian. Me next at number eight. Tanya, nine, then guess who had what everyone considered to be the best place? Beverley!

For the last few days since we'd been practicing in the theatre, she and I had shared the dressing-room on the top floor. It was the largest, with skylights, and long rows of dressing mirrors and sinks, and rails for costumes, plenty of room for a whole chorus.

"You won't mind, you two, will you? The rooms are being refurbished so not everything's available. To get the space, they've given us the old top floor one," Irina explained.

We didn't mind. It gave us lots of room and during the week as if in some mad way returning to the exhilaration of the early days of our friendship, we had revelled in the chance to race each other up to the top of the stairs. It was a false picture, comforting in a way, but a facade all the same. Perhaps though that racing was an outward sign that the real competition was only just beginning. Our dances were both towards the end of each section so we could easily be furthest from the stage, and it was only natural for everyone to imagine that as best friends we would want to be together.

Weren't we almost like sisters? For the past year hadn't we shared everything? Even when two bouquets arrived for her late in the afternoon, one from her father, the other from Sergei, Beverley thought nothing of giving me George's dozen roses to put up beside my mirror. But then how could she know their significance?

"I don't want them anyhow," she said bitterly. "He needn't think he can buy back my affections. And you won't get any tonight, will you?"

No Beverley, I thought. As you so tactlessly point out, I won't get any. There's no-one to send them to me. Not even your father now.

"Thank you, darling," I said, smiling sweetly while angrily tearing off one poor scarlet petal and cutting the life out of it with my fingernail.

"Let's have the pretty one in the middle," said the photographer, arranging us in a group on the stage.

You know who he meant of course. We were all gathered round with her as centerpiece, so even the photograph taken in advance of the result, would display what everyone imagined was a forgone conclusion. I was at the end of the row. Never mind. In the caption it could say, 'Elaine Higham, pictured far right...'

The ten of us moved around the theatre pretty silently all afternoon. The class was uneventful, just us stretching and preparing ourselves. Except for some gossip from Diana about Sergei dumping Olivia and didn't that prove what we always thought, there wasn't the usual chatter. You could feel the tension in the air, chill layers of it. Chloe said she was beginning to feel quite sick. Candice began complaining how hungry she was.

"How can she mention food?" cried Chloe.

"But I can't eat before the performance, can I?"

"Nonsense, Candice!" said Irina. "Have some protein if you must."

"But," she threatened in her sweet dove voice, "that doesn't mean eating some awful hamburger or you'll never get off the ground."

Complimentary to the last, Irina!

Tanya was avoiding too much activity, trying to rest her ankle as much as possible. It was still playing up and she was terribly nervous that it wouldn't last the evening.

"What will I do? All that work and I slip in a stupid shower," she wailed.

As for me, I felt like steel. Silent, methodical, arranging my make-up and my costumes and my point shoes, putting them in order, and in order again. Not hungry. Not nervous. Just determined. Repetitively organizing and reorganizing. Impervious to everything and everyone.

Beverley didn't look nervous either.

Some of the others wanted to run through their solos. Beverley stayed to watch while I went back upstairs to the dressing-room. The only thing I hadn't arranged ready on my dressing-table were the three red camellias. I couldn't avoid it much longer. Better to do it now too, while I was by myself. Without Beverley to say: "Where did you get those?"

I took the flowers one by one from their box and set them out and stared down at them. How happy I had been that day, just driving with him, how wildly, wonderfully alive. I glanced across at the roses. Scarlet too, but not sent to me. Not sent to me, George. The card was still pinned to their cellophane. Beverley hadn't even kept that. 'Fare well my darling daughter....'

Oh the pain of my desire for him, the ache of it. I wanted his arms around me. Needed him to kiss me. The sight of these flowers made me suddenly realize that the stresses of the competition were nothing compared to my own emotions. I was being eaten alive from inside, crying now, shaking. But it isn't fair, is it? Not to be allowed what you want most in the world? To have it taken away by the person you envy most in the world? I tried to swallow back my tears. Even the scholarship would soon be hers.

No-one can stop you winning, Elaine, except....

The room seemed airless, suffocating, spinning. A drink of water. Yes, water might help. Might calm me. I filled a glass. My hand was shaking. I drank and went to fill it again but somehow the glass slipped suddenly and fell into the sink, smashing, almost exploding into smithereens.

I backed away, trembling. Air. Air. Open a window. The skylight above me was so hard to maneuver. One of its panes of glass was broken, partly fallen away. I had to push it carefully to avoid more falling in. Still I couldn't breathe.

There was a little crack, a splitting sound above me in the remaining glass as the skylight settled into an open position. And in that moment.... In that moment the idea came to me. At that instant. And the room stopped spinning. My tears dried up. My temperature dropped sharply into ice cold. Of course.

Of course, it was so easy.

I moved back to the sink, suddenly logical and calculating. Determined. Just as I had been last night when I walked away from George. The shards of glass lay in the sink glistening like diamonds. Glistening. Familiar somehow. Glistening edges sharp enough to slice away relationships at a single stroke. Yes. Yes. I would take from Beverley what I wanted. Have what you want. Make it possible, Elaine, said the drum, its beat sounding louder and louder.

Take it, take it, take it.

Louder.

Take it.

The glass sparkled. Jagged, piercing. Lethal.

Take it, take it, take it.

And since I couldn't have her father....

Chapter 22

"Come on. Race you!"

For what I knew would be the last time Beverley and I ran as fast as we could up the stairs. As we had every day that week when we reached the top at the same time, we leaned back against the rails, panting, laughing at our idiocy. For me it was a final moment of togetherness, and heavily tinged with nostalgia. Maybe that was why it seemed to last longer than usual, and I began to fear that for once Beverley might not lean down and untie the pink ribbons, that she would break her silly habit of removing her pointe shoes before she went into the dressing-room this one time in honour of the occasion. After all tonight was different. At a moment when her whole future life, and all of Paris might be gained in a single night's competition, what did pointe shoes on or off matter?

She stood there looking at me, laughing, leaning back on her elbows, the contrast of pure white satin and tulle of the set piece costume making her dark hair seem to gleam even more than usual in the light. Her dark eyes danced with the understanding of all our intimate confidences and friendship. How beautiful she was, my friend. But she also had everything I wanted and I could never forgive her that.

"Are you nervous about tonight?" she asked.

I lifted my shoulders dramatically.

"Terrified," I said, and I smiled innocently, the smile of traitors. I couldn't resist glancing down at her pointe shoes but I looked back up quickly to her face in case she read anything into it.

Say something. Quick.

"Did you see them all shaking down there? Chloe was the worst. She looked as if she was going to throw up any minute! Mostly over Sergei!"

"She gets stage-fright really badly."

"How will she cope then?"

At last Beverley leaned down and picked at the knots. Slowly the ribbons unwound, and she flexed her pink-tighted toes as they emerged.

"That's a crazy habit," I said, suddenly jeopardizing my plan in a moment of unexpected compassion.

She shrugged. As always her confidence was hard to bear. It spurred me on. Nothing would go wrong for Beverley because she never expected it to. But she had not bargained for the envy of her closest friend.

She hauled the pointe shoes up by their ribbons.

"I've got more lambswool in these than block," she said, picking about inside them. Then she flung them over her shoulder like a rucksack. They dangled in front of my eyes as I moved to follow her into the dressing-room.

I was chattering furiously, with no clear idea of the content.

She interrupted.

"Is Jonty's arm better? How late did my father really stay that night?"

Suddenly I was struck dumb, freezing near the door at what she'd said and at the sight of her walking so steadily across the floor towards the glass completely unaware of the impending danger. She did not falter once. Wasn't she going to look where she was going? She was just a few steps from her chair, and just inches from disaster. Nearly directly under the window. Surely, now....

"What time? And what did he say to you last that made you walk off?"

Still I held my breath. I squinted down at the linoleum. Had someone brushed the glass away? Had one of the others rushed up? Wendy, borrowing something as usual, or Lillian? Had they unknowingly kicked the danger aside? But I hadn't seen them leave the stage, they were both still down there. No, any second now....

Say something....do something....

"Jonty?" I said, starting to walk gingerly across myself, slightly to the left of her route. I felt a sudden crunching underfoot through the soles of my own leather pumps and the extra insoles that I'd taken care to wear. There was glass from the window still there all right, other less hazardous pieces that I'd put down to make it all seem more authentic. Here it was like walking on sugar.

Beverley hesitated. She'd seen it, hadn't she? Maybe she'd even heard it.

Surely.

But no, her eyes were fixed on her reflection in the dressing-table mirror. She was adjusting an escaped strand of hair.

"So how late, Elaine?"

I went on past her, and sat down in my seat at the end. I didn't dare glance back. I heard her move her chair ready to sit down in it. I kept my voice light as if I really hadn't registered the bit about Jonty's arm. What had George told her? I had to say something.

"Maybe Jonty will come tonight. He did threaten to."

Beverley gave a sudden cry. I looked round.

As if in slow motion she lifted a trembling foot and balanced it against her knee. The huge sliver of glass, the worst piece, was embedded deep into the arch of her foot. Her face began to screw up into ugly twists of pain. She opened her mouth but the scream took a second to hit the air. Then it tore through my head and echoed, spinning back to the door and out and down the stairs, louder and louder until I was sure it would burst my eardrums. I cowered down into my chair, shocked by the unexpected intensity of her distress.

The sound brought people running. Suddenly the room was full of them, some staring in horror, others rushing away for medical assistance, still more clasping poor Beverley from every side, carefully sitting her down without her foot touching the floor again, and shouting, arguing whether to pull out the glass or not. Her face at first frozen in shock suddenly collapsed. Now she was in floods of tears.

"How did it happen?" they were asking, trying to keep her calm.

"There's g-glass or something on the floor." Of course it was glass, stupid girl. She sounded as if she couldn't understand what was happening, hadn't taken it in.

"Where?"

Some of them backed around, staring down, dispersing what was left amongst their feet. One of them pointed up to the broken window.

"Oh my God."

No-one saw me or talked to me or inquired about my feet. Beverley seemed to be all they cared about. Carefully I removed my ballet slippers and put them beside me. I wanted the glass I'd trodden in to stay on them, so that I'd been at risk too. I hauled my feet up off the floor, hugged my knees and stared down at the offending floor. I needed to look vulnerable, and anyway I knew safety in the guise of my pair of proper shoes was within easy reach.

Sergie stormed in.

"What's happened?" He stared in horror when he saw Beverley's foot. "Scissors!" he demanded.

He cut away the tights around her ankle and round the shaft of glass and pulled the material very carefully away. Now you could see just how far in the glass had penetrated. It stuck out from the surface like the tip of an awful glistening iceberg. Blood was only beginning to seep out around it, as if the glass itself was holding back the flow. My stomach started to churn at the sight of it. Beverley would certainly not be dancing tonight, nor for some time to come. But why hadn't she looked where she was going? It was her, her silly habit of removing her pointe shoes. Vain as ever, it was she who had stopped to fix her hair instead of minding where she was stepping. From where I was I wouldn't have seen the danger, I couldn't have warned her.

But inside my head I began to hear Beverley's voice mingling with my own - in Luigi's, planning our great futures over coffee, us humming music in the back of her father's car, our whispering and giggling backstage. Remembered her beautiful clothes she'd passed on to me and her mother's hospitality, and the money, the money her father had so generously given me so that I could enter the competition. I cringed suddenly with horror at what I had done. And at the thought of George. I wouldn't be here if it wasn't for him. I wanted him to put his arms around me and tell me everything would be all right. Now he wouldn't. No, he wouldn't ever again.

And I really hated Beverley then for making me do this to her. Losing George was a worse injury than anything I could inflict on her. All she had was the sight and the physical pain of the cut, though it looked pretty fearsome. At worst, she'd have dreadful debilitating disappointment at missing tonight's once in a lifetime opportunity. After all she had worked steadily towards this scholarship and knew it was hers for the taking. It was waiting to fall in her lap like everything else.

But she would still have her father.

What of the pain I had inflicted on her? What about my pain? But now too, I was suddenly gripped by the fear that I might be discovered.

I glanced at myself in the mirror expecting to see guilt written all over my face. But no evil was apparent there, nothing to give me away. Only in my eyes did I detect something different, a strange piercing quality, not penetrating outward, but a kind of opaque blindness, as if a barrier had come down and now I was probing backwards, seeing dangerously deep into my own soul.

I went on silently rationalizing, finding excuses for what I'd done. Beverley must feel some relief surely, a huge release of tension, that she didn't have to endure the performance, that all those pirouettes didn't need turning, and the arabesques no longer needed balancing, that some chance slip could not now ruin everything. Anyway, I thought, justifying my wickedness completely, her parents would afford to send her abroad eventually, wouldn't they? And didn't George think of dancing as a pretty little hobby? It wasn't a serious career for Beverley, was it?

"Who could have done this?"

The mothers all pointed vigorously up to the skylight. Suddenly Sergei glanced along at me. I blushed bright red. If anyone could guess, he would. He looked away again quickly. Perhaps he didn't like what he saw.

But all he said was: "Don't move, Elaine, for goodness sake. Keep your feet up."

"I am," I said meekly, hugging my knees and clutching my toes tighter.

Still no-one said, Poor Elaine. Are you hurt, dear? Did any glass get in your feet? Was there something the matter with me? Didn't I deserve attention too?

"For God's sake, where's that ambulance?"

"Shouldn't we do something now?"

"Best to remove it surgically," said Sergei. "Safer."

Beverley cries increased.

Now Imogen appeared at the door and rushed in horror to her daughter's side. I hadn't realized she was in the theatre and the expression on her face when she turned away from the horror of seeing Beverley's foot to look up at the window frightened me. I recognized immediately how many of her own hopes she had pinned on her daughter, she, who had longed to be a dancer herself. If she was to use her imagination and guess the truth, Imogen might be really dangerous. She would be out for blood herself.

But someone else came in behind her with a hoover, another mother, and then three more invaded with small dustpans and brushes and they all set to work. All the evidence was being removed, and the floor thoroughly, painstakingly swept and minutely examined for anything another might have missed. One of them climbed on a chair and rubbed a cloth over the remaining glass to release any further loose pieces. I cowered in my chair

219

watching them with enormous relief. These women were my allies. They would want to believe in accidents, wouldn't they? Because suddenly their own daughters were in with a chance.

Dotty arrived and clambered urgently past the workers. She was more afraid for the white satin and tulle of the Meridienne costume than for anything that might have happened to the poor whimpering Beverley who was only the temporary incumbent of all the fine stitching. Taking no notice of Imogen's indignant fury she slit the crutch and one seam and set about peeling the tutu off without Beverley moving an inch or her feet having to touch the floor. She achieved her aim and the hoovering and sweeping finished only just in advance of the arrival of the ambulance men, who were temporarily barred from entering until Beverley could be made to look respectable by the flock of interfering and prudish mothers.

The two men refused to wait. They forced a way through.

"Think we haven't seen a few things in our time?" one said, deftly separating Beverley's mother and Sergei from the crowd and ushering the rest quickly out into the corridor.

The first man knelt down to examine the injury close in. "Christ."

The other unfolded a red blanket.

"Good thing we've brought the stretcher up. Can't walk like that, can we, love?"

Beverley broke into renewed sobbing.

"Think we'll leave this until we get to casualty. Could be into an artery."

Imogen put her arms round Beverley protectively and

scowled angrily at the men. "My daughter was due to dance in the Meridienne scholarship tonight. Don't frighten her. She's upset enough about this!"

"Hell's teeth! Could have been done on purpose then."

Why did that immediately make everyone look at me? Perhaps just because I was the only other one there, but I trembled, waiting for the accusations I knew I thoroughly deserved. But they didn't come. Not even from Imogen. Suddenly there was even concern for me.

"Elaine?"

Had I been Beverley's friend just long enough to earn Imogen's trust?

"You all right, love?" asked the first ambulanceman, as the second ambulance man opened the door, shooed away the peering mothers and began urgently manoeuvering the stretcher into the room.

"I had my ballet shoes on," I said, timidly.

"Bit of luck. Who would do a thing like this?"

Sergei shook his head. "These two girls are favourites for tonight," he said. "Everyone knew this was their dressing-room."

I could have hugged him. Me, a favourite! And now provided with a definite alibi too. After all, he was implying the glass might have been meant for me as well.

"I reckon you should call in the authorities," one of the men suggested as they lifted a whimpering Beverley very carefully onto the stretcher.

Sergei frowned. "What about that broken window?" he said, pointing up at it. "Might be negligence, but the theatre's in the throes of structural improvements. We've been given the free use of it for tonight. They haven't charged us, and they only let us use some of these

221

dressing-rooms as a special favour because we kept insisting we needed more space. It's as much our fault. Can't we delay any fuss? We don't need all that now."

The ambulance man shrugged. "Up to you, mate."

"It's taken five years to get Meridienne back. Any investigation would put them off ever offering this scholarship here again. And it's too late. All our poor dancers will be shocked enough as it is. There's so much at stake tonight."

"What about me?" wailed Beverley.

Sergei looked distraught. "I can't stop things now."

One of the ambulance men nodded over at me.

"She looks frightened out of her life."

Oh God, and did I look guilty?

"They're all so nervous," nodded Imogen. She left Beverley briefly to come across and plant a quick insincere but charitable kiss on my trembling cheek. "Dance well," she said. Her voice was strained. "Now everyone else has a chance." She knew well how much she had lost. Beverley would have won, and through her daughter all her own dreams would have been realized. I felt rather sorry for her, but the fear of discovery was stalking me.

"How can I go on now? I am too worried about Beverley, Imogen." I knew so exactly what cards to play. "I couldn't possibly dance tonight. I must come to the hospital with her."

"No, no, you mustn't. You just think about tonight. That's right, Beverley, isn't it?"

Beverley, covered now with the crimson blanket, levered herself up onto her elbow.

"No, don't come," she said.

It should have sounded generous. Maybe it was my

imagination but wasn't the tone of her voice different? Her mother must have heard it too because she turned back to her in surprise. Beverley had a weird look in her eyes and in spite of Sergei's words, or perhaps because of them, I could have sworn she'd suddenly guessed it was me who had wrecked her chances.

"Merte, Elaine," she said, but she didn't smile. She always smiled when she said that, but this time she didn't. Then she looked at her mother, "I need to talk to Daddy right away. Immediately." And she lay down again and said, "Can we go now?"

Was she saying she knew about me and George?

'How late did my father stay, Elaine?' She might have thought he'd gone to see Melanie and she'd been about to question me, hadn't she? And I hadn't answered. I'd prevaricated. Maybe the truth had suddenly dawned on her. She wouldn't be able to prove anything, but after this she would do anything to get back at me. She would accuse me anyway. Convince everyone. She'd already threatened George with publicity, and for George that had immediately been enough to separate us. And if I was in close to her, she certainly was close enough in to me to understand better than anyone now what I would give to win the scholarship from her.

Imogen glanced back to me. And for a second her eyes lighted on and registered the box the red camellias had been in.

"Right," said one of the ambulance men. The stretcher was lifted up. "Let's go."

At the door Imogen, leading the way, turned for a brief moment and looked at me with puzzled eyes. I watched them all carry her daughter out after her with a mixture of shame and elation.

One of the stage hands came in after that with some electrical tape and bound the broken and cracked glass in the skylight together. Even the glass that wasn't damaged.

"You supposed to switch dressing rooms," he said. "The manager's nearly had a heart attack at the thought of an insurance claim."

"But all my things are set out ready," I said. "Everything's been thoroughly swept. You've taped it. I'd rather not."

"But - "

"Please? I won't have enough time."

"Okay," he said, "I'll say you have," and left.

Silence.

My elation increased and took control. All I had to do now was dance as I'd never danced before.

About half an hour later Sergei returned. He did not bother to knock. "The glass. It was you, wasn't it?"

"What on earth do you mean?"

"Don't lie to me, Elaine."

"It was the window! You saw it!"

"You're so stupid, you know?."

"I heard you two," I said accusingly, "making plans. Talking about flats together."

For a moment he seemed taken aback. "That's my job! I am responsible for everybody in the competition."

But I knew his motives. "You wanted Beverley to win so that she'd go to Paris with you. She told me exactly what happened that night by the swimming pool. Well, now maybe I'll be going instead of her."

"Will you!"

"And if you're so responsible you should never have

224

sent us up to this dressing-room. You're trying to shift the blame onto me! It was the window!"

"How very convenient! Child! You're a idiotic child."

"Why did you kiss me then?"

"When?" I saw the memory register suddenly and he turned away, eyes glistening, bright with fury. "You just looked like Beverley for a moment," he said sourly.

The sting of it, that dangerous sting.

He swung round. "What if that glass has severed Beverley's tendon? What then?"

"But it's your own injury that frightens you, isn't it!" I said, trying hard to sound as patronizing as possible. "After all you're so out of practice, without her who else will want to be partnered by you?"

He looked as if he might kill me. "Don't expect any introductions from me if you don't win, then," he hissed.

I stared at him. "What do you mean?" My voice would hardly obey me. Suddenly it was only coming out as a whisper.

"I'd arranged an audition for us with - Oh forget it!" he snapped furiously. "You can go to bloody hell on your own."

He slammed the door behind him.

I just stood there, trembling, too angry to cry. Who needed him anyway? Who needed anyone?

But then I thought hysterically, what if someone had heard us quarrelling? Worse, what if he talked to the judges, or told Irina or the organizers or the theatre manager what he suspected? What if they believed his theory about the glass? What if I was arrested? What if I was disqualified? I waited apprehensively, wondering who else would rush in.

I stayed there for ages, facing the door, waiting.

After a while when nobody came I convinced myself that Sergei's accusations would have gone unnoticed. Most people would have been on stage doing the warm-up while we'd been arguing.

I did not go down to join them. I stayed in the dressing-room alone quietly, trying to calm myself, and slowly stretching, and gathering my energies back together.

Eventually I heard footsteps. Who would it be? I braced myself.

Diana put her head round the door. "Poor you. Did you tread on any?"

"No. Well, some, but I had my ballet shoes on."

"What a shock. Will you be all right?"

"Yes."

"Move down to our room."

"I'd rather be by myself."

"What about warming up?"

"I've done it up here."

She glanced nervously down at the floor. "Is it safe?"

"It's been vacuumed and swept."

She wasn't keen to step in all the same. She glanced at the clock above my head. "Only thirty-five minutes to go."

"Yes."

"We're all wishing each other luck."

I smiled. "Thanks, Diana. You too."

"I think you'll win," she said warmly.

I opened my eyes wide and feigned disbelief.

"If only," I said.

"Yes," she said. "I bet you do. Merte, then."

"Merte, Diana."

After she'd gone I sat down at the mirror, switched

on the rim lights and reached for the pan stick make-up. What I'd done was childish, so spiteful and childish, Sergei was right - but it was effective, wasn't it? And sod him. I didn't need him to use his influence. I'd make it on my own. And I didn't need love, did I? George's or anybody's. I'd done without it all my life. Why worry now? The face of a cool, calculating, ambitious young woman stared back at me, head held high, auburn hair oiled and quite sleek, figure the best it could be. I'd been copying Beverley long enough to know how to make myself look almost pretty.

"Merte, you," I whispered. "Merte, Elaine Higham."

Chapter 23

You could hear them, the buzz of them, those people in the audience, like a threatening swarm of bees. It was full, the house out there.

I was standing backstage. We all were.

A hush, then applause followed by silence, and a voice, Irina's, with that strange humming microphone quality added to it. She was in front of the curtain, talking to the audience, welcoming them, introducing the judges one by one. Three lots of tremendous applause.

"Due to unfortunate circumstances," she continued - Beverley's absence needed explanation of course. "Sadly one of the dancers, number ten in your program, Beverley Soames, is unable to appear tonight, so that the competition will be between just nine entrants, not the original ten. Such a pity...."

Then she began talking about the Meridienne Ballet company, how after five years they were offering this glittering prize again, how the evening might produce a star of tomorrow, what a wonderful chance this would be for the winner.

Back in the wings I was wishing she would hurry up and the curtain would rise. The time has come, for goodness sake. Let me use it. Stop waffling, Irina.

Hot stage lights. The smell of make-up, clayey, sweet. And resin. And fear. Eight girls, all in glistening white tutus. Christopher though, was in all over gray. Different. It flattered him. He looked very slim and muscular. Maybe it gave him an advantage. After all only one of him, and a strong, talented and excellent figure, interested in ballet - a rarer commodity. It had been the choice last time.

Applause. A ruffle of the curtain confirmed Irina was leaving the stage and returning to the darkness of the wings. The audience settled. The moment had come.

We were all by the stage, waiting to go on, five on one side, only four on the other where there should have been five. It was the one variation on what was the first set piece. In this direct comparison, only our entrance from different wings divided us. There was a simple black backcloth. There would be no curtain fall between. We each had to walk to the center of the stage in our turn. Wendy first. Over in the wing opposite mine she looked terrified.

The curtain rose slowly on the empty stage. There was a moment's delay. Even though she was nervous Wendy was using her brains. She waited until the audience was completely silent and you could hear a pin drop. Then she walked out, slowly, deliberately, every step carefully judged. She looked quite astonished at the applause which greeted her and I thought for a moment she was going to cave in, but she kept her head and took up her position. The music started and she stepped forward confidently into the first arabesque. Wendy was a pretty dancer in spite of her narrow shoulders, and she was dancing beautifully, but like a lot of strawberry redheads physical exertion made her skin go unattractively pink.

"She's doing so well," whispered Tanya, as we watched.

The slow controlled pirouettes. The music, violins singing on the air. Then, the final pose. Well held. She'd done it. Applause again.

Christopher came after her. He waited too, letting the

audience settle before he went on. He'd seen how effective it was.

Meg. Then Candice. How quickly each dance was over. Even in adagio when the steps are gracefully slow, four minutes is nothing. Nothing. No time at all. Diana. Chloe. It was a kind audience out there at least, full of family and friends, all willing their own competitor on with warm and generous applause.

Lillian came off stage beside me, panting.

"It's awful.."

I had no time to listen. It was me now. My turn.

Like Wendy and Christopher I waited for the audience to go quiet. Ahead of me the stage seemed vast. I stepped out into the lights, walked to the center. There was the burst of applause but it sounded very far away like heavy rain falling on a rooftop. I knew I would hardly dare to look out into the darkness it came from so I had planned to keep my eyes down until I reached the center just as I'd seen Beverley do. Do what she'd do, Elaine. Take the audience in the palm of your hand like she would. Allow them to watch you, as if it's your gift, this performance. I felt like a mountain climber on a sheer cliff, without safety ropes though, as if it might be dangerous out there, to look out into that black hole, as if I could easily fall into it.

I took up my position, composed myself, looked up, straight out like Beverley would, confidently, and because I suddenly expected it to, that darkness beyond the dazzling lights seemed to give me power.

And no-one can stop you winning now, Elaine. Dance! Let yourself dance.

The music begins. The first step into the arabesque. The white tulle of my tutu glistens around me.

Shimmers. Olivia's voice begins too. Inside me. Imagine there is one place in the company. Earn it, Elaine. Fight for it. And I can. The balance is perfect. I could stay here all night. Your pirouettes are atrocious....echoes from the past. But no, Olivia, I've learned that lesson well, every one of them will work tonight. It's true. Every turn's a perfect double because it's like I am behind this iron mask of make-up, dark eyes drawn on, Beverley's face over mine. Supported by it. I am hidden inside a complete silhouette of her somehow, as if the lights outline me and I'm her, and that brittle sparkle that I have pursued for so long, giving me her balance, her ability, her aura, I have it, and all the while I can be the dark inside, the fire at the centre.

I can hear the silence of the audience, the hush. They're holding their breath. I can sense their approval, and feel my body working, the pull of the arches of my feet as I point them, the stretch of my arms, the powerful lock in of the balance. The lights are catching the brilliance, illuminating me somehow, making starbursts of deep arabesques, creating outlines and patterns with my limbs. That sensual honed line. But it's all over much too fast. I can't believe it. All the practicing I've done for such a small appearance. Now I am taking my bow and walking elegantly off.

"Super!" cried Diana excitedly. "Really super!"

I bent over and put my head between my knees to relieve the tension. Behind me I heard new applause greeting Tanya. We all watched sympathetically, wondering if her ankle would survive. She was tense but there were no disasters.

So that was the adagio over. A few minutes break. We used it to dip our pointe shoes in the resin, to stretch, to limber up again, amongst the heavy black back stage curtains and the shafts of light behind the scenes. And then we were back to Wendy. The allegro this time, faster, showier, and things weren't going quite so well. Wendy missed a pirouette, and you could see her lose her nerve, but she made it through to the end. These quicker steps showed off Christopher's elevation but accentuated his poor arch, and his beats were not as good as usual. Meg was better in this than the first solo, but Candice was frightened of making mistakes. She was holding back, not attacking the steps at all and landing heavily.

My turn was coming fast. It was as if the evening was speeding up. Diana was doing really well, her energy, and enthusiasm giving her extra grace. This was her sort of dancing. But poor Chloe had been physically sick and was shaking with fright at the thought of being next and had to be pushed on when it came to her entrance. She danced but something was definitely missing. Then Lillian was on, and suddenly it was me again. But I was ready. Unafraid. Full of confidence. In the wings beside me Tanya was whispering some unintelligible nonsense

"What?" I asked, but there was no time to wait for a reply.

I was on again and in my stride. My jetés were high, my balance was working perfectly, all the pirouettes were coming off, and all through the dance, with the speed of it, I was filled with a kind of magic. And when everything's working, the soul is freed. You're up there with the Gods.

I was nearly at the end. No-one can stop you winning except..... stop it, Elaine, she's not here. She's not here.

Dance!

But for a split second I found myself wishing George was out there, out in that blackness. In the auditorium watching. Not with Beverley at the hospital where he was sure to be. God, dance, Elaine Higham! Dance! This is what you want. I stepped into the final posé pirouettes. Every single one of them worked. The finish was clean and confident. As I took my bow though, was it the applause I heard drumming in my heart? Or was it fear of what Beverley would be saying to George right at this moment.

I spoke to no-one in the intermission. Once I'd changed into my scarlet tutu I spent what was left of the time upstairs alone in the dressing-room. The three blood red camellias were pinned perfectly, securely, down the side of my hair. I looked just like the photographs in Sergei's book. I put on the flashy little diamanté earrings, George's earrings. I painted on brighter lipstick to suit the scarlet of my costume and re-did the ribbons on my point shoes.

The two minute call came over the intercom. I looked in the mirror. This was it, the last solo. The last opportunity. For us all.

Back down on the stage there was a commotion. Tanya wasn't going on. Her ankle had given in, and she'd taken so many painkillers she was almost delirious, so now Irina was back out in front of the curtain talking to the audience again. There was an aahh! of genuine compassion and then Irina came off.

And the curtain rose.

Waltz.

Nutcracker.

Prayer....

Solo after solo. And wonderful applause. Warm

appreciation. The audience was full of excited anticipation. So Tanya was out of it now too. I waited in the wings, fiddling nervously with my black fan, smoothing out the stiff red tulle of my tutu, psyching myself up. But I felt connected somehow, powerful. And there was a sense of twitching excitement out in front too. I could feel it as I flexed the arches of my feet inside my pointe shoes. It's me they're waiting for, I thought. My flirty Kitri will finish the evening. The final magic position that everyone thinks is the best and luckiest has come to me.

And it can be a real show stopper, all that scarlet and black....

Chapter 24

Kitri is such a little flirt., casting her eyes up at the audience, playing with them, fluttering her fan to the glissando on the harp, and Sergei is right. In spite of the speed of it, the turns and the flashy relevés and the polished pizzicato pointe work, it's the absolute stillness on the balances and between every single sexy step of this solo that makes it cut together, makes it look easy, gives it brilliance.

Finish! The balance lasts and lasts.....

A pin drop silence then a vast breath of excitement before wild applause. It's hard pulling away from the sound of it, I'm suddenly addicted to the wrap around feeling it's giving me, the comfort. I don't want it to stop. All the same I know better than to let it die away from me. It's still enthusiastic as I leave the stage.

So the competition is at an end and still in my scarlet tutu I am waiting nervously with the others for the announcement. During the last twenty five minutes which has been almost worse than the performance itself, we've milled around behind the scenes not daring to speak to one another, while the three judges, two French and one British, have been making their final decision.

Delia Delaney, their spokeswoman, is on the stage now talking into the microphone, thanking the theatre for their gift of hospitality, for the enormous contribution they have made by letting us be here, (applause) and Irina Caillouet for all her hard work. And Sergei Lesarte. (More applause.) And how delighted the

Meridienne Conservatoire is to be offering this scholarship again. She speaks about the deep friendship between Britain and France.

She's like a dainty little bird. Small boned. Slender little hands and ankles. Her dyed black hair is stretched up and away from her high cheekbones into a tight cottage loaf bun, and a long yellow scarf is thrown back, Isadora style, over the shoulderline of her diaphanous black dress. I love the wildly high heeled black sandals which showed off her arched feet when she teetered onto the stage with a tap-tap-tapping rhythm. She's the most presentable of the three judges. There's a rather eccentric looking Frenchman, Paul Gouter, and another woman, Helene Glisse, or some name like that, large and overbearing. No, I'm glad we're listening to this Delia.

"I'm proud," she says, in a high, clipped plum accent, "as an English woman, to be Artistic Director and Ballet Mistress of what I think is the finest company school in France! In Europe!"

Then she gets rather over-expansive on the artistic heritage of the ballet, how France is responsible for its inception, and of course wasn't that inevitable because they are such a graceful and sophisticated race. That classical ballet fulfills a deep human need for fantasy, how dance is a temporal art, an unbroken arc reaching out to every race and back into the mists of time, connecting us with the origins of our kind. She goes on and on and on. Even the audience is wishing she'd get on with it, they're beginning to get restless, shift in their seats. But for all her capacity to talk she's nervous. And getting more so, the longer she goes on. She's blinking a lot now, hesitating, dipping a little too often to her notes.

236

But I can hardly wait to meet her. I could run right out and put my arms round her narrow little shoulders.

"With the wealth of talent on display here tonight from all over the country, I am quite sure you will agree with me," she says, "when I say that the judges have had an extree...emely difficult and exacting task. The technical and artistic standard has been excellent and it has been almost impossible to choose a winner. Having said that, the dancer we've chosen will, we're sure, have an exciting future with us. All these dancers have a flair for the very exacting world of ballet, but this particular dancer has a special quality which will be so vital for success with Meridienne...."

I know exactly what she is talking about. It's what I've always known I had. Indefinable, but the one thing that no-one else waiting in those wings has any notion of, I'm sure, maybe not even Beverley either, if she were here - a searching for something deep down in the unconscious, a sort of magic that makes me want to turn my steps into something meaningful and worthwhile. While all the rest were technically good tonight, I have danced with all my heart, with all my soul. What Sergei calls giving everything to the audience....

"Without this, no young dancer can succeed. It is prized above all else..."

I have always imagined myself walking down the Champs Elysées, around the Paris Opera, through the streets of Montmartre. Now I know it's all been a kind of planning. All those dreams come true tonight. I will have just two weeks before I go. I almost regret having to leave my mother and brother behind, and the narrow view of the Thames from my bedroom window....

"We wish all the dancers here tonight great success

237

with their careers..."

I can see Wendy behind the scenes near me. She will dance for a while and then get married one day and have all those children and the house she was dreaming of. And Lillian behind her, her father will eventually expect her to follow him into the property business. How straight her posture is, already she appears to be executive material. Further down, beside the proscenium curtain is Candice. She was never going to get off the ground. Now she might stop worrying about gaining a few ounces and eat to her heart's content. Beside me in the wings is Christopher, poor boy, put into this competition to show there's some masculine talent around, but tonight he's been outclassed and out danced. He's standing with his head down. He knows his showing was pretty weak but actually if he works hard... in victory I can afford to be magnanimous.

Diana squeezes my arm excitedly.

"It's got to be you," she whispers, and leans precariously round the curtain trying to spot her mother out front. Further back standing meekly in the dark is Meg.

I have removed my leg warmers. My make-up is perfect. I'm all ready to walk on and bow. I've practiced this moment a thousand times, rehearsed how to say how unexpected it is, that I'll try to be worthy of their trust, and to cry a little. I thought in reality that might be hard, but it's such an emotional moment that there are tears in my eyes already. It's what all the work, and all the sacrifices have been for, all those early nights, and hours of pain and solitude, the perseverance and the exercise; the total concentration, and putting up with no-one loving me. Even giving up George for I've done that too now, haven't I? But tonight everyone out there in the auditorium will love me and it will make all my heartache worthwhile.

"There is no need to keep you in suspense any longer. The winner is....."

The girls' eyes are all on me. And Christopher's. There is no doubt on their faces that they expect me to win and they all know how much I want it. I lean forward, ready to step out.

"Margaret Ryan!"

Who?

Ryan, Ryan.....Ryan.... it echoes away from me, the sound slithering away through the wings like some nasty slippery snake. I have to catch myself mid-step. I just manage it. I turn in astonishment and stare back into the darkness. Meg looks dumbfounded. So is everyone else. There is a shocked split second of silence while the name sinks in.

Then Diana cries: "Meg, Meg, it's you!" and rushes over and drags Meg towards the curtains. Now everyone's around her, patting her on the back, saying, "Well done," and "Good for you," and Meg is being propelled out onto the stage to thunderous applause. And suddenly she comes alive, alive! She begins walking like a dancer, her long neck held gracefully straight and high, and damn it, though my tears are stinging my eyes, I can see what the judges see, the stiff competition I failed to recognize.

Meg is bowing, that strange undeveloped blank page of a dancer, on whom nothing is written, the girl with the perfect body and nothing else, the girl who never read a romantic poem in her life. Meg, who has no imagination, and no answers. They will send her to

Europe, to the Meridienne Conservatoire, and they will train her and produce her and create her. And now I realize that could have been what they were searching for all along, a dancer they could create. No, no, Beverley would have won, but without her, Meg was the obvious choice.

The audience's applause is tremendous, but the sound is hollow to me now, a clattering mocking noise, falling from the circle like a humiliating shower of freezing rain to make all my dreams fizzle out. I can't feel any power in my body, I'm having to hold on to the curtain beside me for support, my muscles seem to have lost all motivation. And worse, my precious gift, the genie of my inspiration, my acquaintance with the Gods, seems to have deserted me and flown out to her, to Meg, as she shakes hands with the judges and bows oh-so-gracefully to the audience. It makes my head spin to see how easily the magic has changed hands.

The curtain comes down for the last time and for a while the stage is full of chattering and congratulations and the rustling of cellophane on bouquets, and the smell of hot bodies and perfume and greasepaint. Bursts of flashlight too. Someone is taking photographs. Mothers are kissing their daughters, the daughters are hugging their fathers, and the dancers are all hugging each other and promising to stay in touch. Even Christopher is being hugged. I stay where I am, near the proscenium curtain, alone, out of the light. No-one is here to hug me. Not even Beverley now.

The chattering moves away slowly like a drifting storm, through the wings, on through the propped open fire door, out into the corridors, away towards the dressing rooms. Soon I am the only one left beside the stage except for an electrician raising the curtain again on the empty auditorium and checking the footlights.

I release my grip on the curtain and test standing unaided. I walk slowly unsteadily across to the fire door and out into the corridor. I must have been in by the stage longer than I thought because most of the competitors are already dressed and ready to leave. Address swapping happened back at Rosehill so there's nothing to hold them here. Some are still wearing their make-up, as if to prove to the people who will be waiting in the street that they were part of the night's exciting proceedings.

"Bye, Elaine," shouts Lillian from the stage door.

I smile my professional smile, and manage a wave, my eyes bright and prickly dry. I have learned to hide my emotions for so long, it comes as second nature now and I have never needed my self control more. I even cope with squeezing through between the hoards of fussing mothers and Dotty's bulging rail of tutus politely and with some dignity.

"See you."

"Yes."

"Sure, soon."

"Catch you later."

"Yes."

Halfway up the stairs, I hear someone calling out of the crowd. At first I don't turn and then the call comes again and the voice is too familiar so I do.

"Elaine?"

It is Jonty. I recognize him down there in the sea of faces. And my mother's behind him. My mother. So he was out in front and he brought her to witness my humiliation too. Tears begin to spike my eyes again and

241

I feel as if I'm shrinking. I can hardly bear to look at her. She must think me such a fool.

"You were far and away the best," Jonty shouts over all the heads. He doesn't care who hears his biased bloody opinion. I don't know if I will ever forgive him.

"Honest!" He smiles his broad happy smile that I haven't seen him smile for ages. "Want to go for a coffee?" Is he doing this on purpose?

My mother shakes her head at him. She looks exhausted. Beyond them is Sergei. His dark eyes are staring up at me too and I remember his words... Don't expect any introductions from me if you don't win.... I remember my reply too and feel ashamed. I know he will never contact me now. He has definitely written me off. And now Irina has come over to him and they talk and she glances up at me. He must be telling her about the glass. I know he is. I glare down at Jonty. I could murder him for drawing attention to me. Now Irina has turned and is talking to Meg. Then to Olivier, and then to Mrs Scobie who stares up at me too. One by one they all stare up at me. I run up the stairs to the dressing-room. I can't wait to get away from them all. I won't stay around to be humiliated. There must be a million other ways to live my life.....

Chapter 25

My brother and I stood waiting at the bus stop. My mother had already gone home. The theatre lights had been switched off. It was late and suddenly bitterly cold. I could have done with a hot drink but it was the last thing I wanted to do, go with Jonty to some grotty late night coffee shop. Directly above me the sky was black, the stars bristling in it, diamond hard. At the other end of the road there was a noisy crowd, some of them lingering beside a pub, some starting to stray along threateningly in our direction.

Jonty leaned against the bus shelter, his hands firmly in the pockets of his jeans.

"I don't understand why you didn't win, Elaine."

I tried to shrug as if I didn't care. Inside I was trembling, freezing cold. I felt as if I would never get warm again. "Meridienne wanted a dancer they could mould into their own style." I don't suppose he understood what that meant or how much effort it took for me to sound so calm.

"You could go to Paris anyway. I'll make Mum give you the money. She's got savings."

I frowned. "What savings?"

"I found a building society book. You can go anytime you want."

"Where was it?"

"Taped to the back of her wardrobe!"

I couldn't resist. "How much?"

He grinned. "Ten thousand."

I gaped at him. "Really?"

"Don't believe me then!"

I knew he shouldn't be telling me this, that it was something he shouldn't know either. But it was a completely new side to my mother I could never have imagined, keeping money concealed, hidden away, secret. Then I thought about the vodka. A whole secret life. Did I know her at all?

"Hey, Elaine! I could come with you."

"Well, that's it. I can't then." But what would there be in Paris for me anyhow? And who? Sergei? So it was easy to blame Jonty. "You've got school."

"Sod school. You think I bother going there?"

I shifted my bag across to my other shoulder, trying to break up the intensity of the conversation. "Don't talk rubbish. If we both suddenly left - "

"Mum wouldn't even notice!"

"Well, I'm not going anywhere. I've done enough damage."

"Damage?"

Of course he didn't understand what I was saying then either, what I was admitting to, what I felt as if I'd been punished for. He wouldn't have believed it of me anyway, he thought he was the wicked one.

"So you can forget Paris," I said firmly.

A bus turned the corner. Its engine made a horrible spluttering sound as it pulled in beside us. Before my brother leapt on behind me, he kicked violently at a cola can lying on the pavement. It spun into the air, ricocheted off a parked car then clattered away, rolling along the gutter as the bus moved off.

"Jonty?"

He pushed past me up the stairs to the empty top deck. He could be so volatile lately, so easily provoked. I had a horrible feeling he was going really wrong.

"Jonty!"

"Fuck off," he said, and swung himself into a separate seat. We travelled the few stops in silence. All I could see was my defeated reflection in the window beside me as we sped past the dark expanse of Wimbledon Common. Somewhere in the distance were the lights of Beverley's house.

I tried to imagine how I was going to get through the long night hours, let alone tomorrow. And I felt weak at the knees at the prospect of going in to the studio. How would I face everyone? There would be a party for Meg's departure, wouldn't there? She lived somewhere in London. I wouldn't go to that either. I couldn't bring myself to watch her basking in her success. Not that she was like that, really. It was me, wasn't it? My jealousy.

Jonty got off the bus too soon.

"Hey! Where are you going?"

He didn't answer, just launched himself off into the night. What was I supposed to do, chase him?

All the lights were on in our house as I walked up the street. For once I was dreading Mum being up. She might actually talk to me. I didn't think I could bear it.

She was in the kitchen.

"Where's Jonty?"

"He's walking back."

"Alone?"

"He'll be okay." What was so different about this night?

She gazed at me in a rare moment of full attention. I thought maybe she'd mention the performance, I mean it would have been nice, wouldn't it, if she'd said something complimentary? But no.

"That George Soames," she said, "haven't I seen him

on television?"

"Almost certainly." I was furious. Why now? Why did she have to discuss him?

"I knew I'd heard his voice."

"I'm exhausted, Mum. I'm going to bed."

"Aren't you interested?"

"In what?" I cried.

"He rang up to speak to you."

Was Beverley getting her revenge so soon? It'd be about the glass of course. To blame me. He'd want to know how I could do such a thing to his precious daughter? He'd tell me Beverley knows now, and Imogen knows, and it really is over, and it was nothing anyhow, was it? Just a kiss, for God's sake, when he was feeling sorry for me. And never to ring him again. Ever.

I knew that was why he wanted to speak to me.

I escaped to my room, and sat on my bed in such deep distress I couldn't even cry.

My mother followed me. For a minute she stared in silence at the photographs of Beverley taped round the wall.

"Aren't you going to call him then?"

"No!"

"As soon as you came in, he said."

"Did he!"

"So aren't you going to call him?"

"Go back to your vodka, Mum!"

She gazed at me, stunned. And then disappeared.

The phone was ringing. I refused to acknowledge the urgent repetitive sound. Then it was like a summons, and I feared it suddenly, for what had such late night calls brought me but bad news? I tried to take no notice of it. It was my mother who answered it.

246

She didn't call me. She spoke and then hung up. She came back and stood in my bedroom doorway again in silence. Then she said: "He wants you to meet him."

I ignored her. She had it wrong, didn't she? I couldn't face him, nor would he want to meet me again. Or perhaps he did. He would want to see the guilt on my face when he accused me....

"He'll be at the end of the street in ten minutes."

It was my mother not me, who was anxious about the time, that I mustn't keep George waiting. She seemed almost excited. Personally I was too tired. I had no feeling left. I said I didn't care if he waited all night. But she found my coat and insisted I put it on and almost chased me out of the house, out into the dark street. And she stood guard at the front door daring me to return, watching me until I walked reluctantly to the corner. I breathed a sigh of relief, his car wasn't there. I could go back, say he hadn't come. And then he pulled up, leaned across and opened the door for me and there was no escape.

I sat close to the passenger door, putting as much distance between us as I could. George drove in silence, a kind of silence that was stronger and more frightening than ordinary no sound. Drove through familiar streets which, because the car windows shut them tightly out, might have been on another planet. Over Putney Bridge, along the Kings Road, and then down and along beside the river. It was late, and the tide was low, just a central stream flowing out towards the sea. The intertwining lines of lighting on the opposite bank made the mud shiny, slippery, sticky looking.

I didn't see why I had to be there! I didn't want to

explain myself to George! Why should I? What was done was done. So I'd injured his daughter! What of it? If he accused me, I might injure him. I felt dangerously aggressive.

It was a Chelsea mews he stopped in, cobbled, dark and private. He made for a particular door, turned to make sure I was following him before he used the key. A kind of morbid curiosity drew me on. Where were we? Was this the flat Beverley mentioned? But if George had something to say, why didn't he say it? Out here would do. In this mews. Let's get it over with.

I followed him in though. Once inside he seemed so sure of himself. I hated that. How dare he bring me here to some personal territory? He put on all the lights, filled the kettle, made us both coffee. Confusingly ordinary domestic sounds added to my anger, the hiss and bubble of the boiling water. The mugs clinking. A splash of milk. The friction of my shoes on the stair carpet as he followed me up.

"I went to the theatre," he said, sitting down in one of the chairs. This upstairs room overlooked the river and was expensively furnished, threateningly classy, with carefully blended colors just like the Wimbledon house, as always with Beverley's family, something you'd see in a magazine.

"Elaine, sit down," he urged, "there's no-one here."

I didn't feel like sitting down. Why should I sit down? I didn't want to give George the chance to stand over me. Instead I perched on the arm of one of the chairs, the furthest one from his, not caring whether it was the done thing or not, and took a sip of the coffee. It was too hot and tasted bitter.

"I wanted to get there early, come round backstage

and see Beverley before she went on, wish her luck. But I was delayed and arrived after it all started, after the announcement."

He had come to the theatre then. Would it have made any difference? Would I have acted differently if I'd known he would be there? But of course he would be there. I'd understood that, surely. This was Beverley's father, for goodness sake, and he'd made his position very clear as to who's side he was on. He would want to witness his daughter's success.

"I thought I must be in the wrong seat because there was no sign of Imogen."

He was scanning my face waiting to see my reactions.

I kept my expression deliberately bland.

"At the end of the first half I went backstage to find out why Beverley hadn't appeared. Of course I rang the hospital immediately. They said I should come, Beverley wanted me there, was asking for me."

I'll bet. I'll bet she was asking. She couldn't wait to tell him, could she? Couldn't wait to say what I'd done to her.

"What is it about you, Elaine?"

"Me?" Was he directly accusing me? How dare he accuse me?

"God knows, I should have gone to my own daughter. Instead I stayed, and I'm hardly renowned for my love of ballet, am I! Anyway I stayed. I sat there in the darkness, watching you, convinced you were going to win."

"Thinking Beverley had been robbed of the chance?"

"No!" He sounded almost hurt at my suggestion. "Even though it would mess things up completely I couldn't miss your moment of triumph."

How funny. I began to laugh. Some moment of triumph!

He looked at me and stood up. "This coffee's horrible. Would you rather have a drink?"

"No."

"I think I need one."

He poured himself a whisky.

But what did he mean, mess things up?

I waited, watching him as he stared down into the glass, as if in its amber contents he could see what he was trying to say. "The adjudicators took an age at the end. I sat there on the edge of my chair, keeping my head down, hoping no-one would recognize me and wonder why I wasn't at my daughter's side. But I was thinking what I would do, reviewing things. Maybe I could set up a flat in Paris for a while, base myself there."

Now that was funny. Beverley didn't even have to take part and still she'd won. He'd set her up there anyway, stay with her, make sure of her success.

"Meridienne will take her then? Later?" Oh yes, Sergei would have organized that.

George looked me straight in the eye.

"You don't understand, Elaine, do you? Beverley's foot is in a frightful state."

I stared straight back at him. I wasn't going to admit anything, nor apologize. Who but me knew how it happened anyway? I had carefully removed my fingerprints. And those fussy mothers had added theirs. It could so easily have been an accident. But let him believe what he wanted to believe, I didn't care.

"And then you didn't win - "

"No." The no came out quickly, smarting over my

tongue - fast, so that we didn't have to stop and debate it. I didn't need to be reminded.

"And everything was all right again."

"Excuse me?"

Was the man mad?

Oh, I see! I was suitably punished, was I? Not winning was divine retribution, I suppose.

"Excuse me?" I repeated furiously.

George smiled, and the little lines appeared beside his mouth. So he found it funny, did he, my humiliation?

"This is so difficult," he said, serious again.

Why, why should I listen to him anymore? Somehow he of all people has no right to question me. And now a great wave of tiredness was overtaking me. I put down the coffee mug and stood up ready to leave.

"Take me home."

"I don't know what drugs they've given Beverley but she's making wild accusations. She wants something done about it, Elaine. Should we do something about it?"

Now I was on full alert again and suddenly frightened, my exhaustion forgotten. The sight of the blood seeping through Beverley's tights flashed into my mind and turned my stomach. I winced away from it. The Soames's were rich and powerful. They knew judges and lawyers and MPs. It was probably grievous bodily harm, what I'd done.

George was walking across the room towards me.

"Do you believe her?" I whispered.

"It's Imogen believes her."

My apprehension increased, surged through me like a powerful electric current, rooting me to the spot. Escape was impossible. I knew Imogen would be dangerous. I knew it! I shut my eyes and waited for the axe to fall.

But George's hand didn't come down heavily on my shoulder where I was sure it would. Instead to my amazement, I felt it caress my cheek, softly, carefully. I opened my eyes and stared at him.

"Am I having an affair with you, Elaine? Beverley swears it's true and I feel as if I am, though I've never really laid a finger on you, have I?"

"No." My voice was shaking. I was shaking.

But he had. Forget Beverley. Forget everything that had gone before. Except those moments. He had touched me. I was the 'woman' Imogen was talking about. In a rush of immature innocence I'd fallen in love with her husband, almost as soon as I'd seen him - I realized that properly now, in a flash like it was a revelation or something. I'd been working my way steadily towards George, hadn't I? Towards this woman in me. And elated I was, suddenly. On a high! Joyful at how far I'd come and severely depressed, frustrated, because now it was something maybe I shouldn't have even thought of, shouldn't have wanted. For George's sake. But looking at him now, at his face, into his eyes, I could see his desire too, the intensity of what he was feeling. He couldn't disguise it anymore than I could. I knew he wanted me too. However wrong it was for me. However idiotic it was for him to be looking at Beverley's best friend. A girl his daughter's age. He couldn't stop it anymore than I could. The danger, that danger I had known would come - it would be now. And I wanted it so much. Anyway he had laid his hands on me before. And he'd heard me laugh, and seen me cry. He'd taken my hand in his and told me that he understood. And all the time he'd been moving closer himself. Closer. He'd held me to him and he'd kissed me in the hall at home. And he touched me then. Yes, he touched me then. But suddenly all of that was not enough, he hadn't been close enough, not yet. Here finally was the real danger that I'd seen coming, something that had taken control way back, and had propelled me - and him - forward towards this moment.

"Elaine," he whispered. "I have no right to feel like this. It's appalling. I can't - "

He stopped speaking but he didn't kiss me.

No, he didn't kiss me. I wanted him to, but he didn't. Instead his hand moved round and freed my hair and stroked it, caressed it as if it was silk or something, and he did it as if it was so important a part of me that he couldn't bear to pass it by.

"Say no, Elaine. Please say no."

"I can't." I was crying.

His fingers moved down, and his eyes followed them. Mine too. I stared at the way he unbuttoned my blouse. I saw my breasts as he bent to kiss them, as if for the first time, adult and actually quite beautiful. I discovered my whole body as he discovered it, seeing it myself as if I hardly knew it was there before, and it had this incredible sheen, my skin, as slowly, oh so slowly he uncovered me, until the clothes I'd chosen carefully at the beginning of this day lay at my feet and I stood before him, naked. And he bent to kiss my nipple again and he stroked my thigh, and I was trembling.

"I remember you standing on the steps at Elfino's. You were trembling then. You were cold."

"I wasn't cold."

"What was it?"

"You." I heard myself speaking, as if I was inside the

pages of a novel, or in a film. As if the right words were just there, hanging in the air, waiting for me to pull them down and use them.

He took my hand and led me into the bedroom, the way I'd always thought it would happen. We stood by the bed.

"When I took you out to dinner you came looking the image of Beverley when I wanted you to be Elaine."

"Did I?"

"And tonight Kitri was such a flirt."

"It was the earrings."

"No, not the earrings."

The bed was wide, its cover pure white.

"You're beautiful."

"Me?"

"You have no idea, do you?" His fingers traced down the back of my neck, down my spine. "Lie with me?" he whispered. As if I could choose. And when he'd kissed me, I did. I did lie down with him. I would have done anything he said, because we were somehow separate from the world. And then he kissed me again, deep, as if he wanted to climb into me, and after a few minutes he drew my knees up and open and he touched me with his hands. I wanted him to, more than anything I'd ever wanted before. I wanted it to be him. No-one else. And he touched me, first gentleness, like tiny birds fluttering, then his finger dipped, drank, dipped, fluttered on the edge again. And then, then came pain, deep exquisite trembling pain, then possession. And deeper. And after a long time he removed his own clothes and uncovered the thing which would take me, the thing I had never seen before on a man, and that was hard and erect and glistening, and astonishingly beautiful. And he was standing there, naked, looking down at me, so tall and powerful. He knelt and touched me again, lifted my hips, pulled me towards him. I felt him entering me and I heard myself cry out, a deep utterance straight from a heart that was suddenly, truly alive, and he paused as if he recognized everything that meant. Then as he pushed higher and higher, a rhythm built up between us, as if he too could hear the sound of that beating drum within me, and somehow now I realized what all my dancing had been for - to know and understand this beat, the light and darkness of it, the magnificence of it, the absolute power of it - and to lend it grace. And still he took me onwards to where my body writhed and shuddered and understood better than I did what was happening, and he whispered anything you do or say is right, and everything we did lit new fires and burned and burned and burned, as if we were up there with the Gods. With one breath I wanted him more, with the next I feared for my life.

And he moved his face across mine and kissed me.

And we began again.

In the shower hours later, in the warm stream of water he washed my skin as if it was silk, and then he wrapped me in a soft white towel. When I was lying in the bed he sat beside me, stroking my damp hair.

"You are a beautiful, sexual woman, Elaine," he said. "And it shows on stage. Use it. Recognize yourself. Understand who you are. Angel and temptress."

Me.

Me.

Chapter 26

I thought I had forgotten everything from that time before I came to England. No, I just hadn't let myself remember the piles of books in his study, the dark patterned carpet, the piano, and the splintery corners of my father's old oak desk. A room I wasn't afraid of - until that night, when it seemed brim full of steamy shadows, with only pale moonlight finely sieved by the fly screen, falling obliquely onto the full length mirror on the wall. Outside jasmine growing by the open window competed with the heavy medicinal eucalyptussyness of the ghost gums surrounding the house. A vast Australian night, expanded, enlarged by the heat, the Southern Cross and the arch of bright stars, magnified. And cicadas, the unending singing of them, each one strumming, tuning in to middle C in the heat and the darkness.

The door is just ajar, I can see her dimly in the mirror, standing there, facing my father, just the tall reflection of her. Her ankles, the floral pattern on her dress curving over her hips. Up there her chestnut hair is pulled into such an elegant french pleat. I can hear her voice, higher, louder, less certain than it ought to be, and my father's too, raised in anger. They've been shouting for days. I want them to stop shouting. To stop arguing.

To stop.

In spite of the heat I'm shivering, my nightie's sticking to my skin. They're screaming at each other and in the mirror I see him raise his hand. I want to scream too only I can't, there's no room left for me, for my screaming, so I put my weight against the heavy door to push it open and there's this sudden earsplitting explosion of sound, it cracks the air apart, and there's a shriek, and the mirror shatters, and the shards of glass burst outwards and fall to the floor catching the light as they drop, flashing silver in the moonlight. Falling, landing. Tinkling like notes in a musical box. And she cries out: That's it, she's leaving, that's the last time he's treating her like this and she's not going to stay here to be murdered, or humiliated again, she'll go to her mother's house in England, he can do what he likes. She's going to get the children up now. I can hear his footsteps pounding towards the door, and I draw back in fear and run back to bed and pull the covers up over my head. Any minute now I'll see his face.....

Suddenly I was awake and my head was throbbing against the pillow in the darkness. And it was a strange room, and a strange bed and it was as if I was falling through that black hole I'd imagined earlier in the evening, with nothing to hold on to. Only there was.

Because George was holding me.

"Ssh, Elaine, ssh," he whispered, "it was just a dream. Only a dream." His lips were so gentle on my forehead. Dry and sweet against the dampness that had broken through the surface of my skin. He pulled the cover up over me, stroked my face with his fingers, gently exploring the contours of it, my lips, my eyes, in the darkness. And for once, for once, I felt secure enough to let go. To sink back into dreaming....

Light fading on the path leading down from the house to the old swamp. There's something eerie about the bush air, a dank, sour smell that intrigues me. There's something weird about the sounds too. A whip bird's whistle swells and then snaps through the trees, then a raven chortles and that sound echoes between the ancient rocks, and breaks through into a sky above me which isn't really there at all. The trees are twitching. The air feels so still, it's waiting to burst. I'm aware of a violent tension in my mother, a strange losing out feeling.

This feels like my favourite and most frightening place on earth, this valley where she is walking in silence with my father and where he suddenly snatches her hand and pulls her away from me. "No!" she says, breaking free, then urgently: "Wait here, Elaine. Don't dare move," and she disappears behind the trees with him. I stand alone. Waiting, afraid to walk on, or even to shift away from the ants that have begun to encircle my feet. Their eyes are shiny and round. The whip bird's whistle swells and snaps again violently. Then there is a kind of humming sound of talking. And something is happening. A kind of breathing. I look up from the ants and see, though my view of them is obscured by trees, I see my father pressing my mother against a tree, pinning her arms above her head, pushing, pushing against her. And her face is all screwed up and beautiful. Whatever is happening, whatever it is, I want it to be happening to me too. Why can't I be with her? It's frightening not to be to be part of it too. I want to be owned by it, consumed by it like she is. I don't want to be on my own. But I am.......

I know, I understand what was happening now. Near the dream's surface I am, floating, understanding....

Diving again. A cotton dress, loose fitting to keep me cool. I love its bright stripes, it makes me laugh, all different colours. I can see how my toes inside my new red sandals are being powdered gray with earth. It's working its way in fast, this bush dust, because I'm having to hurry to keep up, I'm small, my legs aren't long enough. My father has firm hold of my hand, it's lost inside his, and my mother's there, I can see her a little way ahead of us, and she's humming, singing to herself. There's that warm antiseptic smell of eucalyptus and a great sense of well-being. And dappled light. Thin shafts of it, broken up by the canopy of trees. Harsh, hot sunshine cracked into pieces. It sprinkles all round me, on the bracken, on the tree trunks, on the air almost, so that we seem to be walking through a galaxy of stars in broad daylight, my father and I. When I say, Look at the stars, Daddy, he smiles down at me. He's wearing a wide brimmed hat and he seems as tall as the trees, and the sunlight dapples him too. And I trust him. I love having my hand in his. We'll always be walking through these stars together, nobody will ever die, this day will never end, nothing will ever change...

I opened my eyes, registered a little daylight. Things did change. Life wasn't full of stars at all. Outside instead the whirring of early morning traffic jams, the urgent sound of a car horn. A jumbo jet droned along above the river towards Heathrow. Beside me George's breathing was even and comfortable, and reassuringly ordinary. His arm lay across me, the weight, the reality of it, pinning me down. The skin felt older than mine, muscular, different, time smoothed somehow. For a long time I studied the face, its bone structure, the lines and the dark jawline stubble, the eyelashes, and I listened to his breathing and remembered the rhythm and passion of the night. Astonishing how peaceful the whole man was now - that established look I'd always liked. He sighed suddenly and slid his leg over against mine. Even asleep, he seemed so totally aware of me. I hated missing a moment of him, but drowsy and contented I drifted back into unconsciousness.

When I opened my eyes next he was leaning over me, and for an instant I saw not his face but my father's, and then I blinked and it was George. Then to my astonishment, my father's again, and I held onto that image and fixed it in my mind. And now I had it at last, knew it, it seemed far less important. I almost didn't want it. Didn't need it. Not anymore.

So I let the face be George's again. I reached up and wound my arms around his neck and pulled him close. But it was different this morning.

"Kiss me?"

The little lines beside his mouth creased. "Feel safer now?"

I smiled up at him.

"No more nightmares?"

"No."

"Just me!"

"George?"

He kissed my nose. "What?"

"I want things to stay dangerous. Us."

He laughed out loud. "So do I."

"Make love to me again. I want you to do what you did last night. That was exciting. I want to feel alive. Real." And I thought, I'm showing him me, I'm allowing it. And that made me feel very powerful. Really powerful, and I think I suddenly understood my life then, where I'd come from, and that I had a future. It had been there waiting, this sensual woman inside me, like Jonty's violence was waiting for him.

"I knew you'd like it," George whispered, running his hand down over the contour of my breast. He sighed. "I could see from the first moment you'd be sexy, Elaine. A much more exciting woman than my daughter, for all you copy her."

I froze, appalled at him guessing my secret. I could feel myself stiffening up, pulling away.

"You do," he said. "It doesn't matter but you don't need to. Just be Elaine."

"I'm not very interesting," I whispered, retracting further into the old shell.

"Oh but you are! You're the kind of woman who will deceive men for the sake of it."

Am I? "But I love you."

Those little smile lines deepened. "For now," he said, shaking me a little, releasing the tension. "So let's seize the moment."

A game it was we were playing, I knew it, but the best game there would ever be. The ultimate game. No rules. No fair play. More than love, the magnificent force of desire. He kissed me and....

And it was as if... I was experiencing it all for the first time again, his touch....as if it would always be....new, the way.... he took my.... breath away.... the way I could....the way I....was feeling ....whole. As if this was.... the way.... my life worked.... And each time.... would be.... a kind of.... creation.... of me.... A new.... universe.... New stars.

New sta..ahhhsrs...........

I stood at the window watching George drive away. Out there under the Albert Bridge the river was shining silver.

Silver points of light. Silver...silver....
Silver.

I went down to the kitchen and made myself coffee.
Upstairs again I began hovering around, not able to sit
down, far too excited. Sore too, unexpected that, though
it wasn't important. Because if George had been there to
start again, I would have forgotten that and begun again
willingly, just to feel that surge of power between us.
The rhythm. My new strength. He wanted to completely
understand me, he said. How I sleep, how long? If I will
mind if he snores a little, moves around in his sleep. And
he was talking about us going away, what it will be like.
In the next couple of days, he said. In the midst of a
political life, he wants it to be beautiful for me. He'll take
me shopping. Buy me anything I want. Abroad, he said.
Where?

The door clicked downstairs.

He'd forgotten something. He was coming back. I
laughed, wanting him all over again.

"Hello, Elaine."

"Imogen!"

She walked up the stairs past me and into the sitting
room as if she owned the place. Did she? It was quite
possible.

She stood there looking at the towelling dressing
gown I was wearing and she smiled. "One size fits all,"
she said.

"George isn't here."

Why did I say that? She knew already. It was me
she'd come to see, wasn't it?

She began inspecting the room, picking things up,
fingering them. Looking for clues perhaps. How dare
she touch things here? "Sent you flowers from that

Croydon shop, didn't he? My husband is so predictable."

I stayed silent, refusing to be provoked.

"Aren't you going to offer me some coffee?"

I didn't answer her then either. I didn't want her to stay. Why should I make her coffee?

But if I'd thought she was dangerous before, Imogen was suddenly seeing how much more she had to lose.

"The glass sliced the edge of the tendon in Beverley's foot."

I couldn't help wincing. A shaft of sympathy pain shot through my own foot and up my leg.

"She won't be able to walk properly for months, but of course you wouldn't care about that."

Would she have believed me if I'd said I did?

"Now you think George is prepared to give up everything for you too, don't you?" Her voice sounded so intentionally calm, as if she really wanted to scream, but she was clever, Imogen, and never to be underestimated. Right then she was implying she'd done this scene a million times. And in case I hadn't noticed, she said it plainly.

"Oh, Elaine, I've been here so many times before."

And she smiled so sympathetically. I could fall on her mercy, she was saying. She might yet manage to forgive me.

But she would say that, wouldn't she? I didn't react. Anyway I didn't believe her, because she'd never forgive herself for letting me in to their lives, or for the harm that had come to Beverley.

She tried harder. "Committing financial suicide just for you, is he?"

George hadn't mentioned it, we'd had other more important things to do. Was he? It hadn't occurred to me until then what he was chancing. But it would be a kind of death perhaps. And Imogen voicing such an idea, was delivering a deliberate sting, a very intentional barb. She had after all been in on my father's death.

"The great sacrifice for love! That's what he's told you, is it? Let me tell you something, Elaine, George has had plenty of affairs! But this one's very carefully timed. His influence in the House is waning. The minister he's responsible to is on his way out. It's a harsh game, politics. You're a means of escape for George, for God's sake. Without him losing face! That's the real truth."

Was I? How extraordinary! Me, exerting a little influence in the corridors of Westminster! But away from it, in her navy court shoes and her fitted cream suit and the rich Liberty scarf knotted at her neck, would Imogen cope with a different George? The only way she would survive would be to hold on to her social standing, her status. She had to be rid of me.

"You're such a child." She almost spat it out, but the woman in me immediately felt more of a match for her.

"He thinks if he takes up with some little bimbo...."

It interested me, her seeing me like that. It made me feel even stronger. She avoided my gaze, turned away.

"He's happy at home, Elaine, with Beverley and me."

"Is he? And anyway do you think I would bother with an unhappy man? Why would I would want to inherit misery? "

She turned and stared at me as if she couldn't believe the words she'd just heard. I was quite surprised at them myself.

She ran a finger across the polished surface of the cabinet beside her. "There are plenty of young men around for an attractive girl like you."

Compliments on all sides! Even from Imogen. I was doing well. I walked across to the window, gazed out at the glistening river.

"Elaine! You're just one of many!"

Such a wild shrill note was creeping into her voice! Poor George. No wonder he wanted to leave. He'd lived with this woman for more than twenty years and there was something so critical and uninteresting about her now. She'd put away all the raw intensity of youth. Just the kind of age, I decided looking across at her, when a man would reconsider who he was with, what he was settling for. Women like her in break-ups like this were featured in the news all the time. And if his influence in the corridors of power was waning, maybe so was her time with him.

But now Imogen spoke more calmly: "He'll do it again. To you as well. I tell you, he's quite predictable. Will you ever trust him? Right now he's using you, Elaine. With the kind of adverse publicity you'll bring, he'll be asked to leave the interest rates he hates behind, those impossible balance sheets and dreaded market forces. He'll use the high morality stakes in politics for his own ends, and be discreetly 'moved on' for the sake of the party."

Well then, he would be better off with me. I could serve that scenario well. Young and innocent, perfect for the part. Besides Imogen was expecting him to see his obligations through. The adventurer was what interested me. Someone really dangerous.

"He'll take up their offer of some other wonderful prestige job right out of their way. He knows well enough how to play their games. He won't appear to be dictating his own terms, and he'll have all the prestige among his friends of attracting a young woman."

She bit her lip as I smiled, because that idea worked both ways, didn't it? Quite an achievement I could attract George away from his elegant wife, from this beautiful woman, for now her anger was showing, Imogen was stunningly beautiful. Undeniably. Almost frighteningly so. A brittle sparkle flashed across her face that I recognized easily. This was where Beverley's looks came from, not from George as I had first thought. No, Imogen had the beauty. And she'd taught Beverley all her style. I'd never noticed it before. The way she treated him, Beverley seemed to think she owned George, but it was this beautiful woman, this wife, who was losing him to me. It was from her suddenly that I realized I wanted the man. He was leaving her.

And she'd always thought me so uninteresting!

But the Imogens and the Beverleys think they deserve their beauty, and that good things are theirs by right. They shouldn't be fooled. Besides now I've discovered we all see glimpses of that, a second when we turn and see ourselves and suddenly recognize a loveliness we never realized we had.

It took Imogen aback, my bemused smile. She was after all trying to offend me, to frighten me, to undermine my confidence.

"George always thinks he'll rediscover his youth! My God, Elaine, he's old enough to be your father!"

Her voice was less sure now, less strident, because what she'd just said was the absolute truth, and her own age was showing. I was doing her a favour though, wasn't I, forcing her to examine what she was? She'd never had a love affair, I bet. Now maybe she would. Maybe she'd regain her own youth.

"I like a man to be experienced," I said brazenly.

"I'm warning you, Elaine, if Beverley starts there'll be a fearful scandal. It wouldn't take the press long. A man in the public gaze - "

And that was the truth too. We both knew Beverley would make sure of it, but by voicing the threat, Imogen seemed to be suddenly contemplating how appalling it would all be and she looked afraid for herself too, didn't she? Her daughter was a danger to her as well! I was winning and I wasn't even having to fight.

"Elaine, for Beverley's sake...."

She'd misunderstood me there, of course. Completely. They all had. Even George perhaps. Beverley was the last one I could do anything for. And Imogen was lost if she thought she could appeal to my better nature. Everything I was now I'd learned watching her daughter. It hadn't improved my better nature. Not one bit.

I'll take him, Imogen, I wanted to say. Like Beverley takes things as her right. I'll live with him, but more, I'll love him passionately, far more than you do.

"He loves me."

Imogen laughed. A cruel, dispassionate laugh, like Beverley used when she wanted to put someone down. "You're so naive. But last night at least you didn't win!"

She stood there for a moment, waiting. Expecting.... expecting what? Me to cave in? Actually there was a sudden power about her I'd never seen before. Or a loss of power in me maybe, as if I could hear myself crumbling a little inside at her reminding me of my humiliation the night before. And a sort of suspicion that maybe George might not love me enough and in the end she might be right about him and that she herself could withstand anything anyone could throw at her. If George left with me she would still triumph somehow.

My silence now seemed to defeat her all the same.

"Well, he's no-one to be happy with," she said, and she turned and went down the stairs. When the door banged behind her I was filled with such an awful sense of foreboding that I began to cry. Strangely enough mostly for Beverley. For her months of not being able to walk. But thinking of her, and talking to Imogen wasn't going to put me off. What I was going to do now might be even worse for Beverley, the worst thing I could ever do to her. All these years she'd been happy. She never expected her life to go wrong. Maybe she'd never get over it.

But I wanted someone to take care of me. And George could afford to do that. He wanted to. And he'd do it with style. More though, I wanted what Beverley had had all her life, a father to love me. Every woman needs a father, and time to grow up. And love's like water. Without a little of it we shrivel up and die.

Chapter 27

I was at home packing. I wanted to be ready when George called. My mother was being quite peculiar, alternating between arguing, and expressing her deep moral disapproval, and then helping me find what I wanted to take with me with a kind of elation that life was opening up for me, that at least I'd found a way out, even if she couldn't. It's was if I'd said I'd won the lottery! And I felt like I had, I was so excited! I think she wished it was her. Maybe she did. And yet... She'd stayed faithful to my father all those years by shutting herself away. But he was dead now and perhaps she was regretting it.

"Why did you leave him, Mum?"

She looked mystified. "Who?"

"When we left Australia."

"Your father? How could I stay? I had you and Jonty to consider!"

That took my breath away! Me and Jonty? What was she talking about? She'd never considered us once!

"I was afraid that you - " She hesitated, took another tack. "He - he might have killed me. He could be quite violent. And I was determined he wasn't going to....." Her mouth closed into a thin resolute line. Was this my mother I was listening to?

His hands.....

"I can remember the night we left."

"Then you knew."

Did I? Perhaps I remembered something, but real or imagined? Or even maybe in her imagination, not mine? And was that what had made her afraid of life? Her fear for me.

"He was a very sexual man." She hesitated again as if she thought I wouldn't understand that.

"Not with me," I said, concentrating on ripping down a photo of Beverley. I threw it on to the bed and reached for another, laying all ghosts. Hers too, maybe.

"I was out in the middle of nowhere," she said defensively, "cut off. Besides there were always the other women."

I laughed, somehow knowing that would be true, but she didn't see the joke. But George was a flirt too of course. He'd had other affairs. He'd told me himself. Melanie, for one, years ago. I liked a man to be established though. And I was fed up with living with my mother. I didn't want to watch television with her for the rest of my life.

"You be careful." She picked up my jacket off the bed and vaguely began folding it. "You're a pretty girl. remember."

I snatched the jacket and threw it in the bag.

"I went along to the High Street this morning."

"You did?" I stared at her in amazement.

"I thought of buying some paint. Doing the house up."

How utterly unnerving! I glanced at my watch. Why didn't George phone?

My mother asked me then what she should do about Jonty. I'd discovered him when I'd come home chucking the clothes out of my drawer and helping himself to the last of my money. When I tried to get it back he threatened to break my fingers. It wasn't worth the fight. I decided not to tell my mother that. If he thought she was frightened of him it would increase his power.

"What can I do about him, Elaine?"

"Talk to him?"

But I didn't know, did I? Besides Jonty was probably lost already.

When the phone finally did ring Mum got to it before me. I went to snatch the receiver from her but she clung on to it.

"In hospital? Where?"

They're either dead modern or miraculously still standing, hospitals. This one was the miracle sort, old bricks, echoes, ancient windows with strings to open them. Polished floors and proper high beds, but somehow crumbling under the weight of serious illness and old age.

"This way."

I could never have been a nurse, I can't stand the sight of sick people. I was appalled when I saw Jonty. His eye looked ghastly, blown up with black bruising, and he had cuts and lesions down the side of his head and across his shoulder. He was conscious and mumbling, not very coherently, but he recognized us at least.

You know something about being in love? When you've just spent a long time with a person and suddenly they're not with you, you need them. Faced with the real world, if this place was a real world, I sought desperately to replace the vision of Jonty's injured scalp with winding George's hair round my fingers, the strong ward antiseptic with the sweet smell of him. Inside myself, in my separateness, all I could do was wish his skin was pressing against mine. And hear the phone ringing at home with me not there to answer it. But then my mother wouldn't have got here without me and my fear for Jonty had made me want to come with her.

She was even paler than he was. She stroked his forehead. which made him wince but it was the first time I'd ever seen her reach out for either of us. "Who would beat him up?" she whispered to me.

"How do I know?" But I thought of those little creeps down by the river.

"Doves damage the kidneys. Has he taken them before?"

"Doves?" My mother stared at the doctor. "Is that what attacked him?"

She turned to me in panic. "Doves?" How could she say she didn't know what he was talking about and not look a fool.

The doctor pressed on. "Mood swings, high temperatures?"

"Elaine?"

"I don't know, Mum. I've been at Rosehill, haven't I?" But I thought of the times I'd pulled Jonty away from that slipway and never once mentioned it. I thought I was doing him a favour. "Was he the only one?"

"There's another kid, but he's not so bad"

"Can I see him?"

The doctor narrowed his eyes. "I guess so. Why?"

It was one of those slipway kids. "Me?" he said innocently, when he saw me. "Me taking drugs?"

But when we were alone he told me someone had turned up with all this stuff, someone they didn't know, but they took it, didn't they, who wouldn't when it was cheap? And then there'd been a fight. He showed me the bruises down his back.

"What's doves?"

"Ecstasy of course." The kid watched me walk away from his ward as if I was completely mad.

"I have to sit down."

I fetched my mother a chair. Her shoes were mine again. Too small for her, but all that could be found in our panic to get here. Settled, she took Jonty's hand and looked up at me.

"If you're going to be away, Elaine, I'm - "

I stared at her. "What?"

"Shall I take him to Australia?"

"Paris?"

"I'm going tomorrow night. If you want to come, meet me at Waterloo."

"I - "

"It might not work, Elaine, but we could try."

"But - "

"It's up to you. The train leaves at seventeen fifty-three."

"What do I do with the lemon cake in the kitchen, Elaine?" asked my mother, when I'd hung up.

"Chuck it!"

It's strange what you take when you're leaving home for good. Most of my stuff belonged to the past. Clothes and things. I thought, I'm like my mother, gathering up little things, picking up trinkets, just stuff to remind me who I am.

The river was sparkling as I walked over the footbridge, but on the east wind there was the chill of the winter to come. No blooms on the Jasmine, just withered threads of the vine waiting for a new season. There was a train, actually standing in the station! Everything had a time.

Maybe mine had come.

It had been quite hard saying goodbye to my mother. I told her I'd ring her, let her know where I was. But the thought of her sitting there in front of the television on her own at the moment with nobody to come home to her at night....

Jonty was still in hospital, thankfully. I didn't know what I would have said to him.

Waterloo was crowded. The last of the autumn evening sunlight filtered through the glass roof panels. The destination displays tap-tap-tapped through their lists. People stared up waiting for the flapping slats to settle. Luggage. Footsteps. Shops. The throb of pigeon wings. Echoing announcements. Beside the news stands the headline boards screamed 'Govt. Finance shake-up'... A front page article in the evening paper with a picture of him said: 'George Soames, one of the government's highly respected financial advisors has decided to accept a prestige post abroad....'

I bought a copy..

I had to queue up for a ticket. Wait. Eventually when I reached the window, I bought just a single.

That terminal you know is all silver and grey. Different from the rest of Waterloo. There's a European feel as you glide down the escalator, even before you board the Eurostar to travel under the Channel. The people are smarter. Leather, a glint of dressy earrings. Theres's something polished about the whole atmosphere. The shine of a wintery mist along the Champs Elysées maybe, or an advance glitter of those silver birch trees that line the horizons in that peculiarly impressionist light. And I thought, France, I'll be walking with him there now, how strange.

The train for Paris would leave in a few minutes. He'd said he would wait by the platform entrance. I pushed my way through the crowd. And he was there, dressed in black as usual, his dark eyes scanning the faces for mine. He smiled when he saw me.

"I thought you'd come. You're an ambitious creature, Elaine Higham."

I didn't get the phone call I really wanted but then in an awful kind of way I'd known George wouldn't ring. Imogen had been speaking the truth. Love hadn't clouded her judgment. And George had his way out without me. Beverley was seeing to that, almost certainly.

But this partnership might work. It was more of an even match. Sergei and I understood each other. What had happened to his undying love for Beverley after all? Now she couldn't dance he wasn't interested. And he knew how far I was prepared to go. We were both ambitious.

A new game.

Maybe a new beginning.

Elaine Higham and Sergei Lasarte. And there was a ring to it, wouldn't you say?

Chapter 28

The stage hand knocks at my dressing room door this time, though it's still wide open. He knocks as if clothes give me respectability. He eyes the dress. "Red!" he says appreciatively.

"Thanks for the tea."

"They've sent a car for you. So you'll have to go now." He helps me into my coat. Picks up the empty mug. "Ready?" I'm gently ushered along the narrow passage towards the stage door because it's late, nearly midnight, and he may like working in a theatre but now he wants to go home to his bed of course, like normal people.

"Night."

I hug my coat closer as I hear the exit bang shut behind me and the bolts shoot across. This should be my night, I'm the star, except there's no-one left waiting, no autographs hunters, I'm too late. But at the end of the covered alley there's a car, and a woman standing by it. In the half light, this wet street night, I'm not sure if it's her. The fitted suit outlines a rounder shape, and the hair is cropped. There's nothing to recognize.... and then I see the shapely ankles and the flat shoes and there's no-one else it could be.

"It's been a long time," Beverley says, as if it were yesterday. I suppose I should embrace her if only in proper theatrical tradition, but how can I?

Weird how the sounds of closing car doors, ignition, the stretch of the seat belts, and power surging into the engine, ordinary sounds, emphasize the awesome chasm of silence between us. Beverley pulls out into the traffic and drives through the familiar narrowness of London's West End. The streets are alive with watery reflections, lights, and streaks of freezing rain. The tyres swish along through guttered drizzle, hiss threateningly over the puddled surface.

"Did you like the roses?" Her words slice into me, their implied meaning crystal clear. The silvery voice hasn't altered but the warmth has gone, and I can only see her profile, I can't read her expression.

What's to say? My mumbled 'thank you' seems inadequate, merely serves to show I might still be intimidated.

"Meridienne's on tour then? How long are you in London?" I'm sure she knows. Of course she does. She's being deliberately formal. Holding herself, and any confrontation she has in mind, holding it back.

"Two weeks." Better. My voice sounds stronger. "Then Birmingham just after Christmas." I fiddle nervously with a diamante earring, and stare ahead into the darkness, drawing strength from the past, that day, the day he bought them, and those red camellias.

"Sleeping Beauty too! The perfect princess part. You do appear to have made it, Elaine."

There's a threat in her words. It seemed only an observation, yet there has to be, it's due, though she sounds so calm. The rain is heavier now, running in sodium lit streams down the windscreen, fighting the wipers. Winning.

The trouble is, that in spite of the bitter taste of adrenaline from the performance high, and the fear of meeting her, and strangely the pleasure of it, I am tired.

"You must be exhausted," she says. "Quite beyond partying. Aurora's a taxing role."

"Mmnn."

"But your first night. You can't miss this celebration - thrilling!"

How do I deal with this conversation? Is she being sympathetic or facetious? And it's backwards. Quite the role reversal. I thought once it would be me saying these things to Beverley, sending her flowers. I would love to tell her what it feels like, that it's everything we talked about and more. I'd love to tell her in the old gossipy way what happens, how different the theatres are, each stage. About the cities, what I see of them, and the long hours of rehearsal, the pain and the fun of it, the slog and the exuberance. But I can't. She knows it all anyway, surely, and remembers it, and she talks to loads of successful theatre people all the time.

"You have such perseverance, Elaine, such ambition."

How does she mean that? There's a malevolence there surely. Has to be. Change the subject. Alter the direction. We turn into the Strand.

"I'm always reading you in the papers, seeing your program on television, your reviews."

"Wonderful excuse to see everything, go everywhere, follow the dance companies, and the theatre."

"And make or break people."

Beverley laughs. "That too."

"And George?" I'm taking my life in my hands but I might as well die now as later, "so, where is he these days? I don't see him on television anymore. And Imogen?"

"They spent less than a year in New York, but you knew that, I'm sure. It made all the papers. Terrible what surfaces when you start digging. When the axe finally fell my mother divorced him and married Philip Hirst - a

278

millionaire with houses in California and Switzerland. She's terribly happy."

How extraordinary! But Imogen would be pleased. Money and image were always her thing. I knew I would do her good! But him. I have to accept my part in his destruction because Beverley lived up to her threats and the media cornered him and tore him to shreds, delighted as ever to bring a successful man down, though never once was I mentioned. That might have been for Imogen's sake, less of a scandal for her. Melanie went down. I didn't. How he achieved my anonymity I don't know. Afterwards I realized that was an enormous kindness. But free, he never came looking.

"And George himself? How is he?"

Beverley glances at me. "Why would you think I have the slightest idea?" Poor George. "I hated the way he was always looking at you, Elaine, as if you were his daughter, or something." Even in the dark now I can feel the ice in her eyes. "Still interested even now, are we?"

There's no point answering that. Instead I look down to see if the scars of the past can be seen, but it's darker down there of course. Her foot slides across to the brake.

"Everyone's waiting for you. It's your night," she says brightly, as she pulls on the handbrake, climbs out and hands the car keys to an attendant to have her Porsche parked. Above me, the gold statue, the flags, the Savoy grandeur bearing down. Glass. Revolving doors. At ground level Beverley's shoes are sensational, Knightsbridge classy, even though they are flat. Real money shows. Nothing changes. Except a slight slowness in the right foot, hardly there, but there. The way it picks up, a restricted flexibility in the arch.

Now we're inside, under the bright hotel foyer lighting, and I can see her face. Still the flawless complexion, but somehow it's lost the radiance. Lost that appalling, compelling assurance. She's been balanced out with the rest of us, become more ordinary, more equal. The hair, while still shining, is ridiculously short, unflattering, and the figure under the smart black suit isn't what it used to be. How could she let that happen?

But then of course I'm a dancer. Different values. She's in the journalistic world now, and her figure's perfect shapely woman, like Imogen's. "Let's join the party," she says, sweeping up the stairs towards the reception suite. But not quite at the same speed as she used to.

"Darlings!" Irina clasps first Beverley and then me to her and steps back to show me off, the new star she and Delia Delaney launched tonight. "Our Elaine, everyone!"

A sea of faces. Smiles. Press. Delia. The choreographer, all the theatre people, invited guests. But in spite of making my entrance well, did I think things would be different? They greet me, congratulate me on my performance, but it's Beverley everyone's in awe of, that the producers and company directors are looking at immediately because they need her. She has more power than ever. They need her good reviews above anyone else's. What Beverley Soames writes and says on television now matters, her opinion brings in audiences or destroys the run. And I can stand them suddenly ignoring me because in a mad way it amuses me. I can say I helped make her new career for her! She made her contacts with the news editors because of me when she

280

was out to break George.

The other company members descend on her, whisk her away, wanting her to remember them in her dispatches.

Only Irina lingers. "What I might have done with her," she says wistfully. "But she makes a wonderful television presenter, and she writes so well, don't you think?"

I watch the foot, rising and falling, that inflexibility.

"She would."

My remark brings a strange look from Irina.

"Perhaps she had good reason to be so motivated," she says. She leaves me and follows Beverley. I feel guilty not because Irina knows anything. It was all pronounced 'accidental' way back. No recriminations ever came and no-one ever speaks of that night.

Sergei comes over with a drink and a kiss on the cheek for me, playing to those who are watching us, who are interested to see what we're like off stage. If we are indeed the perfect partnership they want us to be. They smile at his attentions. Close in, I can smell the sweetness of him. The familiarity of it.

"You didn't wait for me," I whisper.

He shrugs. "Everyone else was ready."

"Did you know she'd be here?"

"Isn't it wonderful to see her. Beautiful as ever."

"Did you know?"

"Know what?" He's lying, for all he looks so innocent.

"Kiss me? Properly?"

Sergei looks shocked. "Elaine! This is a press party."

So what I've been thinking lately is true.

Quite suddenly I am kissed, but not by Sergei. "I

always knew you'd be a startling success! Lovely Aurora, darling."

"Olivia!" I am so surprised by her fawning over me, hugging me, standing so close, sort of owning me, I cannot begin to imagine what to say, except obvious platitudes like how nice to see her. It angers me though that if she thought that, if as she says she always knew, if that was true, why on earth didn't she tell me? All that insecurity, all those insults! It was unforgivably horrible if she saw me in there with a chance. I'm not sure I want to be nice to her now.

"I tried and tried to contact you after the competition. I knew you would do well. Thank goodness Sergei found you."

Perhaps all this attention is actually aimed at Sergei. Was he once her lover? He's never told me. She smiles at him coquettishly while she says to me. "Such beautiful dancing tonight, darling," and begins to regale us about the studio, her new students. Over her shoulder I can see Beverley on the other side of the room, delicately nibbling a canapé, surrounded by admirers. Is she as beautiful? Is she? Certainly Sergie's eyes are following her just as they used to. Before Paris.

Paris. It was my dream city, the gothic towers of Notre Dame, the glittering Champs Elysées, the Opera. And the ballet company. We are a strange match, Sergei and I, but the partnership did work, right from the beginning. And we danced together with an understanding that I hadn't realized would be possible, which easily won us enough status with Meridienne for them to take me on with him - as junior soloists to begin with, since he needed time to get back into practice. It seemed this was what I had been waiting for, a partner-cum-lover. Though often at rehearsal we fight over how a single step or a variation should be done, the physical passion between us shows and gives us fire. People talked about us from the beginning, mentioned us in the same breath. Made us one.

"I saw the Meecham girl recently." Olivia sips her wine.

"Diana?"

Beverley is sipping her drink too. Even at this distance I can see she still knows how to make herself look beautiful, that set of the head, the straight back. And Sergei's eyes are fixed on her.

Three years with Sergei, dancing with him, living with him, making love to him, has altered me beyond all recognition. Given me confidence. Often he and I sit on the floor of our flat in Paris staring at each other as if we have just met, until a kind of urgency moves in on us and sex takes over. I am deeply in love with him of course. It is never anything like my night with George, but it has been passionate and essential, as if we've both needed the comfort the other one provides. And I have no-one else now since my mother sold the house and took Jonty to Australia.

Though lately things have been different. Something's changed.

I turn my attention back to Olivia. She looks older. The dark hair is swept up and back but the pony tail has gone and there are more than just a few strands of gray. "Yes, I met her recently." She smiles into my eyes. I think she really is sincerely interested in whatever it is she's saying. "Diana. In Cologne."

"Dancing?"

"Soloist with Kurt Freidstat's company. She hasn't

changed at all, still as excitable. I haven't seen any of the others. Whether they're still dancing - I thought it was quite amusing that Margaret Ryan gave up. Out of that scholarship group of would be dancers you are far and away the most successful, Elaine."

"Far and away," says Beverley, who has unexpectedly joined us.

Sergei smiles. "And the bitchiest!"

Normally that would amuse me, he and I can be like that. I would laugh except Beverley has suddenly laughed. Laughed! As if there is some private joke between her and Sergei....

Is it me, or has the temperature just soared? Is the room going round for other people?

I catch Sergei's eye and mouth: Can We Go? He doesn't seem to want to notice.

"Another drink, anyone?" he asks, though everyone has a full glass.

Beverley smiles patronizingly at me. "Is Birmingham Sleeping Beauty again, Elaine?"

"Yes," says Olivia, apparently assuming my silence means I'm tired and someone should speak for me. "And Irina says she has plans for Elaine in a new production of Casse Noisette. Will you be reviewing that?"

"Sugar Plum! How sweet." Beverley's sort of laughing again and looking straight at Sergei over her wine glass. "And so old fashioned. I have to admit to liking more contemporary work these days than Meridienne is doing. These antique classics are a bit past it. But of course I'll review if you all want me to. So for Sugar Plum, will I have to come to Paris?"

"Yes," says Sergei. "But Paris will be beautiful."

Beverley lifts an eyebrow and smiles at him. "Really?"

Olivia who's standing next to her, ignores all this and leans in close.

"So what about Elaine's performance tonight? You said you were going to concentrate on her and you wanted those advance publicity photos. What will you be saying?"

I hold my breath.

But Beverley's not falling for that one. Her eyes are fixed on me and I can hear the direct threat in her voice as she says: "You'll all have to wait and buy Sunday's paper!"

So just like George! I know she will do it. When I saw those roses I realized immediately. This weekend she'll take the opportunity to strip away my career, the thing that sustains me, inspires me, and gives me a life and the comfort of admirers around me. She laughed when I said make or break. But she has the power, everyone listens to her. And she'll break me with this review, cut me to shreds. Her timing is perfect of course. Calculated exactly for maximum damage. This will be her revenge, she's waited three years for this moment. Career assassination, the 'motivation' Irina mentioned. But as I stare at her I know suddenly that she isn't going to be satisfied with just that. It isn't enough.

Not nearly enough.

"Take me home now, darling," she says, and Sergei reacts immediately. As if this has all been rehearsed, this scene, like they planned it way, way back. Did they?

Outside it's raining, that greasy depressing constant London rain. There's still the hiss of traffic along the Strand. This city never sleeps. Beside the hotel's revolving glass doors, under its canopy, we are facing each other in silence, Beverley and I. Opposing forces. She's taking Sergei now because I took George. She knows my deepest fear, that loneliness will be the worst for me. She smiles at us both, with that sensational fairytale winning smile. She still has that. He puts him arm round her, I watch his fingers stretch and explore, and I know exactly how that feels, the sweetness of it.

Is she beautiful? Strange, tonight I might forgive her that, though I know the sun still rises and sets just for her. Only perhaps it arcs a little lower now.

Suddenly I don't think appearance – beauty – is so powerful anymore. It seems superficial, like stage make-up, you can draw it on or strip it away. No, it's what's deep down inside that counts. And no-one ever gets close enough to take that away or change it. Anyway it's different, that kind of power, it builds all the time. Increases. Like scales, layer on layer. And it's impossible to damage, because that's what it's made of – hurt.

Sergei glances back at me as he climbs into her car, almost as if he's regretting leaving. But if he wants to go, if that's what he truly wants, let him go. Her hands clasp the steering wheel.

There's a swish of tyres spinning away over the surface puddles, and the rear lights of her car blur, long blood red streaks lighting up the rain....

Beverley Soames:
Her Theatre Diary

Sleeping Beauty
Ballet Meridienne Francais
London Coliseum

I love sitting up in the gods, don't you? Way up in the gallery you get the full picture. The whole stage. It's just right for an antique Petipa-and-pattern ballet like Sleeping Beauty. And definitely a place to see things in perspective.

When European ballet directors decide to come upon the London scene which is so well stocked with excellent local talent, they must fully understand the strength of the competition, and the sophistication of British audiences. Fabulous costumes are a necessity, for touring sets can never match the grandeur of the in-house companies. The corps de ballet must be faultless, the soloists outstanding - and more, much more, the principals must be something really special. Nothing less will do. After all here we are already spoilt for choice.

Meridienne Francais whose Season of Classics opened on Saturday night at the London Coliseum, with Paul Gouter's new production of such an old favourite, would seem to have done its homework very well. Using sets kindly loaned to them by the English National Ballet, they have added enough gorgeous costumes and style to create a Sleeping Beauty worthy of the Sun King's court.

Stephan Fredrick's Carabosse casts a feverishly wicked spell over the proceedings, and as Lilac Fairy, Jeanne Maneau's dancing is lyrical and lovely particularly in the magical transformation scene. Gouter's ravishing and innovative ideas making this a truly French fairytale production, one not to be missed.

But wake up England! This Aurora turns out to be a home-grown ballerina, albeit with Australian roots. Partnered by the magnificent Sergei Lesarte, (see this prince and die!) the twenty-one year old Elaine Higham was on a double first, first night, first principal role. I remember her telling me when I knew her at Orlando's London studios, that she had no idea why she began dancing, and to be truthful, watching her in class then, nor had I.

Time and Higham's unending perseverance and naked ambition have proved me wrong, and your continuing trust in my opinion would be diminished if I did not now acknowledge a vibrant new talent. This Aurora's performance was an absolutely stunning British debut, from the superb Rose Adagio right through the story's drama to the sparkle of the final grand pas de deux.

Higham still has a long way to go. But she's young. And very, very ambitious! She may change partners along the route - it's rumored she and Lesarte are due to do just that. But her dancing is stylish and magical, and as fine as any of our best young British stars. Believe me, if her first lead role is anything to go by, Elaine Higham will soon be up there with the Gods herself.